ABOUT THE AUTHOR

Elizabeth O'Roark spent many years as a medical writer before publishing her first novel in 2013. She holds bachelor's degrees in journalism and arts from the University of Texas, and a master's degree from Notre Dame. She lives in Washington, D.C. with her three children. *The Devil and the Deep Blue Sea* is her tenth book.

ALSO BY ELIZABETH O'ROARK

The Devil Series:
A Deal with the Devil
The Devil and the Deep Blue Sea
The Devil You Know
The Devil Gets His Due

The Summer Series:
The Summer We Fell
The Summer I Saved You

THE DEVIL AND THE DEEP BLUE SEA

ELIZABETH O'ROARK

PIATKUS

PIATKUS

First published in Great Britain in 2023 by Piatkus

1 3 5 7 9 10 8 6 4 2

A CIP catalogue record for this book
is available from the British Library.

ISBN: 978-0-349-44071-2

Printed and bound in Great Britain by Clays Ltd, Elcograf S.p.A.

Papers used by Piatkus are from well-managed forests
and other responsible sources.

Piatkus
An imprint of
Little, Brown Book Group
Carmelite House
50 Victoria Embankment
London EC4Y 0DZ

An Hachette UK Company
www.hachette.co.uk

www.littlebrown.co.uk

For Sallye Clark, the best travel buddy a girl could ask for. Thanks for showing me how the other half lives.

PART I

OAHU

"Argued by many to be the most beautiful of all the islands, it is
not to be missed."
From *Oahu, The Adventure of a Lifetime*

1

DREW

January 21st

A love story is like a bus ride. You can take the express —short and to the point, not exciting but it gets you where you need to go—or you can make it a road trip. Lots of transfers and stops, operating with blind hope in search of the extraordinary.

I don't need *extraordinary*, and I'm not a big believer in blind hope, but a thirteen-hour flight to meet an ex-boyfriend could hardly be deemed *express* either.

Honolulu comes into focus through the window of the plane—the jagged cliffs of Diamond Head looming to my right, white sand and the bluest water you've ever seen.

Come to Hawaii, Six said after the incident, the one that propelled me from mere fame to infamy. *Let your publicist spin the whole thing as exhaustion.*

He's very persuasive, my ex. My best friend, Tali, would use the word *opportunistic*. In fact, that's precisely the word she used. But she has far higher expectations of men than I do.

So here I am, sleep-deprived and stumbling off a plane into

bright sunlight and clammy air, ready to give him another chance. Trying to ignore that there was a *catch* to this whole thing, one he waited to share until I couldn't back out: his family is coming too.

"There she is!" cries a voice, and suddenly Six's mom, Beth, is pushing through the crowd to hug me as if I'm her long-lost daughter instead of the ex-girlfriend she's only met once.

It's sweet, I guess, but I really need to remove my hoody. This airport either doesn't have air-conditioning or considers eighty-five degrees *pleasant*.

"We got here a bit ago," she says, *still* hugging me, "and thought *why don't we just wait for Drew?*"

"Funny," says a grim voice I'd know anywhere, a voice that makes my stomach tighten like it's being sewn too small from the inside. "I don't quite remember it happening that way." I look up, up, up to find Joshua Bailey, Six's brother, looming just past his mother like the Shadow of Death, six foot five inches of glowering male. His eyes meet mine, and we both scowl at the same time. The look he gives me is one part loathing, one part assessment. It's the way you'd look at someone if you were hoping to make her death look like an accident.

"You're sweating," Joshua says, running a hand through his light brown hair. He makes the human ability to cool off when overheated sound like a personal flaw.

"And you look like you're dressed to attend an estate planning convention," I reply, letting my gaze raise from his khakis to his neatly pressed button-down. God, he's such a dork.

A hot dork, however.

If karma was really a thing, Josh would be hideous, but in truth he has the kind of eyes a lesser female might get lost in, such a pale blue against his dark lashes they hardly seem real, perfect bone structure, and a disarmingly lush lower lip—if you're into that sort of thing. And he's also ridiculously tall and broad-shouldered and muscley, the sort of guy who'd feel like a force of *nature* above you.

Again...if you're into that sort of thing.

He turns to the statuesque blonde behind him. "Sloane, you remember *Drew*," he says, dropping my name like I'm the girl who poisoned the town well...or wanted to steal the family silver, which he apparently believes.

And how are they even still a couple? They were in Somalia together, but Sloane moved to Atlanta last summer and she's way too uptight for phone sex. She probably sends illustrations of her fallopian tubes in lieu of nudes.

She extends an expertly manicured hand to me with a stiff smile on her face. I notice her ironed blouse isn't even wrinkled after a flight that must have been as long as mine and is perfectly dry to boot. One of the benefits of her being half-snake, I imagine, is that it keeps her core body temperature low.

"Sorry about Joel," she says.

I blink then. First, because I'd forgotten Six's family still calls him by his much-loathed given name. Second, because where the hell is the guy who called me just a few nights ago, swearing he'd changed?

I attempt to look past them. I'm five-six, but they're all so damn tall I can't see a thing. "*What?*"

They glance at each other, locked in some silent exchange, and my stomach drops.

"I texted you," Beth says. "Maybe it didn't go through. Oh, shoot. It didn't. Airports always have no signal."

She frowns and starts messing with her settings, still hoping to get the text to go through, apparently. I doubt it'll help much at this point.

"He's in jail," Josh provides, without a trace of emotion.

I give a startled laugh. Because arriving halfway around the world to vacation with Six's family *but not Six* is too ridiculously terrible to be real. "*What?*"

"It's all a big mix-up," Beth assures me, while Joshua rolls his eyes. "The band was searched at the Tokyo airport. One of them had a bit of marijuana in his bag, and they were all arrested. But his lawyer says he'll be out on bail by tomorrow and this whole thing will be settled in three days."

I stare at her. She cannot be telling me I'm stuck on vacation with a retirement-aged couple I've met *once*, plus two people I loathe—one of whom suggested to his mother, when he thought I was out of earshot, that she'd better lock up the family silver until I was gone.

But no one is laughing, and Beth is wincing. If this was all a joke, I don't think she'd appear quite this worried.

I look behind me, as if there might be a way to scramble back on the plane before the Baileys have seen me, but that would require time travel, something I haven't yet mastered.

A camera flashes, and Josh's gaze jerks in that direction. Heads are turning, a crowd is gathering. It's the fucking hair. I have one of those vaguely ethnic, Eastern European faces you see everywhere in New York—high cheekbones, pouty lips— but the long platinum blonde hair is what gives it away every time. I put my hood back on but it's too late...once they know you're in the airport, it's game over.

"We should go," Josh says, glaring across the room. "Someone better hold Drew's hand so she doesn't get trampled by all the normal size humans."

"Extreme height is correlated with early mortality," I reply, craning my neck back to maintain eye contact.

He raises a brow. "That's Marfan's syndrome. And you sound hopeful."

"Only if it could take place without ruining the trip."

I see the smallest twitch of his mouth, but it doesn't leave me feeling victorious. I think he just gets excited when people bring up death.

WE GET through the crowd to baggage claim where Jim Bailey, Six's father, waits. Unlike his wife, he's a man of few words and —thank God—not a hugger. He places a hand on my shoulder, nods, and asks what my bag looks like just before the crowd surges.

I told myself I wouldn't need security here, but I'm not five minutes into this vacation and I'm having second thoughts. Phones are held in the air, filming me, and things are waved in my face to be signed—a boarding pass, the inside of a book, a Sbarro receipt, an arm. I feel the first signs of encroaching panic: sweat dripping down my back, heart thudding in my chest, the sense that I'm about to suffocate.

"How drunk were you in Amsterdam?" someone shouts and someone else is asking if I'm here to go to rehab. Pretty much everyone alive has seen the video of me falling off a stage by now. *Drew Takes the Plunge!* was *The Daily Mail*'s headline. So very clever. Within hours, there were gifs, memes, stitches on TikTok. You haven't truly made it until the whole world unites to ridicule your personal crises.

I take a step back as the crowd swells, but people shove forward. The air grows too thick to breathe and just as I'm about to succumb to the panic, a hand wraps around my bicep. Josh pulls me from the crowd as if he's plucking me from heavy surf.

I'll go back to hating him later, certainly, but in this moment, as he shepherds me all the way to the waiting van, I've never loved anyone more.

The van door is flung open, and I dive inside. People already surround us, and are now filming the van itself. Like... who will ever want to watch that video? *Did I show you the taxi Drew Wilson was in?* they'll ask their friends later. And those friends, if even vaguely rational, will say *Why the fuck would we want to watch that? Why would you film the outside of a cab?*

I wind up shoved to the very back, which is less than ideal given I get carsick, but there's not really time to reorganize everyone.

With a lurch, the van accelerates away from the curb. Joshua's broad, khaki-covered thigh presses against mine and he smells annoyingly good. Like soap and deliciously *male* skin. It's clear I've gone too long without sex if the smell of Josh's skin is doing it for me at a time like this. And he flew here all the way from Somalia. Shouldn't he reek of airplane and sweat like I do?

Beth starts reading to us from her guide book about Oahu. Can a human voice actually make you ill? Because I feel like hers is. And there is no air coming from the vent near me. I press my face to the window like a dog.

"The medical care is apparently excellent," she announces. "Some of the best in the country." I can't imagine why this is what she wants to read about. Sure, there are three doctors in here—Jim, Sloane and Josh—but I'd put that fact neck-and-neck with *here's the cab Drew Wilson was in* on the interest scale.

"Are you about to get sick?" Josh asks me, sounding pretty horrified for someone who is *ostensibly* a doctor. I have my doubts: he seems more like the guy you hire to wipe out a group of civilians by drone.

I take shallow breaths through my nostrils. "I hope not." My eyes fall to his laptop bag. "Open that up a bit more, just in case."

He manages to look even more disdainful, a feat I didn't imagine possible.

"You get carsick," he says flatly. "Why didn't you say anything?"

"I don't know," I reply. "Maybe it had to do with the swarm of teenage girls who were chasing me."

"She's just like you, Josh," Beth says, turning to beam at her son as if *either* of us will take that as a compliment. "She does what needs to be done."

His eyes sweep over me with disdain. "Practically twins," he says, lip curling. Then he adds, under his breath, "Except I don't *twerk* for a living."

"And I'm not a jerk to people I just met," I hiss.

"Apparently," he mutters, "you don't remember the day we met all that clearly."

My jaw tightens. I didn't ask *him* if he'd finished high school. I didn't suggest to my mother that *he* might steal the silver.

"Put your head between your legs," he says. "And don't throw up on my pants."

I bend my body over and put my head down, just as Dr. Bedside Manner suggested.

So far, Hawaii is proving more exhausting than my real life.

2

JOSH

It's a lesson I should have learned from children's television programming: every lie, even lies of omission, even lies meant to spare someone, will come back to bite you in the ass eventually. I just never thought they'd all bite me in the ass at the same time.

Mere hours ago, I was at the end of a very long flight, looking forward to some time with my family in Hawaii. Well, looking forward to time with my *mother*, anyway. I expected to find her with her health restored—that last round of chemo behind her—and my father by her side, pretending to be a decent human being, while my brother drank too much and acted like the selfish prick he is.

But only my father is living up to expectations so far, because my mother is clearly not well and my brother couldn't even bother to show up. I'm starting to wish I'd never stepped off the plane.

The van arrives at the hotel at last. By some small miracle, my brother's diva girlfriend has managed not to vomit, but I climb out as fast as possible anyway and head to the Halekulani's open-air lobby.

The place radiates serenity, all bleached stone and quiet elegance, the kind of hotel where no one speaks loudly and it's as if you're the only guest. There are no lines at check-in, no nonsense. In under a minute, we are being led (quietly) through a maze of well-kept gardens and gently gurgling fountains to the elevator in our wing of the hotel. My mother has reserved us three rooms, side by side, on the fifth floor. She wants maximum togetherness at all times.

"Let's meet down by the bar at six," she says when we reach our respective rooms. "They do a sunset show."

I open the door to our suite, which consists of a bedroom with a plush king-sized bed, a living room spacious enough for a table, a desk and a couch, and a long balcony overlooking Diamond Head. In Dooha, I sleep in a tent barely tall enough to stand in. Simply having a bathroom nearby would be a luxury...and here there are two, complete with Japanese toilets that do everything but pull your pants down for you.

I can't begrudge my mother a single thing. She wanted this trip to be perfect and I suspect I know why. I just wish it wasn't...so much. There are kids at the refugee camp using wheelchairs constructed of bike tires and hospital chairs. How much equipment could we have purchased with the money this is costing? How much food?

"You really had no idea," Sloane says. She isn't talking about the room. She's not even *noticing* the room. She's only thinking of this—*us*, when "us" wasn't even a thing until two hours ago.

I run a hand through my hair. *Jesus, what a fucking mess.* "No," I say, forcing my mouth to move into a smile. "But it's great to see you."

It's not all that great, really.

My mother's decision to surprise me by inviting her was... definitely a surprise. Sloane and I were a fling, nothing more, and then she left Somalia, which fortuitously brought things to an end. Now I've got to pretend I wasn't relieved, on top of everything else I'm pretending.

She folds her arms across her chest. Somewhere between the airport and here, she's put together what's happened. "Why did you let your mother think we weren't over," she asks coolly, "if *you* thought we were?"

I shove my hands in my pockets. It's hard to explain how hung up my mother is on the idea of Joel or me settling down. I think she blames her screwed-up marriage for our aversion to relationships, and she isn't entirely wrong. "I didn't want to upset her right before she went through chemo," I reply. I thought I'd gracefully exited the thing with Sloane, gracefully sidestepped the conversation with my mother. And now I'm back in the middle of both.

The bellman enters and we fall silent while he sets each suitcase on the bench at the foot of the bed. When he leaves, she crosses the room and unzips it, saying nothing. The inside of her bag looks like it's been styled for a photo shoot. Everything is pressed, perfectly folded. That's Sloane to a T. Neat, precise, methodical.

By contrast, Drew's bag is probably bursting at the seams. I picture frilly panties and bras and negligees exploding like confetti from a cannon when she opens it. I have no clue why I'm picturing Drew's panties, or why I picture them all being sheer and extremely non-functional, but it's a troubling development.

Sloane opens a drawer and then closes it. "Is this going to be okay? That I'm here?"

No, I think. There is so much that is not okay at this moment that I feel like I can barely take a deep breath. "Of course," I tell her, because the only option is to say *Hey, not really, would you mind flying back to Atlanta instead?*

Her lips press tight. "Then do me a favor: please don't spend the entire trip fawning over your brother's girlfriend."

I give a startled laugh. "*Fawning*?"

"You talked to her more than you did me at the airport," she replies. "And then you rushed into doctor mode in the van."

"I asked her not to throw up on my pants. It was hardly the height of medical care."

Her lips press again, as if she doesn't agree but knows further argument is pointless, and I step onto the balcony. There is no longer enough air in this oversized room. I suspect it's going to feel that way until we leave.

My hands grip the railing and I glare at the perfect view. What the hell am I going to do? The issues with my mother would be enough to make me feel like I was drowning without an unhappy ex sharing my room for the next two weeks.

The balcony door beside mine slips open and Drew walks out, pulling her endless blonde hair free of its ponytail. She's removed the hoody she wore earlier, stripped down to the tank beneath. I see ice-blue bra straps, a hint of lace under the shirt's thin fabric. Collarbone, bee-stung lips, so much exposed skin. She always looks like her clothes can't quite contain her.

And in response I feel that same fizzle inside me, that bizarre, unwelcome spark I've had before. My gaze darts to the hint of lace beneath her shirt and darts away.

I'm better than this. And for the next two weeks, I'm going to have to be a *lot* better than this.

"Pretend I'm not here," she says, with knowing brown eyes that seem to see right through me.

"I plan to," I reply dryly.

3

DREW

Joshua. So far, he's exceeding any and all expectations.

Because I expected him to be a dick, and my God he's *killing* it.

I leave him standing outside, staring at Diamond Head as if it's done something to him. I picture him mentally crafting a list of things he hates:

1. Drew

2. Threats to Mother's silver

3. Dormant volcanoes

4. Drew, again

The bed—white, fluffy, oversized—calls to me but I don't dare lie down. I'm way too tired—there's not a chance I'd get back up before I have to meet the Baileys down at the ocean-front bar. Instead, I shower and wander the grounds, trying to stay awake.

My phone buzzes in my pocket while I'm perusing one of the shops in the center of the hotel. I know it's Tali before I even answer the call, because she's the sort of person who writes down what flight you're on and checks to make sure you landed safely. She's going to be an amazing mom.

"Did you make it in one piece?" she asks.

I go outside and sit on a bench, groaning a little. How am I so stiff from *sitting* all day? "Barely. And I'll give you one guess what Joshua said. First *thing* out of his mouth."

"Don't steal the silver?" She's heard, obviously, about the first time I met him. Her soft giggle lightens my mood just a little.

I kick off one flip-flop and dig my toes into the grass. Even the Halekulani's grass is quieter and more elegant than anyone else's. "He would have, I'm certain, if they'd traveled here with it. And seriously, why is silver still a thing? It's something people put in their *mouths*. If I don't want a diamond you've put in your mouth, I sure as shit don't want *metal* you've put in your mouth. But anyway...no, he did not bring up the silver. He said *You're sweating*, the way someone else might say *You're bleeding*. Like...it was a thing decent people don't do."

She laughs. Tali is one of the most bubbly people I know, and now that she's carrying what's politely referred to as a honeymoon baby, though the baby was in there before any honeymoon occurred, she's positively giddy. "And I'm sure you responded with your customary restraint," she says.

I lean backward, staring absentmindedly at the pretty white dress in the window. It's delicate and girlish, nothing I would ever wear. "I was *lovely* to him," I reply. "Sort of. It's all vague because I'm tired but I'm almost certain I behaved like an adult. Anyway, how's my future godson?"

"You're as bad as Hayes. We don't know it's a boy. But to answer your question, *she* is a monster who, according to the lady at Whole Foods, is stealing my beauty. She literally said that to me. *I can tell you're having a girl because she's stealing your beauty.* Have you told Davis you're not going to rehab?"

Oh, right. My manager pulled a lot of strings to get me into some swanky rehab center in Utah, which would make him sound like a prince among men, except he did it without asking me, and I don't need rehab. We're still on our six-week break from the tour, so for once he can't threaten me with phrases like *breach of contract*.

I pull my hair off my face. "He'll probably figure it out when I don't get off the plane."

"I wish you'd fire him. Why is your life so full of men I want to punch?" she asks. I brace for her to ask about Six, brace for the moment when I have to admit he no-showed on this trip—which only sounds forgivable if I explain that he's in *jail*—but she's still focused on my awful manager. "Please call Ben. He's a brilliant lawyer. I know he can get you out of your contract with Davis. And my husband trusts him—you know Hayes doesn't trust anyone."

"He trusts *you*," I remind her.

I can hear the smile in her voice. "I guess that's a good thing, since I'm his wife."

Tali and Hayes? They're that road trip sort of couple. The ones who don't know what's coming but are in it for the long haul. Marriage thrills them both, and watching them terrifies me.

Because anything that thrills you will hurt that much more when it's lost.

THE BAILEYS ARE all gathered by the time I get to the oceanfront bar for the hotel's nightly sunset show. Sloane is still dressed like she's here to learn about tax loopholes for rich douchebags, but Josh has changed into a t-shirt and khaki shorts and I can't entirely explain the small jump in my gut at the sight of him there, sprawled in a chair he's too big for, with his very well-defined biceps on display. It's sort of like when you hear about someone's fetish and feel simultaneously disgusted and titillated by it.

I take the empty chair next to Beth, who smiles at me as if I'm her favorite person. "Has anyone heard from Six?" I ask.

She shakes her head, a flicker of worry in her gaze. "He won't be able to contact us until he's out on bail tomorrow," she says. "His lawyer is keeping in touch, though. I just hope he doesn't miss all of Oahu, but we'll figure it out."

I blink at her. She said *three* days at the airport, but we are in Oahu for *six*. I'm beginning to worry Beth is one of those relentlessly optimistic people who hope for things fruitlessly, continually readjusting what they wish for, only to conclude it was *all for the best* in the end when nothing works out.

"Even if he misses Oahu, there are other islands for you to see together!" Beth says, patting my hand. "It will be fine. We're just happy you came." I nod, but the truth is I'm so tired I feel numb, so tired my body is simply shutting down from fatigue— it's seventy-eight degrees and I'm shivering—and I'm alone, on vacation with strangers. I'm also still reeling from the conversation with Davis just before I came down from my room. *I don't give a shit if you need rehab, Drew,* he said. *I only give a shit if it looks like you need rehab, and it definitely looks like it. So you'd better get your ass on that plane.*

Things, in a nutshell, feel slightly less fine than I'd like.

The mai tai I ordered as I walked in is delivered and Sloane raises a polite brow, as if to say *Are you sure that's a good idea?* I wonder if the Baileys will still be happy I came once I push Sloane into a volcano.

Beth orders several things for the table, and chatters about the many, many plans she's made for the trip. She is everything my own mother is not: cheerful, accepting, willing to overlook the occasional felony. Six has a chip on his shoulder about his father, who thinks playing guitar is a hobby no matter how much Six earns doing it, but he doesn't say much about his mom. Maybe that's how you know he's got a good one: she's like the foundation of a building, attracting little notice, there simply to hold him up.

All guesses, however. I don't actually know a lot about good moms.

Beth notices I'm shivering and tries to make me take her wrap, which is when Josh's attention focuses on me. His eyes sharpen, as if he'd forgotten I was here at all and remembering is unpleasant, and then his lip curls in sheer disdain. *Put her in a van and she vomits*, he's thinking. *Take her outside and she can't regulate her temperature. Aside from stealing people's silver, what does she do well?*

It's just like spending time with my family, which is why I generally don't do that. And under normal circumstances I could shrug it off, but it's harder to do right now when I'm this tired and this disheartened. Tonight, it doesn't feel like a blip. It feels like disappointing people is how I'm destined to spend my entire life.

I'm relieved when we all go our separate ways. I stumble into my room, eager for bed, but am drawn to the balcony instead. A full moon hangs low over Diamond Head. It seems like the sort of crap I should photograph and post on Instagram to prove to the world I'm occasionally sober, but I'm too tired. Yawning, I turn to go inside when something catches my eye: a solitary figure, standing on the sea wall. Joshua. He's probably out there wondering how he can harness the power of the sea for evil, but then he looks down and stares at his hands, as if the weight of the world is on his shoulders and I feel something a little like worry.

What had him so distracted tonight? And why the hell is he not with the girlfriend he hasn't seen in months?

It certainly appears I'm not the only person feeling lonely on a romantic trip for two.

4

DREW

January 22nd

Twenty-three hours a day, I'm the girl who doesn't give a shit. I'll do a line of coke off my breakfast bagel, wrestle someone in a bath of Jell-O, jump off a cliff when everyone else is worrying about the depth of the water below.

There is only one hour when I'm *not* that girl, and it's this one. Four AM. It's ten back home, so it would make some sense that I've awoken, but I'd have woken anyway because it happens without fail: my heart beating hard as my eyes fly open, scanning a dark room that is, more often than not, unfamiliar. Realizing I am terrifyingly alone and have failed at everything, even the things other people want to laud me for.

It's the hour when I admit that I'm a fake, that this person who appears in magazines and performs for thousands isn't me at all. She doesn't have my name, she barely looks like me anymore, and she isn't even someone I *like*...yet the only way I can succeed in life, the only way I can get what I want, is to pretend to be her even harder than I already have.

After thirty minutes of lying in bed, wondering if things will ever get better, I rise and dress to go for a run. I don't love running, but there are a lot of buffets here and Davis will kill me if I gain weight.

I take the elevator down and wander the paths out to the street. It's silent now but for the babble of the fountains, the occasional murmur of someone at the front desk. There's something inherently reassuring about it. About the whole city, and perhaps the whole island: the weather is mild, the trees bear fruit. You could lose everything and somehow survive. I have more money than I could ever spend, but the idea still appeals to me.

"Please tell me you aren't planning to run before five in the morning in a strange city," says a low voice I'd know anywhere, mostly because only one person is *that* contemptuous of me, twenty-four hours a day.

I turn to find Josh there, looking at me in a beam of moonlight. His eyes are like a summer storm; that furrow between his brows deep as a trench. I feel the oddest tug in my stomach at the sight of him...and ignore it.

And I'm not letting Josh add himself to the long list of people who feel free to correct and criticize me. How the hell is it any of his concern what I'm doing, anyway? Is he worried I'm out prowling, getting ready to steal silver from someone's one-bedroom condo?

"Fine," I reply with my sweetest smile. "I'm not planning to run."

And then I turn and start to run.

I head down toward the main drag, popping my headphones in as I go. I pass a long, long row of ridiculously expensive stores, the kind of places I could now afford to shop if I didn't hate shopping.

My soundtrack is this fairly mellow band from Sacramento. Mostly acoustic guitar, but I love the way they go from subtle to big, from comfortable to goosebumps-on-my arms.

It's the kind of music I used to write, back before I got my first record deal and discovered I was never going to be performing my own stuff. I don't even play guitar in concert now. *You're too hot to stand there just playing an instrument,* my manager explained at first. *People want a show.*

Maybe I should have insisted on doing things my way, but I was twenty and broke and scared if I kept holding out for more, I'd wind up empty-handed. I doubt many people would say it was a mistake, given where I am now.

The shops come to an abrupt end, replaced by a little beachfront park where a massive, twisty tree looms just off the sidewalk. I jerk to a stop and stare at it. Under the glow of the full moon, it looks magical, like something created by Disney.

"It's a banyan," says a voice behind me. I gasp in surprise and round on Joshua.

"Did you *follow* me?"

His tongue prods his cheek. "I certainly wouldn't run this slowly by *choice.*"

"Why?" I bark. My foot begins to tap. This was supposed to be my time to myself. Or at least my time away from people who accuse me of class A misdemeanors. "There's no one even out here."

"Right. I forgot how much safer it is outside when it's dark and there are no witnesses." He sighs heavily, pinching the bridge of his nose. "You do realize that most attacks on female joggers occur in the morning?"

I lean against a lamppost and start to stretch. I'm already getting stiff. "Sounds like someone's been researching the best way to attack female joggers. And we just passed Tiffany and Jimmy Choo. The brokest, most dangerous guy out here right now is probably *you.*"

"Uh-huh," he says. "And on the off chance you're wrong,

Drew, how exactly would you defend yourself? You're about three feet tall."

"I'm five-six," I growl. "*And* I'm in amazing shape. I could fight off ten guys your size."

This is perhaps a slight exaggeration. But I definitely kicked Max Greenbaum's ass, mano-a-mano. Possibly less impressive if we weren't nine when it happened, and if he hadn't been really small for his age.

His brow lifts. "Ten guys?"

"At *least* ten. All at the same time. Tarantino movies are a pale imitation of my fighting skills."

He steps into the sand. "Then show me," he says. His shoulders are relaxed. "Let me see you defend yourself."

The crickets chirp, the breeze blows, and moonlight glances over his smugly perfect face.

"My hands are registered lethal weapons. And you're underestimating how bad I want to kick you in the balls," I reply. "I wouldn't push this."

He tips his chin and his mouth almost curves into something less severe. "Yeah? Because you're acting like someone who isn't sure."

Now that he's called my bluff, I have to go through with it, though to my surprise I don't actually want to hurt him quite as much as I thought. I mean, yeah, I still want to hurt him. Just... less. Also, he's a foot taller than me. It will be a lot like trying to beat up a redwood.

"The last guy I fought wet his pants. Is that really something you want to risk?"

"Feel free to just admit you're far weaker," he says, folding his arms across his broad chest, "and we can proceed with the run."

Okay, I rescind my previous statement. I totally want to hurt this guy.

Fast as a flash, my leg swings out. It's been a while, but I can still do a decent roundhouse kick, if nothing else. But just as I'm about to make contact, he grabs my leg. Two seconds later, I'm on the ground and he's kneeling above me.

I don't even know how he did it, but I do know my whole Max Greenbaum victory feels a little tarnished now.

He pulls me up by the forearm. "So, is there anything you'd like to say?"

"Yeah," I reply, brushing myself off. "You seem to enjoy throwing a female on the ground a little too much. No wonder Sloane looks so unhappy all the time."

His face reverts to its previous severity. Maybe I aimed a little low, but *I'm* not the one who invited her.

"I'll take that as your concession speech," he says. "And you might want to take it easy today, by the way. Lounging isn't really on the Bailey vacation itinerary, ever."

"*I'll* be fine," I reply. "Worry about yourself."

I pat my pocket for my inhaler though I have no intention of using it in front of him, lest he add *asthmatic* to his ever-growing list of my flaws. And then I turn toward Diamond Head and start running, knowing I'll have to go longer and harder than I ever planned, just to prove to Joshua Bailey I don't need his advice.

5

JOSH

There is absolutely no way she intended to run six miles this morning. She looks like she's going to keel over as we stop in front of the hotel. "Are you going to stalk me every day?" she demands, breathing so heavily she barely gets the words out.

"I hope not," I reply. "This barely counted as a workout."

She is currently leaning over, palms pressed to her thighs, as she tries to catch her breath. She looks up to glare at me and I get a glimpse of very ample cleavage before I remember myself.

"Look," I say, "all you have to do is promise you won't run alone at five AM anymore."

She straightens. In the early morning light, flushed and bare-faced and doe-eyed, she looks a lot younger and a lot more innocent than she probably is.

"You are way too scared of strangers, and I would just like to point out that, from a legal perspective, the specificity of that statement renders it useless. Tomorrow, for instance, I could run at 5:05."

"It's really a wonder no one's beaten you to death," I tell her wearily. "And I'm not talking about strangers. I'm talking about the people who know you best."

She smirks, flips a middle finger at me, and walks off.

I'm free of her at last, but I can't go to the room yet since Sloane will be asleep—not that I'd want to go there if she was awake. I took the couch last night, which didn't improve the situation between us. It just seemed like the right thing to do. I can't pick up where we left off last summer, not when she'd be thinking it meant something. Not when I know I'd be extracting myself again at the trip's end, which is the kind of shit my father and brother would do.

I go to the lounge chairs by the pool and watch the sun slowly emerge from behind Diamond Head, thinking about what a messed-up situation this is. All the secrets weigh on me even more than they did yesterday.

Babysitting my brother's pain-in-the-ass girlfriend is not what I need right now.

I think of her running in the dark by herself and stifle a quiet groan. And telling me she could fight ten guys at once when she barely hits my rib cage. My brother has brought home some troubling women before, but Drew Wilson is— hands down—the worst.

AN HOUR later we're seated at breakfast when Drew strolls up, her plate from the buffet heaped to overflowing with carbohydrates.

"Well, good morning, Joshua, Sloane," she says with exaggerated cordiality, setting her plate down across from Sloane and pulling out a chair. "Aren't you going to eat?"

"I have a philosophical objection to buffets," I reply.

She rolls her eyes. "I'm not even fully seated and you've managed to make breakfast dull," she says. "What's the problem? Too much pleasure?"

"It's a waste of food," I tell her. "Half of it ends up in the trash." I know she won't understand. It's not as if this buffet is actually taking food out of other people's mouths. It's just easier not to see it. It's easier not to think about the kids at the camp, how one breakfast like this would be something they'd remember the rest of their lives.

Drew gives me the most exaggerated smile possible as she shoves half a chocolate croissant in her mouth. "I plan to eat way more than normal this week if it makes you feel any better. They won't be throwing out *that* much."

"American excess is repellent to people who've actually witnessed true poverty," Sloane says, looking pointedly at Drew's plate, her voice rife with condescension.

"Oh, yeah?" Drew asks, her eyes darting from the expensive purse hanging off the back of Sloane's chair to the mug in her hands. "How's that oversized cappuccino, by the way? *American excess* is often quite tasty, I find."

Excellent. Sloane has decided to be as judgmental as possible, and Drew has decided to bait her. Just what this shitshow of a trip needs.

My parents arrive with plates from the buffet, oblivious to the growing tension at the table, and my mother pulls out her trusty guidebook—*Oahu, The Adventure of a Lifetime*—which she opens before sliding it my way.

"The hike for today is called Pillboxes," she says. "There are these small military bunkers built into a mountain. Amazing views."

The Baileys have never taken a relaxed family trip once so this doesn't surprise me, but the trail looks steep as shit. Not impossible, but also nothing my mother should be attempting at the moment.

"Mom," I say carefully, "this looks like a lot to bite off. Maybe today can be more about relaxation?"

"I'm fine," she says, refusing to meet my eye. "I think that first picture is deceptive."

I look to my father for backup. He's the last person I want to be siding with, but desperate times call for desperate measures. He's too busy checking his email to notice.

Sloane taps on her watch with a frown. "I may have to bow out. I scheduled a manicure for ten."

Drew's eyes cut to mine and she smirks. *Oh, so the buffet is 'American excess',* her expression says, *but not a manicure in the hotel spa?* Her gaze flicks to Sloane's wrist. *Not that $400 smartwatch?* I knew she wasn't going to let this go, and what sucks is, she has a point.

"Dad," I say, willing my voice to be calm, "what are your thoughts?"

He glances from me to the book and sighs. "Beth, Josh is right. We'll take a look when we get there, but let's think about just going to the beach instead."

A shadow comes over my mother's face. I want that shadow not to confirm every one of my suspicions. She flicks it away soon enough, but I can't quite forget I saw it.

And in the meantime, Sloane is looking between me and Drew again, as if we are an exceedingly difficult equation she's determined to answer. "I'll reschedule my manicure," she says. "It's fine."

Sunlight strikes the table in a blinding flash of heat and several birds swoop in, attempting to steal food from the plates. My father ignores it all, back on his phone, and my mother, for once, can't summon the energy to shoo them away. Sloane, on the other hand, jumps up from the table as if the three small birds are something out of a Hitchcock movie and pulls antibacterial gel from her pocket.

And Drew is laughing at the whole thing, licking chocolate from her perfect lips.

I close my eyes, wondering if there's any way to escape our luxurious vacation and just go back to work.

6

DREW

We are taken by van—I ride in front this time, which makes sense because a) carsickness and b) I'm the dateless fifth wheel on a couples' outing. Beth has the driver drop us off in Kailua, which isn't even the same *town* where our hike begins, insisting the walk will be scenic. It's a lot for anyone, and Beth just finished her final round of chemo two months ago. I don't understand why she's driving herself so hard—certainly, they've got the money to come back later on when she's feeling better if there's something she regrets missing out on.

For twenty minutes, we walk past white sand and blue, blue sea with two small looming mountains jutting out of the water just ahead—the Mokulua Islands, per Beth and her guide book. Everyone but me is sipping their water—I chose not to bring any solely because Joshua *reminded* me to, which irked me. Hopefully, the Sour Patch Kids I brought instead will be a decent substitute.

We turn off the main road to face the mountain at last. It's undeniably beautiful, those jagged green cliffs going up and up

—and I have no desire to go even a step farther. My only hope of getting out of this involves convincing everyone not to climb.

"That mountain is steep," I suggest.

"Unlike most mountains," says Josh, even more snide than usual, and I picture him pinned beneath me with my hands around his neck.

Drew, I can't breathe, he'd say.

I know, I'd reply. *All part of my long-range plan to steal your silver.*

"I wouldn't mind just sitting on the beach instead," says Sloane. When Jim and Beth agree with her, relief whistles through me. I'm going to get out of this and I'll never have to admit anything to Joshua.

"I'm happy to do whatever you guys want," I chime in.

"*I'm* going to hike it," Joshua says to me, eyes holding a gleam that is perhaps twenty percent more evil than their normal gleam. He pulls out one of the *four* water bottles he stashed in his daypack and splashes some on the back of his neck. "But you're probably tired after this morning, so you should definitely rest."

My arms fold over my chest. "I'm not the *least* bit tired." This is absolutely a lie. I took so much ibuprofen this morning I risked an overdose, and I still feel like shit.

He sweeps a hand toward the trail in a *you first* gesture, and I stomp up the dirt path. The trail is steep as hell. I move as fast as possible to get away from him, but he catches me with ease, his long legs unfairly capable of taking three strides for every one of mine.

"How's it going, slugger?" he asks about five minutes in.

"Amazing," I reply, quickening my pace. The sun is beating down on me and my shirt is glued to my skin. I really wish he'd give me one of the water bottles from his daypack. "How 'bout you? I mean, at your age...don't you have to worry about stuff breaking?"

"I'm thirty-two," he huffs.

"Huh," I reply a little breathlessly as I hoist myself up a step so large I have to hold onto a tree to manage it. "I'd have guessed older. Maybe it's just because you and Sloane seem so dead inside."

"Speaking of old," he says, as our steps fall into a rhythm again, "nice fanny pack. Did it come with a motorized scooter or do you have to buy that separate?"

"It's for my inhaler, asshole."

He's silent for one blissful moment, and there's no sound but the small rocks slipping under our shoes. When he speaks again, his voice is absent its normal disdain. "How bad is your asthma? You seemed fine this morning."

"Don't get all excited," I say. "This hike isn't hard, so it's unlikely to kill me off."

"There's still time," he says cheerfully. "My mom has planned a *lot* of hikes."

I stifle a laugh and then sigh heavily as he barrels right past the lookout point—trust Joshua to make this hike as unenjoyable as possible—and in the process of giving him the finger I accidentally make eye contact with two girls walking down the hill. I see recognition in their faces, and my spine stiffens. It's the fucking hair again. I might as well wear a neon sign that says *Notice Me*.

"Excuse me," says one of them from behind us, and I force myself to turn, ignoring the slow sinking in my stomach. "Are you Drew Wilson?"

There are two ways an interaction like this can go: I politely tell them I'm in the middle of a hike and can't stop, and they'll spend the rest of their lives talking about what a bitch I am to anyone who will listen. Or I can give them everything they want, and they'll talk about how nice I was, though they thought I'd be thinner.

It's really not even a choice.

I plaster a cheerful smile on my face, while Josh's eyes bore into me from behind with the power of a thousand suns. "Yes, hi."

They ask for a picture. A separate one for each of them, and I oblige while they ask me questions about the next album—about which I know nothing aside from the fact it will suck. They show no signs of leaving until Josh makes impatient noises behind me.

"Is he your boyfriend?" one of them asks, sweeping her appreciative gaze over him.

"Him? No. Satan isn't allowed to take a companion on the Earth's surface, as far as I know."

They leave at last, and when I turn back up the hill, Joshua is standing there with a brow raised. He hands me a bottle of water, thank God. "Satan isn't allowed to take a companion, huh?"

"So I've heard," I reply carelessly. "I'm sure you're more familiar with the rules."

His tongue darts out to tap his upper lip. I see a glimmer of amusement in his eyes, but he stoically manages to repress it. He nods at the girls and sighs. "They're already posting those ridiculous pictures online."

I shrug. "Do you want one too? You can post it on Instagram and talk about how I was nice, but then mention I'm not as pretty in real life."

He looks back at me, his eyes brushing over my face. Lingering on my mouth. "I don't have Instagram."

I smack my forehead. "Oh my god. Are you serious? Tell me how old you are again, because even my great-grandfather has Instagram. Although he fills up his IG with infographics about the Russian Revolution, so he doesn't get a lot of likes."

He grunts and starts up the hill again. "Why the fuck would I want Instagram?"

"You could post pictures of Somalia," I suggest. "*Here's a pretty sunset. Here's a child with a gunshot wound.*"

"Sunsets only happen once a day," he says darkly. "So it'd be option two more than often not. Glad you find it so amusing, however."

"Jesus," I sigh, scrambling after him. "Has anyone ever suggested you lighten up?"

Rocks go sliding downhill as his feet turn toward me. "Certain things bother me."

"I've noticed," I reply, taking another sip of water. "Mild pleasure, societal advancement, what else?"

He turns to look at me with an expression that makes me feel an inch tall. "Spoiled princesses making fun of other people's misfortunes," he says, and then he stalks off, leaving me in a haze of dust and mild regret.

Six would have laughed at my joke, I think defensively, trying to ignore the small knot in my stomach that suggests Joshua might have a point.

He's waiting at the first bunker, studying the view as if he plans to lay siege to it later.

"I'm sorry," I say quietly because I really hate apologizing. "I was being an asshole."

He looks at me for a long moment. "Yeah, you were. But you're not the first person who's suggested I could stand to lighten up."

"So we were *both* wrong? That's what you're saying?"

His mouth moves, slightly. "Yes, exactly. *That's* what I was saying."

"Smile," I instruct, holding up my phone to take a picture of him for Beth. He folds his arms across his chest, his mouth flat, and the only part of his face that moves is a single eyebrow saying *Why are you taking my picture? I only stand for photos when required to do so by the US Passport Office.*

I take the photo anyway, just to spite him. He looks like a

brooding, virile Viking on the cusp of pillaging a village or declaring *prima nocta*.

"Though you're hideous," I tell him, "you could potentially take a decent photo if you were capable of smiling."

He raises that brow once more. "You think I'm not *capable* of smiling?"

"You're not even capable of smiling right now when I'm *accusing* you of being unable to do it. Your face only has two expressions—mildly disgusted and really disgusted."

There's a low, warm noise from his throat. One I might almost confuse with a quiet laugh. I want to not be pleased by that. "I wouldn't confuse the way I look at *you* with the way I look at *everyone*," he says, turning up the hill and heading toward the second bunker.

Asshole.

For ten more minutes, we climb, and when we finally reach our destination, I'm absolutely spent and ready to throw myself from the peak and hope for the best. Instead, I turn and grab the first foothold to scale its side.

"What the fuck are you doing?" he demands.

I continue to climb, though the footholds are far apart and I'm not especially gifted with upper body strength.

"I want a selfie from the top," I reply, "so I can prove how healthy I am and show up all those dickheads saying I need rehab."

"That definitely *sounds* healthy," he mutters, following me up with no sign of effort.

When I reach the top, I take in the view. The ocean is the deepest blue imaginable, a royal blue crayon plucked straight from a new box and brought to life. In the distance, a kayak moves over the water toward the Mokulua Islands, small as a grain of rice from here. I close my eyes for a moment and picture it—the only sound the roar of the wind, no one gawking at me. There are times when I think I could live like that, on some barren island alone. At least then I could fall down without half the world saying I need rehab, or have some premenstrual bloating without *TMZ* suggesting I'm pregnant.

My eyes open and I discover him standing way too close. "What are you doing?"

"Just making sure you don't fall off," he replies dryly. "I understand you do that sometimes."

I lower my phone and stare at him balefully. I thought he might be the one person alive who hadn't heard about Amsterdam. "You've been saving that up all morning, haven't you?"

He gives a small laugh. "Since the start of the trip, actually."

My mouth moves and I struggle to hold it still. "Well, I'm glad we've gotten it out of the way."

And then I laugh. Joshua is still a fucking asshole. If he hadn't made the comment about the silver, I'd probably want to be his friend anyway.

7

JOSH

Man is not as evolved as he'd like to think—when it comes to sex, we are essentially puppets, wired by our primitive brains to seek reproduction of the species at the expense of all else. Infants will stare at a photo of a symmetrical face longer than they'll stare at a photo of their own mother. Show men around the world a variety of female bodies, and no matter what they *claim* to like, they physically *respond* to the exact same proportions.

So, yes, I did a double take the first time I saw Drew Wilson on the cover of *Maxim*. I imagine the number of straight men who did a double take at that cover was—well, all of them. It's meaningless that the mere sight of her was enough to take me directly from thinking about the surgery I'd be performing that evening to thoughts of bare skin and soft lips and breasts barely contained by a little pink dress.

But that doesn't mean I have to do a double take every time she comes into view.

I'm poolside—forced into a chair next to my father, who's droning on about the evils of managed care—when Drew appears. She's in a t-shirt and shorts instead of some skimpy bikini, thank God, long blonde hair piled beneath a hat.

My mother pats the chair beside her. "You look like you need a nap, young lady," she says affectionately. Drew seems to make her motherly side go into hyperdrive, for reasons I can't understand.

Drew smiles but there's something uncertain in it, something fragile. It's almost as if she doesn't know how to react when someone is kind.

"I was up before five today to run," she says. "Between that and the hike, I'm pretty beat."

Sloane, reading beside me, stiffens. I didn't mention to her that I ran with Drew, since she's already weirdly jealous. She seems to be putting it together now.

"Well, you sit down here and take a little rest then, hon," says my mom.

Drew nods and then her hands go to her waistband and I stiffen in sudden panic. Drew is removing her clothes and my *God* that's nothing I need to see. I know I should stop looking, for my own sanity, but I just don't.

The shorts slide off. My gaze travels involuntarily along the smooth bronzed skin of her toned thighs, and up, up up to the curve of the perkiest ass I've ever laid eyes on. White bikini bottoms tied with string. A single tug and she could be freed from them.

She then pulls off her hat. Her hair spills down while she pulls the t-shirt over her head, revealing a bikini top that barely contains her curves. She is lush and soft, and before I can stop myself, I'm imagining her under me and wanting it so fiercely I think I'd give up anything to make it happen.

I have to drop a book in my lap to hide the fact that my cock is reacting to her like I'm new to puberty.

I squeeze my eyes shut, but the image of her is still seared in my brain.

I'm worried it's going to stay there.

8

DREW

January 23rd

I manage to sleep a little later the next day, but it's still dark when I head out to begin my run. Josh's bedroom door clicks shut as I approach the elevator. I'm no lawyer, but I'm fairly certain he's meeting the legal criteria for stalking.

He leans against the back wall of the elevator and closes his eyes.

"Why are you so tired?" I ask. "Please tell me you were murdering Sloane and hiding the body all night."

He opens one eye. "What makes you think it would take all night?"

Joshua Bailey, making a second joke in twenty-four hours. I laugh at the unexpectedness of it more than anything else.

"It must take a lot of time," I continue. "Movies make it seem easy, but, like, sawing through all that bone takes some upper body strength."

"Jesus Christ," he says, stepping off the elevator and walking ahead. "The way your mind works frightens me."

It's absolutely black outside; no noise but the crickets and the fountains and our soft steps falling into line with each other's. We reach the road and start to run. This time I don't bother trying to stay ahead of him or falling behind. I clearly can't outrun him anyway, and I've had worse company. Davis, for instance, ran with me once and spent the whole time talking about the importance of keeping my weight down.

"I get it. I've thought about murdering Sloane too," I tell him, picking up where we left off. "Although just an FYI, *wanting* to murder someone is not a legally justifiable defense. I checked into it after we met for the first time."

He scowls. "You talk about murder a lot. You might want to lay off the crime dramas for a bit."

"I don't need to watch crime dramas," I reply. "My mother and my stepfather practice criminal law."

His gaze jerks toward me. "*Your* mother?"

I sigh. Everyone assumes simply because I sing about sex on occasion that I must be the product of foster care or a single mom who supported the family via prostitution.

"It's flattering, how shocked you are by that."

He shrugs. "I just figured you were raised by someone...a little more shallow. Like, an aging model or a pageant winner, someone who'd have you out there auditioning at age five to model swimwear for sexy toddlers in the newspaper."

"Ads for sexy toddlers," I muse. "Is that what you use for porn in Somalia?"

"Only when the internet's slow," he says, and I give another startled laugh. I just made the world's most distasteful joke and he doubled down on it. I respect that.

"Wow," I say.

He smirks. "I think I even grossed myself out with that one."

We pass the banyan tree. There are surfers out this morning, pulling boards off the large rack in the sand and heading into the dark water. "I can think of nothing more terrifying," I say as we pass, "than surfing when it's pitch-black outside."

"I can't imagine waking up this early by choice," he replies, which has me wondering, once more, what kept him up last night. I'm fairly certain *Sloane* does not stay up all night for sex. She'd want it rigorously scheduled, with as little touching as possible and a wet towel at the ready to promptly clean up the mess.

Was it satisfactory, she'd ask at the end. He won't ask her the same, because her release is not critical to the continuation of the species.

"I'm trying to imagine you and Sloane having sex," I reply, mostly because I know it will make him uncomfortable.

He stumbles and catches himself. "What?"

"Don't worry, it's not sexy. I picture more of a Ken doll, Barbie doll situation, with you two rubbing your smooth parts against each other. Or two robots fucking, in some kind of simulation set up for scientists to observe. I'm not entirely clear on why scientists would *need* to observe robots fucking...still working that part out."

"Please stop talking," he begs, but I see that twitch to his lips.

I can't imagine why, but that smile he's repressing is the first thing about this trip that's really made me happy I came.

BY THE TIME we approach the hotel, daylight is starting to break and I'm utterly destroyed. He thought he was running slow on my behalf and I was too proud to admit we were running at least a minute per mile *faster* than I have ever run.

We reach the gardens and he turns toward the pool. "I'm heading this way. I like watching the light come up over Diamond Head."

"Can't you watch it from your balcony?"

Something passes over his face, a hint of trouble he doesn't want to share. "Sloane's a light sleeper."

He isn't exactly inviting me along, but I follow him to the lounge chairs facing Diamond Head and the bay anyway. He glances at me, undoubtedly irritated I'm crashing his sunrise party, and that irritation only encourages me.

The light is just creeping out from behind the volcano as we take our seats, but I'm already starting to shiver in the early morning air. My soaking wet sports bra is now pressed to my skin, growing icier by the moment. If there were no witnesses, I'd just remove it. Instead, I wrap my arms around myself. He glances over and frowns.

"Why do you never bring sufficient clothing?" he asks. "You were cold the other night too."

My eyes roll. I should have known that even the viewing of a sunrise would involve a little criticism. "Was I supposed to run carrying a sweater and change of clothes?"

He unfolds himself from the chair, lean and graceful for his size. I'm not sure how he's in such good shape, living where he does. I doubt there's a SoulCycle. "You could have left a sweatshirt at the front desk," he gripes. "Hang on."

Once he's gone, I slide my wet bra off underneath my shirt —a complicated maneuver, and one for which I feel not enough credit is given—but he returns just as I'm pulling it through the top of my tank.

His gaze flickers below my neck before it comes back up.

"I was cold," I argue.

His gaze drops to my chest and jerks away nearly as fast. "Yes. I noticed."

"Maybe you should look at my breasts a little less."

He blows out a breath, staring at Diamond Head. "Asking a man not to look at your breasts is like asking him not to watch volcanoes explode. The human race would die off if we were capable of ignoring that kind of thing."

The feminist in me wants to tell him how wrong that statement is, but I feel a tiny fist in my core clench with the kind of desire I'd almost forgotten existed. I should be uncomfortable with the idea of Josh looking at my chest, but strangely, it's the opposite. I could create a lot of fantasies about this weird exchange if I were going to allow myself to do it. Part of it is his size—I picture feeling overwhelmed by him in bed, overcome. And part of it is just *him*, and that thing boiling inside him, just below the surface. I'd like to see what happens when the lid is removed at last.

A waitress approaches with a tray and a pile of towels. She hands Josh the towels, which he then hands to me. While I cover myself up, head to toe, like a mummy, she sets two cappuccinos on the table between us. I thank her and wrap my hands around one, savoring the warmth while he signs the check.

I'm now perfectly happy and toasty and the sun is finally breaking through the clouds to the east. "This is perfect," I say with a sigh. "Even the stupid sunrise part."

"So glad the pop princess is finally impressed. I was scared I'd disappoint you."

I grin at him. "Are you sure it's not too much happiness? Too much *American excess*? Shouldn't you suffer a little more to better serve all your starving Somalians?"

He sighs wearily. "You really hold a grudge, don't you?"

I laugh unhappily. He doesn't know the half of it.

~

THE BAILEYS ARE GOING golfing today, and then on to Pearl Harbor. The only way they could make this sound less appealing is if they were throwing a trip to church or a seminar on microfinance in the middle, so I politely bow out to get a hot stone massage and lie out by the pool.

I've just reclined in a lounge chair when my phone rings and I see Six's name, calling by video. He must finally be out of jail.

"Babe," he groans, running a hand over his handsome and deeply-in-need-of-a-shave face. "I'm so sorry."

Bringing drugs almost anywhere in Asia is a rookie error and he should have known better, but it's hard to get mad at him when he's just spent over a day in jail, is missing the trip, and looks so miserable. "I'll probably forgive you," I reply, pushing my sunglasses on top of my head. "Was it bad?"

He shrugs. "Mostly it was boring. So what am I missing?"

I turn the camera, showing him the pool with the sea behind it. "It's amazing."

"Cool. Now let me see the better view," he says. "Let me look at you."

I smile reluctantly, turning the camera back to face me.

"You're wearing an awful lot of clothes," he suggests.

I roll my eyes. "I'm only in a bikini. I'm also in public."

"Go to the room and remove it for me," he says. "I just spent a day in foreign prison. Don't I deserve a reward?"

I wait until the waiter passes before I answer. "A reward for ditching me on a trip with your *family*? No. And as I recall, we had a deal about this trip: *no sex*, remember?"

It's the one rule I made while giving in so easily otherwise. And I'm not sure if that extends to phone sex, but it seems like a slippery slope.

He shakes his head. "Lower the camera, at least. Let me see my second favorite things in the world."

"What's the first?" I reply. "I assume it's my brain."

"Of course not," he says, smirking. "Not until I figure out how to get my penis in there, anyway."

I snort laugh. That's always been the issue with Six. He's too damn charming to stay mad at, even when he's, you know, awaiting *trial*.

And this is why he's perfect for me: he's just enough fun without ever being someone I might let myself trust.

9

JOSH

January 24th

I wake the next morning on the couch, realizing I've just heard the slam of her door. She's so loud normally I can't imagine how she made it that far without waking me. There's always a thud or a squeak or a muted *Oh, fuck* from her room if she's up, which I find both amusing and irritating. I dress and brush my teeth, planning to catch up with her on the road, which isn't exactly difficult. She's ridiculously slow.

I get downstairs and find, to my surprise, that she's still here, stretching against a pillar near the lobby.

"Were you *waiting* for me?" I ask.

She jumps in shock and I place a palm on her bicep to steady her.

"Of course I wasn't waiting," she sniffs. She turns back to the pillar and continues to stretch. "Sometimes I like to warm up."

She's full of shit. She was totally waiting for me. I hate that I'm pleased by that. I'm doing this out of duty and nothing more, and she's putting up with it because I won't give her another option. It's not as if we are going to be *friends* when this trip is over.

We run the same route as before, down past the shops and the park and on toward Diamond Head. I know she ran farther and faster the first day just to spite me, but she's got to be the only female I know who would just *keep* doing it, day after day.

When we're done, we go to the chairs by the pool again. I have no idea why she's coming along, but hopefully she can refrain from discussing sex robots, which I'd never heard of and now can't stop picturing.

I get her warm towels because she's incapable of remembering to bring a sweatshirt, and soon she's wrapped up, sipping a cappuccino and watching the sunrise beside me.

"Do you think anyone lives up there?" she asks, nodding at Diamond Head. "There's probably palms, a pineapple tree. You could build yourself some kind of hut, live off fruit."

I glance over at her. "Why you'd want to is the bigger question."

She frowns before she turns back to stare at the mountain. "It would just be nice to have no one talking about you," she says. "I get tired of having to be nice all the time."

"*All* the time?" I ask. "Is that what we're going with?"

She laughs. "Almost all the time. Just not to you. Trolls don't deserve kindness."

I follow her gaze to the hills, thinking of the unhappy woman who waits in my room, the issues with my mom. "I guess I can see the appeal," I admit quietly. "Probably not a lot of Sour Patch Kids up there." I still can't believe she brought *candy* on that hike instead of water.

She makes a face at me. "Of course there are. Those hills are full of Sour Patch Trees. It's like you know nothing about Hawaiian agriculture. You'll see."

And just like that, she's included me in her imagined life,

living in the hills. I don't know if she even realized she did it, but I wish the idea appealed to me a little less than it does.

WHEN I RETURN to the room, Sloane is up and dressed.

"You were gone for a long time," she says. I can't tell if she's insinuating something or if I just feel guilty for avoiding her.

"I was worried I'd wake you if I came back too early."

She doesn't react at all, emotionless as ever. Her seeming apathy is what led me to think the fling in Somalia was meaningless, and I'm still not sure it *wasn't*. Her interest in me seems driven more by my *lack* of interest than anything else.

"Do you know when your brother's going to be here?" she asks.

In theory, he should get his passport back any day now, though the truth is you never know with Joel. It would not surprise me to discover he wasn't in Japan at all, that he'd actually been on a bender, one hotel over, the entire time. "Possibly tomorrow."

"Good," she says, and then she brushes her hands against each other, as if she's successfully solved a thorny problem.

I'm pretty sure the problem is me, and I'm pretty sure having Joel here isn't going to fix a goddamn thing.

10

DREW

I wonder how little I would actually do on this trip if I wasn't competing with someone.

My morning run? It would be three miles long at most, were it not for Josh. My breakfasts? Half their current size if I weren't trying to be as *excessively American* as possible for Sloane's benefit. And when Beth says she's arranged for us all to surf—she's rented a board for Josh, gotten an instructor for me and Sloane—the only thing that has me agreeing is Sloane saying *I think I'll pass* in that snooty way of hers.

To be honest, I can kind of understand Sloane's apprehension over this whole surfing thing. The ocean is mostly something you attempt to survive, not master, and here, where the surf break appears to be a mile from shore, it feels almost suicidal. I only want to be that far from dry land if there's a champagne-stocked yacht involved. But I hate the way Beth deflates a little when Sloane says no, and I want to feel *cooler* than Sloane, though it's hardly a competition. She's currently wearing a shin-length linen dress and heels for breakfast on *vacation*. If she has a stylist, her only instructions must be "boring" and "no, more boring than that."

At the appointed time, Josh and I wander to the beach. He's clad only in a pair of black swim trunks, still damp from the pool and clinging to his thighs. They've slipped to the top of his narrow hips, low enough to show off that perfect v of his abdomen, which I swear to God is pure muscle, not an ounce of fat anywhere to be found. He tucks the rental board under his arm and moves toward the water, leaving me to wait for the instructor, who arrives late and clearly has no fucks to give. Normally, I'd appreciate the fact that he's treating me like everyone else, but I'd prefer someone who seems at least vaguely invested in keeping me alive.

He shows me how to pop up on the board. I practice twice, he yawns and says, "Whatever, it's easy," and then we are off. Josh is now a tiny speck on the horizon, approaching other tiny specks.

"We're not going that far, right?" I whisper.

The dude, whose name is Stan, all but rolls his eyes. "Yeah, unless you've discovered a new way to surf that doesn't involve waves."

Gosh, I sure hope Stan wasn't expecting a tip.

We paddle, and paddle—requiring more upper body strength than I probably have.

If he were nicer, I'd tell him I find the ocean slightly terrifying, and that I find things that *live* in the ocean similarly terrifying—the movie about the surfer who got her arm bit off took place in Hawaii, after all. I'd also like to mention that I want to keep all my limbs, which doesn't feel like the sort of thing I should *have* to mention, but bears repeating.

A wave crashes over my head for what feels like the hundredth time, knocking the board out from under me and dumping me in the ocean. It seems as if we're making no progress, and I want to weep from the ache in my arms when Stan heaves a sigh and pinches my board between his toes. "I'll tow you," he says, not hiding how *tiresome* he finds the fact that

I cannot propel myself with ease, using only my upper body, for extended periods of time.

When he finally stops, we are really, really far from the shore, and nearly as far from Josh.

"Okay, lie flat on your board," he says. "We're gonna catch this next set."

"*We?*"

"Sure, I'm gonna surf when you do," he says. "That's why I do this job."

"What if I fall, though?" I ask.

He shrugs. "You won't. That board's like an ocean liner. But if you do, just float until I get back."

Right. Just float in the middle of the shark-infested ocean alone 'til you get back. Excellent plan, Stan.

He pushes me while shouting frantic instructions about paddling and standing. I only make it to my knees because the board is less like an ocean liner and more like a flimsy piece of plexiglass going god-knows-how-fast over rushing, uneven water. Fortunately, he's still there, though he looks a little disgruntled. "That was a perfect wave you just missed."

"I'll try to stop being so bad at surfing, then," I reply. "Surfing, something I've never done."

He is looking into the distance, not listening. "Get flat," he says. "Hurry. This is a good set."

This time I manage to get up, for all of two seconds. Stan gives me a thumbs up as he blows past me on his tiny little board, and just the act of looking at him is enough to send me right over the side.

When my head comes back up, I'm alone and there's an endless ocean on three sides of me. The shore is so distant it almost seems like a mirage and I feel panic setting in.

God. *Don't do this here*, I beg. *Do not* do this here. I take shallow sips of air and try to ignore what's happening—though after Amsterdam I should know this tactic doesn't work.

Passing out in front of thousands of people, and on camera, sucked. But not as much as passing out in the middle of the ocean.

I attempt to get my board right side up, but just as I do, a wave hits, knocking me for a loop, the board tugging dangerously on the ankle strap and flying into the air. I cover my head with my hands as I go under. What happens if it lands on me? What happens if I'm knocked unconscious? No one will even know. No one will even see me.

Don't panic, I plead. My head breaks the surface and I look around frantically—no one is nearby. I see Josh in the distance but he's not even looking my way, and another wave is coming. Stan told me to dive under them, but I can't get on the board in time. Once again, the wave hits, and this time my leash doesn't survive. When I emerge, my board is sailing away without me, heading straight for the glamorous shores I can't possibly reach on my own. My breath is coming short now, and without my inhaler, I'm going to pass out in the water and no one will have a clue.

My head goes under again and when I reemerge, I see Josh paddling toward me *fast*. I have no idea how he does it, but within seconds he's there. He jumps into the water and grabs me from behind, holding onto his board with one hand while the other arm wraps around my waist, keeping me safely above the surface.

"What happened?" he asks.

"I panicked," I weep, placing a hand on his board and trying desperately to get air into my lungs. He's the last person I want to freak out in front of, but there's no helping it. "I get asthma attacks when I panic." *Deep breath in.* "It always happens at the worst times. And now my board is gone. And..." I'm still trying to get air in and out. I squeeze my eyes shut tight trying to control the quiver in my lower lip.

"You're okay," he says, his voice low and calm in my ear.

"You're absolutely fine. If you can talk, you can get enough air. I'm gonna get you back to shore now, okay?" His certainty reassures me, even if nothing is solved yet.

With the arm he has around my waist, Josh slings me onto his board.

"Just sit up unless I tell you otherwise," he says. "If a wave's coming, I'll have you lie flat."

"But—" I begin.

He places a hand on my knee, warm and huge and reassuring. "All you have to do is sit there. Pretend you're back lounging at the pool."

"Do I have a drink?" I ask. I'm still crying, and it's so goddamned embarrassing. But he laughs.

"Yes, you have a margarita, but they forgot the salt," he says. "So you're trying to get the waitress fired."

"Of course I am," I whisper. "The salt's the best part."

He laughs again, and then he starts to swim toward shore, pulling me with him. I am still trying to suck in air, still wondering what happens if I pass out.

Stan is paddling toward us, dragging my board alongside him.

"I've got her," he tells Josh, as if I'm some tedious pet he's been assigned to watch.

"The hell you do," Josh replies, placing his hand on my back. "Give me her board."

"I told you, man, I got this."

"Give me the fucking board," Josh snaps, reaching out and snatching it from him. "And next time, don't leave someone who's never been out in her life a half mile from shore in heavy surf."

"Fuck you, man," Stan says.

"Come repeat that on shore, asshole," Josh replies.

Stan gives him the finger and paddles off, and I find myself laughing quietly, and still crying a little, as Josh climbs on the board and begins to tow me in.

"Found that amusing, did you?"

I nod. I still can't breathe but if I could, I'd have a big old laugh over Josh putting that kid in his place.

We reach the shore at last. He helps me to my feet, shoves both boards toward the sand and then bends, as if he's going to pick me up. There are people everywhere, staring at us, and I know how this will unfold if I let him do it.

"Don't," I plead. "They'll say I was drunk."

His eyes meet mine, looking at me as if he's starting to put something together.

"Okay," he says, wrapping an arm around my waist, and helping me out of the water. My legs are shaky and I'm pretty sure I'd be on my hands and knees if he wasn't holding me up. I stumble onto the sand toward the Halekulani, with him still holding onto me.

A group of teenagers walk toward us. "Don't even think about it," Josh barks at them, and I'm oddly grateful, even though this will end up as another story about what a bitch I am.

We get through the Halekulani entrance and he leads me toward the chairs where his family was sitting, though only Sloane is there now.

"Where's your inhaler?" he asks, his arm still around me.

"I'm getting better," I tell him, straightening, attempting to put distance between us. I can already feel Sloane's illogical resentment from thirty feet away. I didn't even finish high school and am known only for having a nice ass and singing barely literate songs about sex. It's not like Josh would choose me even if she wasn't around.

"Stay," he replies, holding me tighter. "And I'm getting your inhaler. Your breathing is still really shallow."

"It's upstairs in my toiletry kit."

We reach Sloane and I drop into the chair, doubtful I could have stood for a second more. "What happened?" she asks. "You haven't even been gone thirty minutes."

Josh holds out his hand for my room key and I place it in his palm. "The instructor ditched her in the middle of the water so he could *surf*," Josh says tightly. "I'll be right back."

Sloane raises her sunglasses, looking from me to Josh's departing back. She appears irritated by my inability to survive a half mile offshore alone. "Why did he have to come back *with* you?" she demands.

My tongue prods my cheek. I don't want to tell her anything, but Josh will be back in a minute with my inhaler so there's no point in lying.

"I had an asthma attack," I admit, closing my eyes. "Or a panic attack. It's hard for me to tell them apart sometimes."

She stands up and walks over to me. "Sit up," she says wearily. She reaches back and adjusts my chair so it's fully upright and at the same time flags down a waitress. "Can we get a cup of coffee, please? As fast as possible?"

"This really isn't..." I begin.

"Stow it," she says. "I noticed when you walked up that your lips were blue. I thought you were just cold. Why would you go out there without your inhaler?"

I shrug. "I didn't know if it was waterproof."

"It's not," she says. "So you get a waterproof bag. Or take a dose of albuterol before you go out."

The waitress comes with the coffee and Sloane hands it to me. "Drink," she barks.

Her bedside manner leaves something to be desired, but at least she's trying. "Thanks," I say quietly.

"Of course," she says with a sigh. It's a soft sound, full of resignation and disappointment. I can't tell if she's upset that I expected less of her, or upset that she led me to expect it. "I don't especially care for you, but I don't want you to *die*."

It would be easy to take offense, but I've been in her position before—wanting someone I can't make want me back—and it sucks. I just don't understand why she seems to believe she's competing with *me*.

Joshua returns with my inhaler, looking like he sprinted the entire way. "Jesus, you own a lot of makeup," he says, handing it to me. I take it from him, shake it, and place my lips around the mouth, feeling the rush of cool air sink through my throat and open up my lungs. I do it again and begin to relax at long last.

Josh glances at the coffee beside me. "Thank you," he tells Sloane.

She looks up at him. "Just like old times, eh?"

He laughs. "The waitresses in Dooha weren't quite so efficient."

They smile at each other like old friends, and I wonder if this incident is going to help them find their way back to each other.

I don't know why that bothers me.

11

JOSH

Thirty minutes since seeing Drew sinking beneath the ocean's surface and my stomach still remains in a tight knot.

She goes back to her room and I flag down the waitress and order a scotch. I need something to ease this strain in my chest.

I haven't been in a fist fight in at least six years, but I'm still trying to talk myself out of one with that prick from the surf shop. I know I should probably be mature about it and settle for getting him fired once Sloane's not around to overhear, but it won't be nearly as satisfying.

The scotch is delivered and I take a healthy swig of it, willing myself to calm. *Drew is fine*, I tell myself. *She promised she'd lie down.*

My eyes close as I picture it. She will shower first and barely dry off before she collapses in bed—naked, I imagine. She seems like the type. She'll let all that hair of hers soak the pillow. If I were sharing a room with her, she'd forget the pillow was wet until bedtime and then she'd beg me to trade with her. She'd look at me from under those long lashes and smile and say *Come on, please, it's not that wet*. The double entendre would be an accident, but she'd lean into it, letting the word *wet* pop off her lips like a promise. And it would totally fucking work.

Sloane looks at my drink, which is now down to ice. "Too much adrenaline?" she asks.

I set the glass on the table, wondering how bad it would look if I ordered another. "Yeah," I say, with a long exhale. "It was surprisingly stressful to be a half mile off shore with someone who can't breathe."

It was a joke, sort of, but also not a joke. Her smile is muted at best.

"So she has asthma *and* panic attacks?" Sloane asks. "Or is she just confusing one with the other?"

I don't fault her for the question. I already texted Michael, one of my best friends from med school and now a pulmonologist, to ask the same. "Apparently, people with asthma are more prone to panic attacks and one can trigger the other," I tell her.

Sloane raises her sunglasses, graces me with one of those long looks of hers, meant to convey something her words won't, not entirely. "She's messy," she says quietly.

I could argue she's being unfair. I could argue she's punching down, given that lots of people would panic in that situation, and she's clearly had it in for Drew since her first day. But I know what she's really saying: Drew is more complicated than she appears, more fragile, more damaged.

I say nothing, because I know what Sloane is really doing is giving me a warning.

And I don't want to hear why she thinks I might need one.

WHEN SLOANE finally goes up to the room, I grab my phone to pull up the video of Drew falling offstage. I haven't wanted to see it, but there's something in my head. Her saying *It always happens at the worst times.*

She's in a tiny white dress, platinum blonde ponytail swinging. With all that makeup, she looks more like a doll than the girl I know. The crowd is chanting for her to sing *Naked* and she smiles but it's forced. Even through a long-range lens, you can tell it's forced.

She isn't stumbling at first. She's just wide eyed, staring off to the side of the stage as if she's thinking of making a run for it. For a moment the camera zeroes in on her face, and there is absolute panic there, her chest rising and falling too fast.

The music starts and she misses her cue and then she takes one step out on the catwalk, and another, as if she's lost or doesn't know where she's supposed to be, before her eyes flutter closed. The microphone falls to the stage with a discordant crash and she falls right over the side.

She had a panic attack.

And she'd rather let the whole world think she was drunk than tell the truth.

12

DREW

"So what I hear you saying," Tali says once I've finished updating her about the trip, "is that Joshua rushed across the ocean to save you, lifting you into his brawny arms."

"Oh my God. Stop." I'm out of the shower after the incident in the ocean, still shaken enough that I needed to hear a friendly voice, and Tali is pretty much the only friendly voice I know of. I pull off my robe and climb into bed naked.

"And for the first time in your life," she continues, "you felt found and seen, and a piece of you, *a secret piece you hadn't even known was there*, recognized he was what you wanted all along."

Tali just published her first book last summer and is now at work on the second. She can romanticize almost anything.

"*Jesus*," I groan. "Are you just reading to me from your next book?"

"My next book is even worse," she says with a reluctant laugh. "It's so much worse, you wouldn't even believe it. Pregnancy is making me so dumb—I couldn't remember our phone number the other day and Hayes said *Well, let's hope he gets my brain and your looks*. But I want to hear more about Joshua."

I pull the towel off my head and sink back into the pillows. "I was drowning—please don't turn that into a metaphor—and he decided not to let me die, though he was obviously a little on the fence. It was in no way romantic."

Except I can still see the sheer determination on his face as he paddled toward me, and the fear in his eyes. I suppose, had Tali been watching, she'd *still* argue it was a little romantic.

"Is he good looking?"

I sigh heavily. "He's not *repulsive*."

"Oh my God. You're so full of shit. I'm looking him up. Joshua...what's their last name again?"

"I'm not telling you."

"Ha! Bailey. The baby hasn't taken every brain cell. Bailey, doctor, Somalia...oh. OH. Wow." And then she starts to laugh. "Holy shit. 'Not repulsive'? You are such a fucking liar."

I wish I could see what she sees and I'm also glad I can't. It's probably some picture of him refusing to smile, a brooding Viking with a baby in the curve of one bicep and a puppy in the other.

I snort. "Maybe it was a good picture day for him."

"This guy is a living good picture day." I hear her then laugh and say *Yes, Hayes, you're handsome too*, before she returns to the phone. "And I notice we haven't discussed Six even once. I assume he's still in prison?"

I exhale and scratch the back of my neck. "They think it'll all be settled tomorrow. And don't make him sound like a serial killer. He made a little mistake, and you've got to take the good with the bad, Tali. You put up with Hayes being British, I put up with Six smuggling weed in a guitar case."

"Sure, okay, but Hayes is also sweet, and loving, and okay-looking, which balances out the fact that he's British." I hear a shout in the background and she stifles a laugh. "What balances out Six's many, many negative qualities?"

I shrug, though she can't see me. It's as if I'm trying to

convince *myself* the answer doesn't especially matter. "He's laid back."

"He isn't laid back," she says softly. "He's *careless*. There's a difference."

"Not everyone is going to be Hayes," I reply. "But if he's not here by the time we leave for Lanai, I'll just go back to California."

"Or you could spend more time with hot Josh who doesn't get along with his girlfriend and just saved your life in a dramatic sea rescue."

"Even if Sloane's generally an asshole, I would never move in on someone else's boyfriend, nor would you," I reply. My hair has soaked the pillow. I reach over and grab one from the other side of the bed. "And besides, this is Josh, who also accused me of potentially stealing their silver, Tali."

She laughs. "You are never going to let that go, are you? Cut him some slack. Maybe Six's previous girlfriend stole the silver. Maybe there's someone online claiming you're a klepto."

Except, even if there's some outlandish reason he was such a dick last summer, he'll still be Six's *brother* who lives in *Somalia*. Clinging to my dislike, at this point, seems...prudent.

THAT NIGHT, at Six's suggestion, we have dinner "together" though we aren't even on the same continent.

We convene at nine PM my time, four PM his, me in my room while he sits at the hotel bar with his phone propped up on the center of the table.

I'm yawning even as the conversation starts. "Sorry," I tell him. "I've been waking up in the middle of the night and I can't fall back asleep after."

He grins, raising his empty glass to someone I can't see. "As long as you don't wake me up once I get there. You know how pissed I get when my beauty sleep is interrupted, and apparently Sloane is cranky enough for all of us."

"They don't seem all that thrilled to see each other again," I venture.

He shoves a piece of salmon in his mouth. "Probably because long-distance relationships never work," he says.

That statement sits poorly, given that it's in the nature of our jobs to be apart more often than not. "You seem to be forgetting," I reply with a disgruntled laugh, "that you invited me on this trip because you wanted long-distance with *me*."

"It's totally different," he argues. "Under normal circumstances, Josh only gets to leave once a year. How the hell do you even make *once a year* work? He was only home last summer because they were all forced to evacuate."

I set my drink down. "Evacuate?"

"Some explosion at the camp," he says, already bored by the topic. "A lot of the staff didn't return but Saint Joshua, of course, *had* to go back."

There's a weird twist in my stomach. I knew Josh's work wasn't glamorous, wasn't the height of luxury, but I didn't think it was a place where things *explode*. "So...it's dangerous there? He could get hurt?"

He groans loudly, taking a drink from the waitress and chugging half of it in one go. "Please, Drew, do not join the Joshua Bailey fan club with everyone else. He's totally safe, and I really need just one person in my life who isn't taking his side, okay?"

"I'm not taking anyone's *side*," I reply. "You make it sound like there's a battle going on and you're not even here."

"Exactly," he replies. "I'm not there. And you know what my mother wants to talk about? Poor Joshua and Sloane, and how she wishes they were getting along, while my dad basically just reams me out and then tells me how glad he is *Josh* turned out well. I'm the one who just toured the world and is about to play at South by Southwest, but shit's the same way it's always been: nothing I could ever do will equal what Josh does."

I know what it's like to be the kid who isn't as good, who can't quite win a parent's heart no matter what you do. Scrambling for my mother's approval and failing is such a constant in my life I almost can't imagine there's another way.

I tap my finger to the screen as if I'm touching his face. "Your parents love you," I tell him. "And I'm sure they're proud of you. Maybe it's just that your dad and Josh are both doctors, so they have something in common."

For a moment, Six's eyes are so bleak it breaks my heart. For all his bluster, I've seen this lost boy in him—the one who wishes his father cared—more than once. "He doesn't even try with me, though."

Until his father comes around, nothing is enough for him. And trying to prove yourself to someone who's written you off is like trying to prove an algebraic equation using geometry—it's never going to work no matter how much effort you expend.

I want to solve it, for both of us. But I also wonder if he doesn't need someone a little more complete, a little less damaged, to fix it. I wonder if I don't need that too.

13

JOSH

January 25th

"I like running here," Drew says the next morning, once she's done gasping for breath outside the hotel entrance. The gasping no longer amuses me, now that I know about the asthma. Slowly, she stands up and we walk, side by side, toward the pool. "I'm gonna miss it when we leave."

I like it too. These early mornings with her, which I resented so much at first, are now my favorite part of the trip. And honestly, after experiencing dinner without her last night, I'm wondering just how unbearable this entire vacation would be if she hadn't come.

We all felt the difference. Without her, my mother's attempts to remain buoyant never quite succeeded. The strain between Sloane and me was palpable, as was the strain between my dad and me, and I'm not sure what's worse—my mother's endless attempts to pretend things are fine, or my father's failure to pretend anything at all.

"You can still run on the other islands," I reply as we take our seats by the pool. "I don't think there are laws against it."

She kicks my leg. "Yes, I'm aware that no one has outlawed running on the other islands. I just meant I like the scenery here. I like seeing the moon over the water, the palm trees, the surfers heading out to certain death."

I laugh and rise from the chair to find a waitress for the towels and cappuccino Drew will need any moment now. I wish to God she'd stop taking off her bra when I walk away, however, because even with it *on*, I can see way more of her anatomy than is good for me—the soft curve of her breasts, tight nipples reacting to the cold. I picture leaning over, tugging on one through the fabric, before I can stop myself.

This has to stop. I honestly don't know who the fuck I am around her at times. I think about amputations all the way to the towel bin, trying to rein myself in.

When I return, the bra is off and if I look, there won't be enough gruesome amputations in the world to keep my dick in place. I focus on her face instead, noting the tiniest scar on the bridge of her nose. "How'd you get that?" I ask, tapping my own nose. I'm only mildly curious about the answer until I discover she doesn't plan to provide it.

"Cage match," she says. Her smile is wide, as fake as her hair color. It's as if she's pulling a curtain shut before my eyes. "I won."

Messy, I hear Sloane saying, but I suspect the messy part is *me*. Every time Drew closes herself off to me, I just want to pry further, to dig past all her secrets until I get to the small piece at the center of her that's never been hurt.

"This view will be impossible to beat," she says, changing the topic and looking out toward Diamond Head, its edges now a bright, brilliant orange.

"The other islands might be even better," I tell her. "You never know."

"Listen to you, being all optimistic," she says, accepting a cappuccino from the waitress with a grateful smile. "Maybe there's a bit of your mother in you after all."

My eyes fall closed. "I hope there's more than a bit."

"You and your dad seem to get along," she argues. "Like, every time we're together it's only you he's talking to."

Yes. Talking to me about reimbursement, billing, how irritating it is that people can't pay his cost out-of-pocket. And his business practices aren't even close to my biggest issue with him.

"If it weren't for my mother," I reply, in a moment of unprecedented honesty, "I'd probably never speak to my dad again. Instead, I just moved halfway across the world to prove I would never be like him."

Her teeth tug at her lip. "Haven't you proven it yet?" she asks. "Couldn't you...come home now?"

There's something tentative in her voice, something simultaneously hopeful and worried. I like it, and know I need to crush it at the same time. "That's a very far way off," I tell her. "The camp I run had some issues last summer. We're so severely understaffed, I can't imagine a time when we *won't* be."

I'm crushing that hope for both of us. Because there's a piece of me that wishes I could finally say *Yes, I'm going to come home soon*, and I need to remember how impossible it is. My father got into medicine to make a lot of money and the patients were secondary at best. I want to be a different kind of doctor, a different kind of *man*, and abandoning thousands of helpless people would be the opposite of that.

When the sun is fully out and our cappuccinos are gone, we rise and begin walking toward our wing of the hotel. Her gaze flickers to the white dress in the store window the way it always does.

"I don't know if I'm coming with you guys to Lanai," she

says, just as we step onto the elevator. "If Six doesn't make it, I can't keep being the fifth wheel on your family vacation."

My stomach tightens. She's misunderstood something vital about this trip, about our family dynamic right now. Mostly, I think I just don't want her to go.

The elevator arrives at our floor and we walk down the hall together. She opens her door.

"Hey, Drew?" I say. She looks over at me. "Just so you know, you're not the fifth wheel, right now. You're the glue."

I open the door and slip quietly into my room, feeling as if I said too much. Because I'm not sure if she's really holding *all* of us together, or just me.

14

DREW

Once upon a time I thought fame would insulate me from criticism. I thought it would get me to a place where I no longer answered to anyone. But an all-caps text from Davis over breakfast saying CALL ME IMMEDIATELY is enough to make my stomach lock up, proving it hasn't happened.

If I weren't still floating from what Josh said to me this morning, I'd be in a raw panic. Instead, I think *You're not the fifth wheel. You're the glue.* And then I smile and continue to eat, waiting until I'm back in the room to call Davis—a bit of petty defiance I enjoy far too much.

I slide the balcony door open as I wait for him to answer. *You're not the fifth wheel. You're the glue.* It's the first time in a decade someone has suggested I'm not the source of all their problems. That I am inexplicably the thing holding people *together*. I want to bathe in those words of his. I want to tattoo them on my chest and keep them with me forever. I know it won't last, but I like what I see when I look through Josh's eyes. It almost makes me want to leave while I'm ahead, before I disappoint him.

And disappointment seems inevitable. I'm still *me*, after all.

Even Davis's breathing is angry when he answers. "The pictures of you drunk yesterday are everywhere," he seethes.

"Um...*What*?" I ask. I was prepared for any number of valid criticisms because God knows I make a lot of mistakes. This one has thrown me for a loop.

"I'm not sure how I can make it clearer," he says between his teeth. "You were *drunk*." Being accused of something I didn't do makes me feel like I'm a kid again, takes me straight back to those days when my stepbrother would accuse me of something with so much certainty I'd start to wonder if he was right. Davis and my stepbrother have a lot in common, and they're both capable of making me feel like shit even when I'm completely innocent.

"I don't know what you're talking about," I reply. "I didn't even go out last night."

"I guess it was your identical twin, then, who had to be held up getting out of the ocean yesterday," he says snidely.

My stomach drops—I should be used to people stealing every moment of mine as if it belongs to them, and I should be used to hearing the narrative twisted, but there are times, like right now, when it feels like nothing could possibly be worth it. "I was surfing and I nearly drowned, Davis. I wasn't *drunk*."

"Well, I'm in the middle of booking your apology press tour," he continues, "and you need to watch how things look. The last fucking thing I need right now is you out acting like you aren't even sorry."

"First of all, *apology* tour? To whom do I even owe an apology?"

"All the teenage fans who just watched their role model plunge off a stage? All the ticket holders in Paris and Berlin who didn't get to see you perform? All the parents who supported their teen daughters' obsession with you, only to have you wind up as the *before* picture for the Betty Ford clinic? Do I need to go on, or have I made my point?"

"I wasn't drunk, and you know it."

"I don't care what you were," Davis says. "If I'm trying to fix this for you, the least you can do, the absolute bare minimum, is not start more fires *I* will have to put out."

I stare at Diamond Head, and think once more of escape. Perhaps Davis needs a little reminder that *he's* not the one of us who's vital to the operation.

"Maybe I should just go live off the land," I tell him. "Quit while I'm ahead."

"You just made an ass of yourself in public," he replies, missing the threat or ignoring it. "I'd hardly say you're *ahead*."

I hang up and slide the screen door open only to find Josh sitting outside. He glances at me with his lips pinched tight, guilty and worried at once. "You just heard all that, didn't you?" I ask.

He shrugs. "It was hard to miss. You're extremely loud."

I sink into the chair on my side of the balcony. "Of course I am," I mutter. I'm too tired to fight on my own behalf anymore.

It's silent for a moment before he turns toward me. "Why do you let him talk to you like that?" He sounds pissed and also appalled, reminding me just how bad it must seem to someone on the outside, someone not accustomed to it.

I shield my eyes from the sun to look over at him. "Well, he's under contract, first of all. I'd have to pay out the ass to get rid of him, and he hired everyone else who works for me, so untangling it would be a mess." Saying this out loud makes my situation seem even more hopeless.

"Except you weren't drunk," he says. "When you fell. It was a panic attack, right? So why are you allowing him and everyone else to act like you're a problem?"

I hitch a shoulder in lieu of answering. I don't mind that he knows, but the whole thing is embarrassing. "I'd rather let everyone think I'm a drunk than a complete nutcase. At least drunks can be cured."

"Having panic attacks doesn't make you a nutcase," he says. "There are worse ways to cope with stress. And, by the way, I'm really curious to hear what you think the expression *live off the land* means. Because I doubt there are hot stone massages or mai tais."

"Stones are from the land and I could build a fire to heat them," I reply with a grin. "Stop killing my dream in its infancy. To clarify, though, I'm not talking some kind of *Castaway* scenario where a volleyball is my only friend, I'd rely on my money a *little*."

He raises a brow. "While living off the land. Land like...*this?* A nice hotel with room service?"

"It's on *land*, isn't it?" I ask, grinning.

He laughs, his blue eyes bright and completely free of contempt, his smile wide and almost affectionate. I wonder what he'd do if I woke him at four AM, telling him my world is falling apart. I'm not sure anyone can make it better, but I suspect he'd really do his best.

AT TEN-THIRTY, I meet the Baileys down at the valet stand to ride to Diamond Head. Jim has rented an oversized Jeep that manages to fit all of us, but that's pretty much the only part of the trip that goes according to plan.

At the convenience store, we are mobbed by teenage girls wanting autographs. Josh winds up pulling me out, barreling through the crowd like a lineman. We get to Diamond Head, which—disappointingly—is *not* a dormant volcano, but a volcanic crater, meaning there's not even a chance it will explode. And we haven't even started to head up the path before I'm posing for pics and signing things again, listening patiently while one chick lists the songs on my last album she didn't care for.

"Your face looks thinner on camera," someone else says. "Is it contour? Or are they using Photoshop?"

"Can we go?" barks Josh, stepping between us. He successfully separates me from the crowd, and shepherds me up the trail away from them before walking ahead with Sloane.

I'm in back with Beth, who's moving slowly, while Jim trails behind us, slower still, when I see a group of teens coming down the trail, and feel that too-familiar panic in my chest. At the entrance, I could still escape. But up on that trail, which is about to narrow, anything can go wrong. Sweat dots my brow, slides between my shoulder blades.

"I can't," I whisper.

I can't handle being surrounded, not being able to get away. I can't handle having a panic attack with everyone watching.

Beth stops. "What's wrong?"

"I can't deal with this," I whisper. "Finish the hike, okay? I'll be fine. I'm just going to meet you at the hotel."

And then I race back down the trail, past the entrance, and keep going until I finally find myself on some street where I don't see a single person, thank God.

I can't keep living like this, I think.

It's exactly the thought I had that night in Amsterdam, except there it felt paralyzing and right now it just seems...freeing. I pull out my phone and call my assistant's number. "Ashleigh," I tell her, "I need a haircut and color in Waikiki."

She pauses. "Have you talked to Davis?" she finally asks. "He probably has a certain look he wants for the apology tour."

The apology tour. I still can't believe they're calling it that.

"Which one of us pays you, Ashleigh?" I ask. "And who does my hair belong to?"

"You," she says sullenly. "Fine. When do you want to do it?"

"Now," I reply. "Right the fuck now."

15

JOSH

Those photos of Drew and me walking out of the water are suddenly everywhere, it would seem.

Every five minutes I'm getting a text from a buddy in med school. It's amazing just how many of my friends have made precisely the same joke, some version of *Life in Somalia looks a lot better than I realized*. My colleagues back in Somalia write to say *I see you're making the most of your time away*, or *You're never coming back, clearly, and I can't blame you*.

I could live with the ribbing. But I'm not sure I'll survive Sloane's attitude about the whole thing, because she's getting texts about it too. And even though she knows there's nothing to it—even though she was *there* for most of it—she's absolutely livid.

We arrive at Diamond Head with Sloane's considerable intellect focused entirely on the question of whether I'm *aware* of my brother's girlfriend. It seems a little unfair, as Drew currently comprises twenty percent of the people on this trip. It would be almost sociopathic for me to *not* notice, but apparently if Drew is surrounded by a crowd of jackals pulling at her clothes and her hair and commenting on her weight, I'm just supposed to ignore it. Someone can say *aren't you going to rehab* and someone else can say *I thought you'd be thinner* and I'm supposed to be sitting there on my damn phone, reading an article about the Greek debt crisis or checking out reviews of the restaurant we're eating at tonight.

I did almost nothing to extricate Drew from the situation, but Sloane was still irritated.

Look who's suddenly Sir Lancelot, she said under her breath.

So for ten minutes I have marched forward, determined to salvage a situation I didn't put myself in the first place, and when I finally stop I find my parents approaching.

Alone.

"Where's Drew?" I bark, and I know I sound far too angry and invested, but I can't help it.

My mother blinks. Just once. A tiny processing of something and discarding it. "Poor thing," she says. "She saw those crowds coming down and panicked. She said she couldn't do this."

"And you just *let her go*?" I ask.

My father raises his brow. He's a quiet man, but I know what that look means: *Watch your tone.* As if he has a leg to stand on where treatment of my mother is concerned.

"She said she was fine," my mom argues.

What am I supposed to do at this point? I've got three adults who think I'm overreacting, and maybe I am. But if it was up to me, I'd be going right down the path after her.

We finish the miserable climb—the summit is closed so there's really only one decent view to speak of—and return to the hotel.

I shower and leave for the pool, praying I find Drew there since she wasn't in her room. I'm approaching the elevator when the doors open and a woman walks off, the kind of woman who makes the whole world go silent for a half second. She's got the cheekbones of a supermodel, curves, and a body made up of at least 70% long bare legs, encased in tiny shorts.

It's only when her face lifts up from her phone and I see her eyes—the softest, most luminous brown God ever created—that I realize it's Drew.

Her hair reaches her collarbone now, and it's a darker blonde. She was beautiful before—in the way of a priceless object you'd stand in line to see. Now she's beautiful in the way of something you didn't expect to find, something you've chanced upon and know will change your life. "You cut your hair."

Her smile has a brittle, uncertain edge. "Your keen powers of observation never fail to astonish."

"It's nice," I tell her, and it seems like too much and not enough all at once. "You look...I mean...it suits you."

"Oh," she says, and she swallows as if she's about to cry. "Thank you."

It's only as she turns to walk away that I realize she expected me to say something shitty. That she was already hunching her shoulders like a boxer entering a ring, because she fully expects the world to hurt her all the fucking time.

I'd probably have panic attacks, too, if I had to live like that.

16

DREW

I stare in the mirror for a long time after I see Josh in the hall.

I barely recognize myself, yet I also look like *me* again, like the girl I once knew, the one who had plans for herself before they all got co-opted. Davis is going to have a fit. *Everyone* will have a fit. I care, but not as much as I thought.

I think about the look on Josh's face, the way he said *I like it*, and feel the oddest thing in my chest unfurling. I look in the mirror to discover I'm crying and smiling at the same time.

I'M GETTING ready to meet the Baileys to watch the sunset when Sandra calls. She is married to my stepbrother, Richard, and has a stick up her ass even larger and longer than his.

"I'm hosting a small dinner to celebrate Steven and Maria's anniversary," she tells me. She sounds fatigued, as if the words are being dragged from her unwillingly. "Can you be in New York the weekend of February 18th?"

I want to say no, because I don't want to celebrate their

fucking anniversary and because every visit with my family winds up hurting. But every visit also offers a chance at redemption. The childish part of me thinks *Maybe this will be the time they're okay with me, when I'm not the brunt of the joke, not the part of the family they look on with distaste.* And it never works, which is probably why it always hurts in the end.

"I'll have to check with my team, but I'll try."

"Great," she says, though her tone implies the opposite. "I'd really appreciate it if you'd try to stay sober this time."

Her words flip a switch inside me, one I'm always about to flip when dealing with my family. The fury is almost instantaneous. "And *I'd* really appreciate it if you wouldn't act like a raging cunt," I reply, "but we can't always get our way."

I enjoy her shocked silence for only half a second before my stomach sinks. I took it too far, the way I always do. My family keeps a bucket labeled *terrible things Drew has done* and I've just added to it. I can't seem to stop.

"You know," she says between her teeth, in that voice she uses when her rage is glittering and lethal, "I try so hard for your family while you don't lift a finger and yet when I try to include you, this is how you behave. You push everyone away. Don't be surprised if we just stop trying, Drew."

She hangs up—to go complain to Richard, I'm sure—and I sit here with the phone, feeling ashamed and pissed off at once.

Not two seconds later, my stepbrother's text arrives. They're so unbelievably predictable.

Richard: Did you seriously just call my wife a cunt because she invited you to dinner?

Of course that's how the conversation was relayed. *I invited Drew to your parents' dinner and she called me a raging cunt.* Like that's a normal order of events—polite invitation met with profanity and nothing occurring between the two.

Me: No, I asked if she could not act like one DURING the dinner. Very different.

I laugh at my response, knowing I'm only making things worse. But honestly, how much worse could they be?

Richard: If you ever use that word with my wife again, we're done.

Me: Done with what? All those heartfelt talks we have? I can live without the humblebrag Christmas card your wife sends every year, believe me.

Richard: You know what? Don't come to the party. You'd just ruin it anyway.

I wish that it would all just end here, but it won't. Richard will complain to my stepfather, Steven, who will complain to my mother, who will call me to tell me how wrong I was. This has been the pattern since we moved into Steven's upper east side apartment when I was nine. Richard was in college at that point but would come home on weekends, seething over nothing at all—because he thought I'd looked at his phone, or drunk his Gatorade, or swiped his charge cord. And my mother always took their side. Never once did she suggest that Richard was a spoiled, petty asshole who'd gotten a far better deal than I had. Never, not once, did she say *I'm sorry I ruined our family. I'm sorry I did this to you.* But why would she? She wasn't sorry, and it was so much easier just to blame it all on me.

It still is. That's how I know she'll call, and I'm already bracing myself for how much it will hurt when she does.

17

DREW

January 26th

"Tell me something real, Drew," Josh says quietly, staring straight ahead.

The Baileys leave tomorrow for Lanai, and since Six promised last night he'd have his passport back today, I guess I'll be going with them. I'm not sure what happens to our morning runs and cappuccinos at sunrise once Six is around. Maybe it would have stopped anyway, but I doubt it. Josh and I have both adjusted to the time change and yet here we are, after all.

I turn to look at him, at that perfect, sharp jawline, that luscious lower lip. *God, he could really have anyone he wanted.*

"Something real...The sky is blue?" I reply. "This sunrise is okay? I'm not sure what you're looking for from me here."

"Tell me something no one else knows," he says. "You could tell me how you got that scar on your nose, for instance."

I nod. "There was this hurricane, and sharks were whipped up into the air, so suddenly it's *raining* sharks and..."

His smile is soft. "Fine, you choose the thing." And then he looks at me in a way that makes it impossible to lie and evade, difficult to breathe. I reflexively reach toward my pocket to make sure my inhaler is still there. It's as if, in this moment, he's capable of peering beyond my skin, past corneas and what everyone else sees, and finding my soul.

"I hate *Naked*," I tell him. He raises a brow, forcing me to remember that Josh is a robot and probably only listens to classical music, and only then because he's heard it's associated with improved limbic activity or similar boring bullshit. "It's my best known song. I—"

He laughs. A real laugh. "I've heard your song. You don't need to explain it to me. Sometimes it's like you think I live in a cave."

"Morgue," I correct. "Or robot storage facility. So anyway, there's my thing no one else knows, my deep dark secret. I fucking hate that song. I didn't want it on the first album, but I let it go because I didn't want to piss off the label, and it turns out they were right and I was wrong. So maybe I don't know anything. I have to sing it at the encore and every time it's a little harder."

And occasionally I have to sing it and I have a panic attack instead.

"If it's any consolation," he offers, "I hate that song too."

I laugh. "God, you're such a dick. Now you tell me something. Something no one else knows."

His mouth quirks up. "I'm a robot, remember? It's all on the surface."

I suspect that none of it, not a single thing, is on the surface. I'd like to pry his brain open and look at the contents if it wasn't going to be one hundred percent fatal. "Fine, see if I tell you anything from now on."

He's silent for a moment. He takes a sip of his cappuccino, swallows, and turns to me. "I didn't want to come on this trip. In fact, a part of me didn't want to come home at all."

"Why?"

He tugs his lush lower lip between his teeth. "It's hard for me to be around my father...he doesn't treat my mother the way he should."

I glance at him, waiting for more, but it doesn't come. I assume Jim is cheating, and it's easy enough to believe, probably because there's something restless in him that reminds me a bit of his son—not Josh but the one I'm ostensibly here to reunite with.

"Just being home is hard too," he says instead. "It's hard seeing how much better life is for everyone. All the stuff..." He waves his hands.

"The *American excess*?" I ask, mocking Sloane's disdainful tone.

He laughs. "Jesus, you can hold a grudge. But yes, the excess. Not just America, but everywhere. All the food and the services and the stores and the money everywhere you look, and how oblivious people are to it. But then it stops being so shocking after a few days. And I get *used* to the food and good internet and having five hundred channels and a soft bed. I get used to life being so easy. And that's right around the time I have to go back and get used to not having it."

I sigh. "I'm sorry. Why haven't you told your mom?"

His head turns, resting against the back of the chaise lounge to face me. His lips curve into a wistful smile. "Because she's my mom. She wants to make me happy. She wants to baby me. I can't take that away from her."

Then don't go back, I think. *Let someone else go.* But I don't say it aloud, because it would sound like the plea of someone who cares and I really don't. I'll have forgotten all about Josh in a week.

Our cappuccinos are gone, the warmth has seeped out of the towels, the sun is full in the sky, and the first guests have started to filter downstairs toward the buffet, but neither of us move to go anywhere. My eyes close and I don't realize I'm humming until Josh asks what it is.

I shrug. "I don't know. Just a song I'm working out in my head."

"I didn't realize you wrote your own stuff."

"I don't," I reply. "Well, I don't record it. I started off wanting to go in a different direction, but then I discovered that it's more fun to be able to eat and pay rent."

"I like it," he says. "Better than *Naked*, even, symphonic masterpiece that it is."

I laugh, unwillingly. Maybe I won't have forgotten him in a week, after all.

We turn to walk back to the elevators. My eyes drift to the displays, to the white dress, and Josh elbows me.

"You stare at that every morning," he says softly. There's a sweetness to his voice. "Why don't you get it?"

I didn't entirely realize I'd been staring at the dress, which is long and loose and has delicate little ties at the shoulders to hold it up, and I guess I *do* like it, but I shake my head. It's way too innocent for me. Too virginal, too girlish. I'd feel like I was playing a part. *Here I am dressed as a girl Josh would date. I have a medical degree but I'm not a shrew like Sloane. I'll probably quit my practice to give birth to all his children sometime soon. I would never call my sister-in-law a raging cunt.*

I guess I've thought about this dress more than I realized.

"It's just not me," I tell him. "I'd feel silly."

His teeth sink into his lip. "It looks like you to me."

I smile at him and my heart gives a weird little kick when he smiles back. Josh sometimes makes me feel like I still have the ability to change everything.

I am strangely ebullient, practically floating, as I enter my room—where a pile of luggage and two guitars sit in the middle of the floor.

"Surprise!" says Six, crossing the room and pulling me into his heavily-tattooed arms.

"Wow," I say. "You're here!" Somehow I can't quite inject enough volume, enough joy, into my voice.

He pulls back, holding my face in his hands, observing me. "Babe, what the fuck did you do to your hair?" he asks.

And I fall from that cloud I was on and land right back on earth with a sharp, unpleasant *splat*.

"Come here," he says, lying across the bed and holding out his arms. I've always liked how easy it is for Six to be affectionate, but now I think it's simply that it's so meaningless for him. I feel awkward as I slide onto the bed and put my head on his chest.

His lips press to my forehead and then he pulls back just enough to seek my mouth. "I've missed you," he says. "I'm so glad you stayed."

He kisses me and then rolls me onto my back, using a knee to push one of my thighs out of the way. There was a time when I'd have gone along with it, but today it feels as if my limbs have turned to metal, as if there's a cage encircling my chest. *I don't want this*. The moment I think it, I panic a little, as if it's already gone too far. "Six," I say, pushing against his chest. "Stop."

His laughter is silent, a huff of air against my neck. "Babe, come on. Is this about the stupid rule?"

No, but also...it's not *not* about the rule. I mean, he agreed *willingly* when he was trying to get me on this trip. I told him I wasn't coming along as his fuck buddy. "You agreed," I say, trying to push him off me. He's impossibly heavy and doesn't budge. "Are you already reneging the minute you get here?"

He gives an exasperated exhale and rolls off me. "It's five days into the trip," he argues, "and you said we'd see how it went."

"You haven't been here," I reply stiffly, climbing from the

bed. "Three FaceTime calls aren't what I meant when I said we'd spend time together and reassess."

He climbs off the bed. "Fine," he says a little sullenly. "Whatever. We'll spend time together."

He's only been here a few minutes and I'm starting to wish he hadn't come.

~

THE ENTIRE FAMILY takes a pool day at last. Beth is so thrilled to see Six she can hardly remain in her seat. She keeps tearing up and saying *I'm so happy you made it*, as if this is the only vacation they've ever had together. But every time Josh looks at his brother I see signs of strain, and Sloane—watching it happen—is just as unhappy. I still don't understand what Josh meant the other day about me being the glue, but it's clear Six isn't. If the Bailey family was spinning out a little, Six's arrival has only increased the speed of it.

Once the excitement diminishes, Jim goes back to talking exclusively to Josh, and Beth's conversation with Six takes on a frenzied quality, as if she's trying to distract a toddler from crying for a lost toy and knows she can't quite succeed.

Josh finally gets up and goes to the pool alone. I suspect it's simply to get a break from his father. I'm still watching as he climbs the ladder to get back out, sun glinting off those nice broad shoulders, dripping over his perfectly flat stomach. His swim trunks are hanging low and I find myself riveted by that trail of hair below his belly button, by the pale skin beneath his tan line and the hint of a tattoo just to the left of his hip. I picture dragging the trunks slightly lower to get a better view and suddenly I have goosebumps in eighty-degree weather.

Lunch is ordered and just as we're finishing up my mother calls. I'm not entirely surprised—this is the pattern, after all.

I've upset Richard and he had to run and tell on me as fast as he could.

I walk over to lean against the railing by the sea wall, because I don't need the Baileys overhearing that even the woman who brought me into the world thinks I'm a useless screw-up.

She bypasses the whole *Hey, how's it going?* part of the conversation entirely. "Did you really call Sandra the c-word?" she demands.

"Cancer?" I ask, squeezing tightly to the rail as a family passes by. They don't even look at me twice. I wonder how long my anonymity will last.

"You know which word I'm referring to."

"Yes, we both know," I answer dryly, "because only one *c word* fits."

My mother gives a heavy sigh. That sigh of hers is so familiar to me that I hear it in my sleep. I heard it in my head when I regained consciousness in Amsterdam. When I die, I won't hear anyone grieving, I'll just hear my mother's long-suffering sigh, as if my death is simply one more thing I've done wrong.

"Maybe your merry band of misfits throws that word around without a care, but normal people don't. You lash out at people and just assume all will be forgiven, Drew, but it adds up. Eventually people are going to stop letting things go."

I slump into the same chair I sat in this morning with Josh, watching the sun come up. "Yeah, I've noticed how you all let things go. Which is probably why Sandra asked me to *stay sober for this one*, as if I've shown up rolling at every other family event we've ever had. And I *don't* assume all will be forgiven. I just don't give a shit."

It's not the first time I've said something like this to her. There's a part of me that wishes she'd just call the time of death on our entire relationship. Block my number, cut me off, stop trying. It seems easier. Less painful.

"I cannot talk to you when you're like this. But let me just explain this one thing to you: you're in a downward spiral. It's obvious to everyone but you. And when your career ends, we're all you'll have to fall back on so you might want to be very careful about who you push away."

I hang up the phone, my heart aching, my head full of all the same vengeful thoughts I've had for years: *I'll show them. This album will be so big they'll eat every word they've ever said and they'll never open their fucking mouths again.*

Except...except...there is no album. I hate every demo the label has sent, and even if I liked them, they still wouldn't be *mine.* They wouldn't be my words, my heart. They wouldn't even be my taste in music.

My stepfather, Steven, texts not even a full minute after the call with my mother has ended.

I spoke to your mother. She said you claimed you "don't give a shit" about the family. I'm not sure who told you it was okay to speak to a parent that way, but I'm here to tell you it's not.

I type my reply: **I don't know who told you it's okay to fuck someone else's wife, but that's not great either.**

I laugh. Josh says I'm good at holding a grudge. He has no idea.

A chair scrapes the cement of the pool deck as it's pulled up beside mine. I look over to find Six there. "I feel like getting drunk," he says. "My family is on my last nerve."

At last, we are in the same place and on the same page.

THE COOL AND also tedious thing about Six is that he always *knows* people. Drop him in the middle of the Amazon, and he'll have some friend there who knows about a party somewhere else, and even though it means wading through a mile of piranha-infested water and getting in a truck driven by a human trafficker, you're going to that party.

So *of course* he knows of a party here, and *of course* it's clear on the other side of the island where some huge surf competition is occurring.

After a very expensive Uber ride that goes on way longer than I expected, we arrive at an oceanfront house that looks out over the Banzai Pipeline.

"You better text your mom and let her know we might not make dinner," I tell him. "They had reservations for seven but it's going to take us an hour to get back."

He swats my ass. "We are definitely not going to that lame fucking dinner. I'll let her know."

The house is full and the deck is too. It's a music crowd here and I suppose if I ever wanted a shot at morphing into a real musician, the kind I *wanted* to be, it would make sense for me to talk to these people, but I suspect none of them would take me seriously.

I get a drink and fight my way out to the deck to watch the competition. It's a single huge wave, curling and unfurling, and the surfers look like ants as they rise up inside it. My heart pounds in terror simply watching them, and that seems like a reasonable response. Until today, I've never been to a beach so dangerous that signs warn anyone who isn't an experienced surfer not to even *approach* the shore.

I'm leaning on the deck railing watching the competition when a guy walks up beside me and introduces himself. He's apparently the drummer for a band called The Sweat Monkeys, of whom I've never heard. "I'm pretty sure we're getting a spot at Coachella next year," he says with feigned ambivalence. He looks over to make sure I'm suitably impressed. I do my best.

"That's awesome," I reply. He has no idea who I am, clearly, but it's fun to be anonymous again, to go back to being some random hot girl an unknown drummer is trying to impress.

"I can get you backstage, you know, if we get the spot," he says.

I headlined there last year, but I simply bite down on my smile. "That would be really cool."

I tell him I'm getting another drink, but instead I just wander down to the dunes where the hardcore competition viewers sit with binoculars.

And one of them is Juliet Cantrell.

It's rare for me to be starstruck these days, but with her, I am. She has the career I wish I had—the one I should have held out for. She writes her own stuff, she chooses her own producer. No one makes her take cocaine before a show to perk her up. No one books her into rehab without asking her first.

She's watching the competition, focused on it. I should probably leave her alone but I find myself creeping closer until suddenly, I'm right there and she's blinking up at me, shielding the sun with her hand.

I give a small wave. "Hey, I'm Drew."

She peers up at me and then her eyes go wide. "Holy shit. Drew *Wilson*? I didn't even recognize you. I'm Juliet."

I laugh. "I know—you have my dream career."

She raises a brow at that. "Hold on to the career you have. I guarantee your bank statement's a lot more interesting than mine."

I glance at the spot in the sand beside her and she scoots over to make some room for me.

"You're chilling in Hawaii on a Wednesday afternoon," I reply, sitting cross-legged. "You can't be doing all bad."

She laughs. "Fair enough."

She picks up a pair of binoculars and peers into them before handing them to me.

"It's terrifying," I say more to myself than her. They're so tiny compared to the water. It looks as if they'll all come crashing down when the wave breaks, but somehow no one does.

"It is," she says with a sigh, biting her lip. Her worry isn't like mine. It's not general and vague, it's specific.

"You're here to see someone, huh?" I ask.

She gives me a wary look and doesn't answer for a moment. "Yeah, but he doesn't know." She sighs. "That sounds stalker-y. It's just someone I grew up with."

"Don't you think he'd want to know you're here?"

Her eyes fall closed, as if even the question is painful. "He definitely would *not* want to know," she replies.

"I guess that's why your songs are so angsty," I say, and she laughs.

"I'm curious," she says after a moment. "What is it about my career you envy? You make more money and you're way more famous."

I think for a second before I answer. I would *like* to be less famous, but that's not why I want it. "I'd rather be well known for singing my own shit than famous for singing someone else's," I finally reply. "I don't even get to play guitar now except as a stunt."

She raises a brow. "You must have enough money at this point to do whatever you want."

My shoulders sag. It sounds so easy falling from her lips. But I know it wouldn't be. "It's hard to extricate yourself. Even if I could get out of my management deal and my recording contract, I wouldn't know where to start."

She looks like she wants to argue but then shrugs. "If you change your mind, give me a call. I might know people who can help you out."

A shadow falls over us then and I look up to see Six there. "Hey, Juliet," he says, reaching down his hand to me. "Babe, we've got places to be. I've got a friend holding a luau back in Honolulu."

There was a time when I'd have gone anywhere with him, when I'd have dropped anything to see him. Now, I find myself tempted, as I take his hand, to tell him to go alone.

~

IT'S late and I'm drunk.

Dusk had barely fallen when I started telling Six I was ready to go back to the hotel and suggesting we might be able to meet his family for dinner after all. But it's hours later and we are still drinking. I've lost count of how many stops we've made along the way—there were bars, there was shopping, there was even some family's pig roast on the beach. Now we're in a club, and the flashing lights hurt my head and I'm so tired I can barely manage the words *Let's go* for the hundredth time, yet here Six is, still buying everyone shots.

"I'm sleepy," I tell him.

"Barkeep!" he shouts. "I need a Red Bull and vodka for my pretty friend here."

The mere thought of it makes my stomach turn. "Gonna go to the bathroom," I slur.

He hands me a shot. "Take one for the road. I've got plans for you later."

I've heard him say that before. I'm too drunk to remind him that isn't the deal, too exhausted to explain that I care about him but I'm not sure this is working, that I worry I'm getting his mother's hopes up about something that will never happen.

Or maybe I should stick it out. He hasn't even been here a full day and I did say I'd give him a chance. And tonight was fun, until it wasn't. *At least he wants me around some of the time*, I think. *It's more than I can say for my family.*

I leave the bathroom but my stomach starts to swim so I

push through an exit for fresh air, standing with my head pressed to the wall, taking shallow breaths.

When I'm finally okay, I turn to go back inside only to discover Six has my ID.

The doorman won't budge, even when I tell him I was just inside and that my boyfriend has it. "Then your boyfriend can bring it to you," he says. "No ID, no entry."

As much as I love not being recognized, it had its benefits.

I pull out my phone and attempt to call Six, and when that fails, I text him. There's no answer, of course. He'll see it eventually.

I sink onto the nearest bench and scroll on my phone, opening a text from an unknown number which I'm strangely thrilled to discover is from Josh. *I have his number now*, I think. It feels like a gift, one I'm likely to abuse.

Are you guys okay? You missed dinner and my mom is worried. Please reply if you see this.

Fucking Six. He said he'd call them. I *told* him to call them. I wish I'd never come out tonight. I'd honestly have had more fun with Beth and Jim, even with Josh and Sloane. Okay, maybe not "fun" but if I'd just stayed, I wouldn't have spent the past hours begging to go to bed, and I wouldn't feel like I'm about to throw up.

Sorry, I reply. It's all I can manage at the moment.

Suddenly the phone in my hand starts ringing. That same unknown number. Josh's number.

"Hey," I whisper. I wish we were sitting by the pool watching the sun come up. I wish he was sitting on this bench beside me.

"Where are you guys?" he asks. He sounds worried, not mad. I don't know why that makes me want to cry.

"I'm stuck outside this club," I tell him. "Six has my ID and they won't let me back in."

"And you're sitting outside on the *street*?" he asks. *Now* he sounds mad, but it's just because he has some weird belief that I'm fragile. I spent the three years after I dropped out of school sleeping on people's floors or at the train station. Sitting outside in Waikiki is *child's play* compared to life back then.

"I texted him," I say, closing my eyes. "It's fine. He'll get me in a second or I'll Uber back."

"Are you drunk?" he asks. I hear a zipper and wonder if he's undressing. For a moment, I picture him pulling off his shorts and it has the well-worn quality of something I've pictured before. I see abs like artwork, that fine trail of hair leading to boxer briefs.

Jesus, Drew, I can't believe you noticed his happy trail with that level of specificity. "Bad Drew," I say aloud.

"I don't know if that's a yes or no," he says.

I blink. "To what?"

"Never mind. Your inability to string words together answers my question. Where are you?"

He sounds slightly breathless, distracted. I wonder if he's asking me all this while he's getting busy with Sloane. That is not an appealing thought. "I can't really picture Sloane having sex," I tell him. She seems like she'd demand all surfaces be wiped down with bleach or ammonia before commencing, perhaps run a few quick labs to make sure they're both disease-free.

"Drew," he repeats, sterner now. "Where the fuck are you?"

I lean forward to look at the well-lit sign above me, and nearly fall off the bench in doing so. "The Tik Hut." I look again and realize one of the 'i's isn't lighting up. "Tiki Hut. I just want a glass of water. They won't even let me get a glass of water. This is America. I should be able to get water."

He's preoccupied, talking to someone. I sit, listening to the sounds he makes—his deep voice, a car door shutting, the seatbelt warning. I bet wherever he is the air isn't quite so muggy. I bet there's a bottle of water. I bet if I'd come here with him, he'd have been worried when I didn't return. He'd have looked for me.

"So tell me what happened," he says gently.

"Happened with what?" I ask. I'm going to be too hungover to run tomorrow. And it might be our last chance.

"Focus, Drew," he says. "What happened tonight? Why did you guys blow off dinner? I'd expect it of Joel, but not you."

"Because I called my sister-in-law a cunt," I whisper.

To my surprise, he laughs. "You did *what?*"

"I called my sister-in-law a cunt. But she is one. She's *such* a cunt, Josh, you would not believe."

He laughs again. "So you decided to blow off my parents and go on a wild drinking spree because you used the word *cunt*? No offense, but I pictured you as someone who'd say that word fairly regularly, and with ease."

A group of guys slow as they walk past and I put my head down. "I didn't call her a cunt, actually, I asked her not to act like a *raging* cunt, so I didn't call her a thing. It was just a simple *request*. And then..."

My eyes fill with tears. Goddamn shots. They're the only explanation for why I'm on the verge of crying right now for at least the third time.

"And then..." he prompts.

I want to say it all. I want to say that my stepbrother told me I'd ruin the party, that my mother said my career was ending and I was going to need them, that even my asshole stepfather who destroyed my family thinks he gets to chime in. I want to say all of it and hear a single person agree with me, but the truth is that when everyone is telling you you're a piece of shit... you're probably a piece of shit. I'm silent for so long he has to prompt me again.

"My family kind of piled on," I whisper.

"Get in the car," he replies.

I look up to see the Jeep the Baileys rented directly in front of me. He came here to get me. And the zipper was the sound of him dressing because he was already in bed, and he *still* came here.

I don't know why that makes my throat swell. I cross to the passenger side of the Jeep. "You didn't have to do this."

He hands me a bottle of water and then leans over to buckle me in. "Yeah, I did. Has anyone ever suggested that you are alarmingly unconcerned with your own welfare? It's late. Anything could have happened to you out here."

"No one even recognizes me now that I've cut my hair."

He sighs. "I wasn't talking about the fact that you're famous, Drew. I was talking about the fact that you're pretty."

I laugh. "Oh. MY. God. *You* actually paid me a compliment?"

He rolls his eyes. "Shut up. And no. I didn't pay you a compliment. I didn't say anything you haven't been hearing since the day you were born. That's not a compliment. It's just, like, a line item on a list of assets."

"You paid me a compliment."

He laughs. "Whatever."

The breeze whips through the Jeep and I lean my head back and look up at the sky, slamming the water. It's ice cold. *Josh is kind of a keeper*, I think. I consider telling him, but even *I'm* not drunk enough to think that's a good idea.

That he came to get me, though, feels like the first embers of sunlight coming out behind Diamond Head, warming a cold gray sky. I hope tomorrow I manage to hold onto this feeling, that I remember what it's like when someone actually cares. And then I hope I get on a plane and get my ass back home, because I know this situation can't lead anywhere good. Josh isn't mine, and even if I wasn't with his brother, and he wasn't with Sloane, he's too smart and too good to ever fall for someone as damaged as me.

18

JOSH

I can't believe my brother hasn't fucking *noticed* she's not with him. I can't believe she puts up with a man who doesn't notice that much. Is there any polite way to tell your brother's girlfriend she can do so much better? To ask what the hell she's thinking?

"My dad had a Jeep," she says. Her eyes are closed. "It was such a piece of shit, and so old, but I loved it."

She's never, not once, mentioned her father. I feel like she's finally letting me peer behind the curtain and I don't want her to pull it closed again.

"Yeah?" I ask. I take a left when I should turn right. I don't want to get back to the hotel too soon.

"We'd go for a drive, and he'd sing these stupid songs and I'd hold the six pack. My job was to open a new one for him just as he emptied the one he had in his hand, and then we'd split the last one."

My stomach sinks. I thought I'd get some cute childhood anecdote. A tiny pigtailed Drew being driven to soccer practice or going to McDonald's. "You'd split it? How old were you?"

She shrugs. "Nine? Ten?"

I glance at her and take an extra turn. "Drew, that's...kind of terrible."

She shakes her head, her eyes still closed. "It isn't though. You're just seeing it as, like, a responsible adult. *Drinking bad. Spinach good.* Like that. But as a little kid it was just fun. He liked having me around and I felt...I don't know. Special. He was the only member of the family who liked me just as I was."

"You're talking about him in past tense."

"He's dead," she says with no emotion whatsoever. She could be reporting his year of birth, his eye color. "Drunk driving accident."

"I'm—"

She starts to laugh. "Oh my God, your face! I'm kidding! I mean, not about the dead part. He's extremely dead. But he wasn't drunk driving."

I wait another minute just to make sure this isn't a joke too. "Drew, I'm so sorry. I had no idea."

She hitches a shoulder, leaning back to close her eyes again. "It was a long time ago."

I turn toward the Halekulani at last, feeling slightly ill and thinking about Sloane's quiet warning the other day—*She's messy*—and knowing there was some merit to it. Reaching beneath the surface with Drew is like reaching blindly into broken glass. But the way she's so cavalier at times, the way she acts if nothing matters, it also seems like resilience, like the thing you'd do if you thought caring would destroy you. It worries me but I admire it at the same time.

I pull up to the valet and open her door. If it was up to me, I'd just carry her upstairs, but just because *I* didn't recognize her earlier today doesn't mean other people won't. I place a hand on her shoulder to wake her, leaning over to unbuckle her seatbelt.

Her long lashes slowly flutter open, and suddenly our faces are inches apart and we're way too close. My gaze dips to her mouth before I can stop myself. I imagine leaning closer, pressing my lips to hers, and for a moment there's something in her eyes saying she'd let me.

Fuck. I'm imagining taking advantage of my brother's drunk girlfriend. It's got to be a new low.

I take a step backward. "Can you walk? I can carry you, but I'm worried someone will take a picture."

"I'm *invisible* now," she says in a stage whisper. I think they probably heard her one town over.

I laugh to myself. "Yes, super invisible." I help her out of the Jeep and wrap my arm around her. She can't walk a straight line even with my help, so we cut through to the pool area, where it's dark and vacant, rather than go through the lobby.

"Are we going to swim?" she asks, giggling.

I scoop her up like a child. "No, I'm just trying to get you to the room without witnesses. Do you have your key?"

She shakes her head no, resting her head against my shoulder and then she sniffs my shirt. And sniffs again. "You always smell so fucking good," she says. There's a hint of a groan to her voice and my body reacts before I can stop it.

"I need to be bathed in boiling water," she adds.

"Man, you get weird when you're drunk," I say, but I'm smiling. "I didn't expect that about you."

"You just thought I'd be all sleazy, didn't you?" she asks. "You thought I'd be like the *Naked* video. Dancing around with only the naughty bits blurred out."

I wish she hadn't reminded me of the video. Yeah, I hate the song, but no straight male hates the video, and I don't need to be thinking about what *wasn't* blurred out when she's in my arms and my hand is inches away from her breast and she's groaning *You smell so fucking good* against my neck.

When we reach my door, I set her down gently. "I need you to be really quiet, okay? Sloane's in the bed, so I'm gonna put you on the couch."

She nods but all my caution was unnecessary—there's a light on in the bedroom. Sloane must be up and she probably knows I left, which will go over about as well as everything else I've done this week.

Drew falls onto the couch without appearing to notice the blanket and pillow already there. She curls up and kicks off her shoes and just like that, she's out cold. I get a second blanket from the closet and am pulling it over her when Sloane walks in, fully dressed.

"She smells like a distillery," she says, arms folded across her chest.

"I thought you'd be asleep."

She walks into the bedroom and I follow, feeling too tired for a fight but knowing we have to discuss it.

She's got her suitcase out and it's already packed.

"Sloane," I say, running a hand over my face. "What are you doing?"

She swallows. "I'm going home."

"It's the middle of the night," I argue. "Look, go to sleep and we'll discuss it in the morning."

"I need to get out of here," she says. "I hate what it's turning me into and I should never have come in the first place. I know that now." Her shoulders sag as if defeated and I hate that.

"I'm sorry," I tell her. "I'm so sorry this wasn't what you wanted."

She shakes her head. "Don't apologize," she says, and she forces a small smile. "I knew the deal from the beginning of the trip. You told me how you felt but I chose to ignore it."

I sink onto the edge of the bed. "You seemed so ambivalent in Somalia. I had no idea it meant anything to you."

"I know," she says. "I'm not sure I thought it meant anything myself until I got back to Atlanta. I turned it into a competition with Drew, rather than admitting to myself that coming here in the first place was a terrible idea. And competing with Drew was my second terrible idea, because that's a competition I was never going to win."

"Drew had nothing to do with this," I argue. "Obviously. She's here with my brother."

She takes her toiletry kit and shoves it in her carry-on. "Is she, though? I was hoping once your brother got here it would change, but it hasn't," she says. "She's at the center of every room for you. She's the center of every conversation. She's all you can see."

"Sloane..." I begin, running my hands through my hair. What she's saying is ridiculous. "I don't know what you think is going on between me and Drew, but you're wrong. There is absolutely nothing there."

She puts her bag on the floor and pulls it over to where I sit. And then she stops and wraps her arms around me, pressing her cool lips to my cheek. "I know you think that's true. I just hope you work it all out before a bad situation gets worse."

There's no arguing with her, clearly, and I'm not sure I would anyway. Because the truth is that I like having Drew here, all to myself. I wish my fucking brother had never shown up at all.

19

DREW

January 27th

I wake up half on and half off the couch with the sunlight blazing through the window.

For a moment, I wonder if I'm on tour, because it's very much like the morning after a show. My mouth feels like I shoved it full of sand, and my brain is howling like a wounded animal that deserves to be put out of its misery.

Not on tour.

Hawaii.

Fuck my life.

What the hell happened yesterday? I see flashes of things—eating tacos at some total dive with a bunch of surfers, getting beers with our Uber driver, and a pig roast with some random Hawaiian family. I'm pretty sure I offered to let one of them get married at Tali's beach house. I seem to recall even showing photos of her wedding.

I bury my head in my hands and groan.

"There's Advil on the table beside you," says a voice. I

squeeze open a single eye and see Josh sitting at the desk, tapping away on his trusty laptop.

"Why are you here?" I ask. My voice is rough, like I smoked a carton of cigarettes.

"Why am I in *my* room?" he asks. "Great question."

"Shit," I whisper. I struggle to push off the heavy blanket on top of me and sit up, burying my head in my hands again. I'm sweaty and filthy and I want to be placed in a medically induced coma until the alcohol is out of my system. "Shit."

More snippets of the evening are coming back to me now. We were in the rental car. And I was remembering my dad singing me those stupid Russian songs from his childhood in his piece-of-shit Jeep and drinking the whole time, and I think I might have told Josh about it.

I reach for the water he's set out for me on the coffee table. "Whatever I said to you...can we just pretend I didn't say it?"

He closes his laptop and turns in his chair to look at me. "Why?"

I close my eyes. "I don't...discuss my father, okay? With anyone. And that's all just...it's shit I don't want out in the world."

"Hold on. Let me see if I can stop that telegram I just sent *The New York Times*," he says.

If I wasn't in quite so much agony, I might laugh. But I'm in no mood. "Don't tell Six," I whisper. "And please, please don't tell Sloane. She's already got it out for me."

"You didn't say anything worth repeating, Drew," he says. "Don't worry about it. And she's gone, anyway."

My head whips up to look at him. "Gone?"

There's a quick flash of worry in his eyes before he glances away. "She headed back to Atlanta. It's for the best. You might have noticed there was some tension."

"No," I say with a half smile. "You two hid it really well."

He doesn't smile back. "My mother is devastated. I told her earlier and she burst into tears."

My stomach drops, and not simply because I hate the idea of Beth being upset. Between the bar last night and waking up now I had decided to leave. But if Sloane's already gone and Beth's upset, how can I possibly leave too? "Doesn't she see that everyone's better off this way? Like, why waste all that time on something that isn't going to work?"

He shakes his head and for a moment there's something grim in his face, something he doesn't plan to share. "She wants to see us all married," he says quietly. "I think she blames herself for the fact neither of us are inclined to settle down. Thank God *you're* staying, at least."

I swallow, unable to meet his eye.

He looks at me, then. A long look, like he knows exactly what I'm thinking. "Drew, promise me you're going to stay. I can't get into it but...this trip is really important to my mom. If you leave, too, I'm not sure she'll be able to rebound from it." My stomach drops farther. I don't think any reasonable person would argue that it's better not to know the truth. But I imagine Beth struggling to stay chipper through the rest of this trip and feeling like a failure because neither of her grown sons can keep a girlfriend, and that seems worse. "Please," he adds.

"Okay," I whisper. "And I'm sorry...about Sloane."

His tongue darts out to wet his lip and then his teeth sink into it. God, I hate when he does that. I hate it so fucking much. "I'm not. I just wish my mom wasn't upset."

"You're probably a little sad. I mean, come on, you dated the girl for a while. As unfeeling as you are, there must be something there."

His mouth moves into an almost smile. "Unfeeling, huh? That's how you see me?"

I rise shakily to my feet. *No*, I think. *I don't see you that way at all anymore.*

ONCE HOUSEKEEPING ARRIVES to let me into my room, I enter to find Six's clothes spread over the floor like Hansel and Gretel's trail of bread crumbs, straight to the bed where he's in nothing but boxers.

There was a time when the sight of him like that might have appealed to me.

At this exact moment, he just looks a little unclean and a whole lot selfish. I check my phone: he didn't reply to last night's text for two hours. It took him *two hours* to wonder where I was and check his phone, for fuck's sake.

And that's exactly what I wanted: someone who was never going to depend on me, and someone I'd know better than to depend on. But I think back to last night, to that moment when Josh appeared in front of me in the Jeep. The way I felt found, and safe. And it felt a lot better than this does.

Six is dead to the world, so I close the bedroom door and sit on the couch with one of his guitars. Frustratingly, it's not well-tuned but I leave it alone and start trying things out, this song that's been in my head for the past few mornings. The words aren't quite there, but the chorus gives me chills, and I'd sort of forgotten what that felt like—the quiet thrill of creation, the moment of realizing I did something, and loving it enough that it almost doesn't matter what anyone else thinks.

An hour before we're due downstairs, I put his guitar away and wake him.

"Hey," he croaks. "What happened to you last night? Where'd you sleep?" His worry is coming about twelve hours too late.

I could tell him his role in the whole thing but I'm still tired, and it hardly matters at this point. "Josh picked me up. You had our room key so I slept on their couch."

He sits up, suddenly stiff-spined and tense. "You called *Josh*? Jesus Christ, Drew, all you had to do was—"

"I didn't," I reply, unduly irritated. I cross the room and get my suitcase from the closet. "*He* called me, looking for you. You told me you were going to text your mom. She was worried."

"Right," Six says, rolling his eyes. "And I forgot. Thank God Saint *Fucking* Joshua was there to step in and save the day."

I've been in his shoes so many times—when I've screwed up and someone has fixed it for me, and made sure to let me *know* they had to fix it for me. It sucks to be the screw-up. It sucks to be the one people roll their eyes over, about whom everyone's saying *Well, what did you expect?* to each other.

But I'm not willing to sit here agreeing with him that his brother is a dick for coming to get me, for fixing problems he, in part, created. "Well," I reply, "he really *did* kind of save the day."

I set the suitcase on the bed and walk onto the balcony to take in Diamond Head. I hate that I won't really be able to hold onto this trip. Memories are like artwork left in the rain. They blur and smudge until all that's left is your weak interpretation of it, your best guess as to what it was. One day I'll merely say I watched the sunset here, but I probably won't remember the way Josh made me laugh. I won't remember him saying *Tell me something real*, as if what I said and what I felt and what I thought actually mattered.

I'm going to miss this place, I think, taking it in for one last moment, *and it won't ever be the same without him.*

"THERE YOU ARE," says Beth when we arrive in the lobby. "We were worried last night."

Six shrugs, unable to even pretend he cares about the

inconvenience. "Sorry," he says, sounding not at all sorry. "Time just got away from us."

"Time got away from *you*," Josh corrects. "*She* wasn't the one who was supposed to text Mom."

"Joel, we had reservations and this is a family trip," his father begins. "We expect you to—"

Beth stops his lecture with a gentle hand to his forearm. "Jim, it's fine. He made a mistake and he won't do it again. Besides, we've probably overscheduled the kids. They deserve to have a few nights out without us old folks along."

She's covering for Six. She's forgiving him quickly so that no one else can hold him accountable. All this time, I've felt like Six and I were in the same boat, the unloved black sheep of the family whose every misstep is magnified and whose every good deed still manages to be cast in a poor light.

But we aren't the same at all. We are both black sheep, but Beth loves her son so much she won't even let him suffer when he's in the wrong. And my mother doesn't love me enough to protect me, even when I'm in the right.

He grins at me now like we've gotten away with something. "Maybe I need a wife to keep me on the straight and narrow," he says, wrapping an arm around my waist. "What do you think, Mom? Should I keep her around?"

I stiffen. Never, not once, in all the time I've known him, has Six even *hinted* at marriage. I can't imagine why he suddenly is now. You don't decide you want to marry a woman you forgot about mere hours before. Josh stands frozen, staring at his brother as if he's even more stunned and unhappy about what was just said than I am.

He opens the van door. Six tries to take the front and Josh snarls, "That's her seat, she gets car sick," and I start to wonder if I've made a grave error by remaining on this trip.

PART II

LANAI

"The tiniest of all the islands, and the loveliest as well."
From *Lanai: The Tiny Jewel*

20

DREW

"It's only eighteen miles at its widest point," says Beth, reading to us aloud from her trusty guide book. "And it has no traffic lights. Can you imagine? *No traffic lights.*"

I flash a pained grin at our van driver, a local who probably doesn't love hearing his home described as some kind of wasteland.

"And there's no hospital," she continues. "Oh my God. Forty-four percent of the population lives below the federal poverty line. Isn't that a shame?"

"Mom," I hear Josh intone, firm but gentle.

"I just think it's a shame," she argues. "Women who are thirty-six weeks pregnant can't remain on the island. It's primitive!"

I cringe and turn back toward her. "So what's the plan while we're here?" I ask desperately, before she says something even worse.

She glances up from her book with a smile, happy someone is finally on board with her agenda. "We'll just relax this evening, and tomorrow we'll golf—you're sure you don't want to come?"

Am I certain I don't want to waste an entire day in Hawaii hitting a small ball while dressed like a fucking idiot? Quite.

"There's also a sunrise hike," she says. "The hotel provides a flashlight and map."

I can't help it—my eyes meet Josh's. The sunrise is kind of our thing now. He raises his brow as if to say *Obviously, we're doing it.*

"Mostly, we're just here for a little rest and relaxation before the backpacking trip in Kauai," Beth concludes.

I blink. I must have misheard her. There's no way she just said *backpacking trip.* I doubt she's ever stayed at less than a five-star hotel in her life, and camping is rarely a five-star experience, as far as I know.

"Um...backpacking?"

"Didn't Joel tell you?" she asks. "I booked us on this amazing two-day hiking trip on the Kalalau Trail in Kauai. It's supposed to be one of the most scenic hikes in the world."

"Mom," Josh says, pinching the bridge of his nose, "I don't know that it's a good idea. A hike like that...it's a lot."

I see a silent exchange occur between his hard stare and her refusal to meet his eye. "We'll see," she says quietly.

"Does anyone actually *want* to backpack?" asks Six. "That sounds like a lot of work for not much fun."

Beth deflates visibly. She's been down over Sloane's departure all afternoon, and Six's lack of enthusiasm is the icing on the cake. I feel forced to salvage this.

"I think it sounds amazing," I gush, "but I didn't bring any gear."

"Oh," she says, perking up. "I rented it all there. You only need your toiletries and a change of clothes."

"Great," I say weakly. As much as I was hoping to get out of it, if it matters to Beth, I'm in. She's been so nice to me this entire trip that I'd suffer through worse for her, and surely camping can't be *all* bad or people wouldn't do it.

"And," she adds, reopening her guide book, "*they* have a hospital in case one of us gets hurt. Unlike *Lanai.*"

I glance backward, but it's not Six I look at. It's Josh. His mouth moves ever so slightly, as if he's trying not to laugh. Suddenly, the backpacking trip doesn't seem so awful after all.

THE FOUR SEASONS Lanai feels exactly how I'd expect a Hawaiian hotel to feel, if it were crafted by billionaires for fellow billionaires. Everything is lush and jungle-y and wood toned. A man-made lagoon stocked with tropical flora and fauna quietly weaves through and around the hotel, exotic birds squawk from cages, and even though the hallways are open to the outside, there isn't a speck of dirt anywhere. The tropical breeze is gentle, not too warm and not too cold. I imagine they've managed to somehow pull strings with Mother Nature along with everyone else.

Our room faces the ocean, of course. Even from the doorway I can see dolphins frolicking, putting on a better show than you'd get at Sea World.

Six wants to play guitar for a while, so I put on my bikini and wander to the beach. Almost no one is out this late in the day, aside from Josh.

I grab a towel from the attendant and wave him off when he offers to get me a chair. "I'm just here to harass someone," I tell him.

Josh glances over—head to toe and away again, as if he wants me here and doesn't want me here, all at once.

"My mom just went up," he says.

"Did you want to be alone?" I ask.

He shakes his head. "As long as you're not down here to tell me a hundred times that you hate that I'm on this trip by myself, we're fine."

"I'm sorry about Sloane." Not that I'm sorry she's gone, necessarily, but I know all too well what it's like to be the third wheel.

"It wasn't your fault," he says.

I glance at him. I didn't think it *was* my fault, but his response, and the way he's avoiding my eye right now, leads me to think *he* does. "I know it's not my fault. I was just trying to express sympathy, robot man. It's what humans do for each other."

"Ah, so we're assuming you're human now? That wasn't the premise I was working off."

It's kind of a low blow. I feel closer to him than any member of the Bailey family at present, but now that Six is here, he's apparently shunted me right back to being the stranger he hates.

"Fine," I reply, standing. "I'll let you sulk by yourself."

"Hey," he says, reaching up to grab my wrist. "Stay. I'm sorry. I'm just a little...testy about the whole thing. There's nothing like having your mother desperately sad about your dating life to make you feel like you've gone wrong somewhere. That's all."

I retake my seat. If he's feeling bad here, it will be worse in Kauai. Does he really want to be the only one sleeping in a tent alone? It's not as if Six won't go out of his way to make him feel like an asshole about it either.

"Okay," I reply softly. "Let me know if there's anything I can do. Like, if you want me to sit out the camping trip or whatever, I—"

He smacks his forehead. "Jesus, no. The one thing that could make this whole shitshow worse is abject pity from *you* of all people."

And there we have it. Just that fast, he's back to being an asshole. I laugh, the sound so sharp and bitter even the birds startle. "Right," I reply. "The girl so pathetic she might steal the silver. Pity from her would be a new low, wouldn't it?"

His eyes go wide. "*What?*"

"I heard you. Last summer. You were complaining about how I wasn't good enough, and then you told your mother to keep an eye on the silver. Don't try to talk your way out of it either. There's really not much room for interpretation in a statement like that."

He closes his eyes and blows out a resigned breath. "I'm sorry," he says. "It...sounds much worse than I intended. And I guess saying I didn't think you and my brother were a good fit doesn't sound much better."

I'd secretly begun to hope he had an excuse, like Tali suggested. That he didn't really think I'm a piece of shit. But no —that's exactly what he thought.

We watch the waves lap against the shore for a moment. I'm going to try to get over the silver thing. It probably wouldn't have bothered me so much in the first place if I hadn't spent so many years subject to Richard's tantrums and accusations —*That thieving Russian bitch was in my room again* was all he had to say about me to ruin my week. Maybe because I was nine when he started saying it.

And maybe part of the problem was I felt like I *deserved* Josh's disdain. Because the truth is that on the night when I first saw him—standing on the other side of a hotel ballroom—he took my breath away. His gaze left me feeling like a bottle of champagne shaken a little too fiercely, and I knew how wrong it was, even before discovering he was the brother of the guy who'd brought me to the party.

"I'm really sorry, Drew," he says. "It honestly had nothing to do with you."

"It's fine," I reply, willing it to be true.

His mouth curves up, a hint of a lopsided grin. "And in my defense, you did refer to me that night as *personality free*."

I laugh half-heartedly. "In my defense, it isn't your strong suit."

Enough, I tell myself. Josh has enough problems right now without me piling on at the moment. *Has* had them, based on the couch in his room last night, already made up for sleep.

I don't know why I feel relieved that he slept on the couch. The idea of him undressing her, or even flirting with her, produces a tiny bitter seed in my chest that I refuse to look at too carefully.

"You and Sloane—" I venture, and then I stop, uncertain what I want to ask or how I can phrase it without sounding jealous. "Why *her*? I mean, she's pretty. I'll admit that much. But she's just...not right for you."

He closes his eyes. "The refugee camp is kind of like being in space. You're so isolated, and it's so stressful at times, and there are very few people who get what you're going through and even fewer who speak English. Things happen."

I give a dark laugh. "Based on all the bedding on your couch last night, I assume they didn't *keep* happening."

He winces. "No, they didn't. My mom invited her as a surprise for me and...it just didn't feel right when I knew it wouldn't go anywhere. You must have thought it was pretty goddamn weird when you got to our room last night."

I shake my head. "Nah. I already assumed you only believe in sex for procreation and would prefer to handle it all with test tubes, if possible."

"Is that what you think?" he asks. There's the tiniest movement of his mouth, a sly look in his eyes as they cut slowly to me. The look he'd have if he were actually thinking about sex and wanting it, and about to get it. And I know, based simply on that look and the smug confidence in his voice, that he is anything but ambivalent and clinical. That sleeping with him would be hot and indulgent and messy and perfect and he would ruin me for anyone else.

And I think I'd be better off not knowing it.

"No," I whisper as I rise and walk away. "Not really."

WHEN I GET BACK to the room, Six sets his guitar down and pats the bed beside him.

"I'm all sandy," I reply.

He grins. "I don't mind."

"I do," I tell him. "I'm the one who'll have to sleep in it. Let's just sit on the balcony."

To my surprise, he rises and follows me outside. He takes the seat beside me and reaches out to grab my hand. The sun is pretty much gone in a sky rapidly turning the color of slate, where a tiny crescent moon blinks to life. "This is pretty amazing, huh?"

"Yeah. Different than Waikiki, but I like it."

"No medical care, though," he says, and we both laugh.

"My God, I thought your mom would never stop."

"I didn't want her to," he says with a grin. "If that ride had been even a moment longer, the word *savage* would absolutely have been used and I'd have laughed so hard."

I grin at him. This is who he was when we first met backstage at Glastonbury. He was cool and funny and he wasn't trying to impress me, which I liked. We just got along. It felt natural.

"Yesterday was fun, right?" he asks.

I glance at him. Yesterday was fun...until it wasn't. "I can't drink like that anymore, Six. And it's not just because of all the rumors about me. I just don't have it in me to drink for eight hours straight."

He picks up my right foot and places it in his lap, sinking his thumbs into the arch. It's blissful. "It's for the best. One of us has to grow up first, right? Who's going to plan out all these trips for us when we're old if we're both still getting hammered all day long?"

I don't know how to respond to that. A year ago, I'd have

been thrilled. I'd have rushed off to text Tali, demanding she agree that Six and I had turned a corner. Now, I don't even want to agree with it myself. I feel as if, in doing so, I'd be making him a promise I'm not sure I can keep.

The breeze picks up and it feels like a warning. A sign I should extricate myself quickly, before it's too late. "You might want to plan these trips with someone who doesn't tend to go missing or who you notice is missing," I reply, softening it with a laugh. "Especially on an island where there's no hospital."

He swallows. "That was shitty of me last night. It wasn't that I didn't notice you were gone, though. I just assumed you were, like, dancing or talking to people. Sometimes I forget you're not like me, that you're more of an introvert. I'm gonna try to be better."

It's the most earnest thing he's ever said to me. And it leaves me terrified, rather than hopeful. I'm not sure I *want* him to try.

21

JOSH

January 28th

The next morning, I'm waiting in the lobby for her with a flashlight. Joel made noises about joining us this morning. I'm quietly relieved when she shows up alone.

"You ready?" I ask.

"You're a little too eager," she replies. "You're not planning to throw me off the cliff, right?"

I shrug. "Not the kind of thing you commit to until you've assessed the situation."

A guide from the hotel leads a small group of us outside, where the world is the deepest charcoal, just shy of absolute darkness. Using the flashlights, we weave past lagoons and pools to reach the path that goes to the beach and beyond. By the time we've begun to ascend the cliff, the sky is lightening into various shades of gray, with the barest hint of a bright orange sun at the horizon's base.

We keep walking, up and up, past sharp rocks and crashing ~~waves~~. I'm less focused on the scenery than I am on making sure Drew, who is quietly humming and paying little attention, is not too close to the edge. Eventually, the sky lightens a bit more and I can finally make out the coastline curving in the distance, and a big rock in the water with a Hawaiian outrigger canoe passing nearby, heading toward the rising sun in heavy surf. I reach out, placing a hand on Drew's hip to get her attention. "Look," I say, nodding toward it. My hand drops, though it felt better where it was.

"How do I get that job for a living?" she asks. "It looks peaceful."

I laugh. For someone with an unfathomable amount of money, she spends an awful lot of time trying to escape it all. "Are we back to your living off the land fantasy?"

She grins. "Maybe. I could just take my big boat out each morning and live at The Four Seasons like those guys do."

"Yes," I reply. "I'm sure they all live at The Four Seasons. And then they go into the hills to gather breakfast from the Sour Patch Kid Trees." She smiles, and though she's barefaced —her hair in a messy bun, her tiny form swimming in an over-sized sweatshirt—she's never looked more beautiful to me.

We reach the overlook at last and take a seat, side by side, to wait for the sun to rise over neighboring Maui, though it shows no sign of happening soon.

"This had better be one hell of a sunrise if there aren't even gonna be cappuccinos involved."

I reach into my daypack and hand her a bottled Starbucks drink.

"Best I could do on short notice," I reply. "The gift shop didn't have Sour Patch Kids."

"Fucking Four Seasons," she mutters, but she is smiling down at the drink like it's something precious. It takes so little to make her happy and I wonder if anyone in her life even tries. She peers up at me. "You're kind of a keeper, Joshua Bailey."

Her eyes are the color of whiskey in the dim light. My gaze

falls to her mouth and away. How the hell can she be with my brother? It astonishes me a little more with every minute I'm near her. "I might say the same to you, but I don't even know your real name."

Placing the drink down next to her, she leans back on the rock, bracing on her palms. "Why can't Drew Wilson be my real name?"

I smile to myself. She'll argue over *anything*. "Well, Drew is a boy's name for starters."

"Not necessarily. And it's better than Joshua. Do you know what Joshua means? It means *diarrhea mouth*. Look it up."

My teeth sink into my lip as I try not to laugh. Her gaze follows the movement like a shark scenting blood, and desire hits me like a hammer, plucking a muscle low in my abdomen.

I force myself to look away. We sit in silence for a moment, watching the sun as it begins to warm the horizon. "My real name is Ilina Andreyev," she says quietly, not looking at me. "It was a little too ethnic sounding, according to my manager. Andreyev means son of Andrew. So I started going by Drew."

"You're Russian?"

She shrugs. "My father was. My mother went to Russia after college and he came over with her."

I sense at any moment this curtain she's opened will be pulled shut. I know I need to proceed carefully, not look too far in, and she might close the curtain anyway.

"Was he a lawyer too?" I ask.

She laughs. "God, no. A musician. That was her first mistake...musicians are the worst."

My smile is muted. *Some of them are*, I think. *Like the one you're with*. "So what happened?"

"She wanted to be an opera singer and he wanted to be in a band, and neither of them were good enough at what they did to make a living from it." She scuffs her sneaker into the dirt and kicks a rock down the hill. "So my mom went to work as a paralegal, and then went to law school, which my dad deeply resented and felt emasculated by, and he drove a cab until he drank himself to death."

My hand nudges hers. "I'm sorry."

She shrugs. "I can't be ashamed of what she does for a living forever."

She laughs and I do too. There's more here she isn't saying, I'm certain. There's more in the fact that she has never mentioned her mother once, until this moment, and that it sounds like she was closer to her dad and lost him young. *Messy*, Sloane says in my head. *Resilient*, I think again.

The sun begins to burst over the horizon at last and we watch quietly, my thigh pressed to hers, her hand resting on the rock just behind me, brushing my back every once in a while.

Someone offers to take our photo together.

"He has this affliction," Drew tells the guy as I hand him my phone. "He's unable to smile. I've started a *Go Fund Me* on his behalf but we haven't had much success because he looks so cranky in the photo."

The picture is taken. I thank the guy and glance at it when Drew is looking away.

I was smiling.

22

DREW

An hour after we return, I attempt to rouse Six for his day of golfing and he says *Five more minutes* and pulls the pillow over his head so I go to breakfast without him.

I sit at the table with Josh while his parents go through the buffet, trying hard not to laugh at him in his dumb golf shoes and belted shorts and polo.

It's not that he looks dumb in golf clothes. It's that *everyone* looks dumb in golf clothes.

"Something to share?" he asks, raising a brow. "Go ahead. Your struggle is palpable."

"You look like an idiot," I reply, unable to restrain my laughter. "Why are golf clothes so dumb?"

His lips push forward, in an attempt not to smile. "Golf clothes are a mark of civility. If you were from a better family, you'd know this."

"Wow," I say, picking up a roll, fully prepared to pitch it at his head. "I can't believe you went there."

"I can't believe you think lobbing food at me in the middle of The Four Seasons will prove me *wrong*."

I close my eyes as I laugh, and when I open them, Six is standing at the head of the table.

"What did I miss?" he asks, and it feels as if I've been caught doing something I shouldn't have, which makes no sense. Six would love a food fight in an upscale restaurant more than anyone.

"I was just saying you look like idiots in your golf attire."

"Josh does," says Six, "because he's too fucking big and he has no tattoos."

"Yes, he does," I reply too quickly.

"One," Six says. "On his arm. Big deal."

Josh actually has two, but I say nothing, as I wouldn't know about the other one if I hadn't been watching him climb from the pool *way* too closely for the last several days.

"What are you going to do all day without me, babe?" asks Six, taking the chair beside me and wrapping his arm around my back.

Josh's gaze freezes on that arm for a moment. A vein pulses in his temple. "You should work on your song," he says, his eyes moving to mine.

Six frowns. "What song? She doesn't write her own shit."

I'm not sure why I was willing to let Josh know but don't want to discuss it with the guy I'm actually dating. Who's a *musician.* "Just something I've been playing around with," I reply.

"Babe," Six says with a laugh. "You don't even play an instrument. Leave the songwriting to the pros."

I feel something silvery and cold slide into my blood. He knows I started out performing my own stuff. With as little as we've discussed about our respective pasts, I know he's heard this much, and he's either forgotten or just feels this strange need to take me down a peg, to put me in my place. And I suspect I know which it is.

"I could play guitar and piano before I could read, as a matter of fact."

"So eleventh grade?" Six cracks. It's mean. It hurts. But my first thought is *Don't overreact.*

Stop being so dramatic my mother must have said a thousand times, whenever I was upset about something Richard or his father had done.

But Josh has gone perfectly still, like a snake about to strike. I've never seen him so furious, which tells me my anger and pain might not be an overreaction after all.

"I know you didn't just say that to her," Josh snarls. His hand is gripping the coffee cup so hard he risks crushing it.

"Settle down. It was a joke," says Six, turning to me. "But babe, lots of people *claim* they can play, but that doesn't mean they can *actually* play. So you see where I'd have to call you out a little."

I climb to my feet. Beth and Jim are approaching, but I'm too furious to stop myself. "I actually play as well as you do," I reply. "And by the way, I've never seen you play an F chord correctly live. Not once."

And with that, I march away from the table. This is normally the point where I'd worry I've gone too far, but Josh's reaction to what Six said is burned in my brain—like he simply couldn't believe the words he was hearing. It leaves me wondering if maybe I haven't gone far *enough*. If maybe I've been letting a lot of people walk on me for a very long time, because the worst things they say about me aren't nearly as bad as the things I say about myself.

So I'm going to let myself stay mad a while longer. And the only thing to do in the meantime is get out one of Six's precious guitars, which he never tunes right, and write my fucking song.

∼

I'm at the beach that afternoon, half-asleep, when I hear the sound of a towel unfurling beside me.

Josh, out of his dumb golf clothes. Shirtless. Bare skin, for a moment, is all I seem to see. He's so chiseled that his abs look like boulders stacked one atop the other with a perfect line running straight to his navel, and below it, leading to that small happy trail I'd love to...*Gah. Stop, Drew, for the love of God, stop*. I roll over and turn to face him, but I try to keep my gaze north of where it was.

"How mad is your brother?"

Josh shrugs. "He was pretty mad this morning, and then he got drunk while golfing, and I imagine he's sound asleep in your room and will have forgotten by dinner."

My lips press together and I squeeze my eyes shut. "I shouldn't have said it," I say softly. "I do that—get my feelings hurt and lash out. Which might have something to do with the fact that none of my family is currently speaking to me."

"Did you call them *all* raging cunts?" he asks with half a smile.

The breeze picks up and I pull my baseball cap lower. "Basically." I blow out a tired breath. "I'll apologize to him."

He runs his hands over his head as if he's frustrated. I'm momentarily distracted by the pulse of his tricep. "Don't. He can be jealous of your career and your fame all he wants, but he doesn't get to speak to you like that. He doesn't get to belittle you. Ever."

I laugh. "He's not jealous. He just has no respect for my career, and I can't even fault him for it when I don't respect it either."

"He wants what you have," Josh says. His head turns toward me. "I can't imagine why, because until you dyed your hair and got a little privacy, your life looked miserable, and I imagine it will go back to being miserable. But it's definitely what he wants. And you take way too much shit from people."

I frown. Josh would never say that if he spent a moment with me around my family. "I don't really see myself as taking shit from anyone."

"You take it from him," he says. "At that party last summer, a friend of my dad's asked for an autograph and Six said something shitty about it, something totally demeaning, and you just laughed."

Look at her rack, is what he said. *If you want to know what it takes to be famous in this country, I offer you exhibit A and exhibit B.* And yes, I laughed. He was joking, mostly, and it wasn't entirely *un*true. I'm not about to delude myself into thinking I got where I am based on talent alone.

"He was just drunk. He makes stupid, tactless jokes when he's drunk. The nice thing about your brother is that he doesn't give a shit about my money, or my fame, so when he's nice...I get to know he means it. And I'd like to point out that you're the one who convinced me to stay on this trip yesterday."

He blows out a breath and pinches the bridge of his nose. "I know. And I shouldn't have. You deserve someone who worships the ground you walk on, Drew. Someone you can lean on. Who cares more about your happiness than his own."

I swallow. I'm not sure what he's describing exists, and it hardly matters, because I don't want it anyway. Life is easier when you don't entirely depend on another person for anything, when you hold a little back.

"I'm not looking for that," I tell him. "It's like driving. Some people want to take the long, meandering journey with no guarantees, hoping they end up in a good place. And some of us just take the express bus: it won't get you anywhere special, but at least you know what you're in for."

He looks like he wants to argue, and I'm relieved when he doesn't.

Because he's the one person alive who could convince me to

take a risk, and I can't stand to let myself love yet another thing I'll eventually lose.

WHEN I GET BACK to the room, Six is awake and wary. He looks at me like I'm a feral animal skulking near his chickens.

"Hey," I say quietly, dropping my beach bag on the desk.

"Hey," he replies. He crosses to the minibar and I'm sorely tempted to ask if he really needs it, but I'm not his mother, after all.

I'm sticky and sandy and I just want to have a shower and not engage in some pointless fight with him. I go to my suitcase and grab a change of clothes.

"You played my guitar today," he says.

I look up and meet his gaze. I'm not going to apologize for it. It's one of his backups, and no one would consider it a great guitar. "I tuned it for you."

"I didn't need you to tune it for me," he snaps.

Oh, believe me, Six. You needed me to tune it.

"Josh spent all of breakfast and half of the golf game laying into me about what I said, by the way," he says. "So that was fun."

Warmth spreads through my chest. I didn't need Six to be scolded, but I kind of love that for once in my life, someone took my side. Especially when I'm not sure I deserved it.

"I shouldn't have said what I did," I reply, grabbing my clothes. "But you shouldn't have either."

For a moment I'm certain he means to argue, but then he puts his glass down and crosses the room, pulling me against him. I'm in my bikini, he's only in shorts, and it's the most physical contact we've had since this so-called vacation started. He hardens and I try to ignore it.

"You're right," he says. "I just—"

"Please don't double down and defend what you said," I reply, stepping away. "Just don't."

He laughs and pulls me back to him. "Okay, babe. Whatever. You're the best guitarist in the fucking world. Are we good now?"

No, I'm not sure we are.

I close my eyes and see a gray sky, bare trees. A driver glancing back at me in the mirror, thinking I'm too young to be on the bus for so long. It's what I remember whenever I'm feeling lost, whenever I'm scared.

Or whenever I suspect I'm on a dangerous path, and I think maybe I am right now. I just don't know if it's Six, or his brother, who's the danger.

PART III

KAUAI

"Home to staggering vistas and lush vegetation, Kauai is, without a doubt, the most beautiful of Hawaii's islands."
From *Kauai: The Garden Isle*

23

DREW

January 29th

"Kauai is believed to be the most beautiful of all the islands," Beth reads as Josh drives us from the airport to Princeville, located on Kauai's north shore.

I stare out the window at the dreamy coast off to our right, trying to ignore my desire to look at Josh, to point things out to him or study his broad hand resting on the console near mine, the flex of his bicep as he steers.

"Oh," Beth murmurs. "For major medical care you have to be transported to Oahu. That's disappointing."

Josh's gaze slides to mine and we both smile. His skin is tan from the long days outdoors, his hair glinting gold, that sensual lip of his looking like it was made to be kissed.

"I'm so excited to see it all," Beth says. "I just wish Josh wasn't here alone. Drew, do you have a sister you can set him up with back home?"

"Only my stepsister-in-law," I reply. "She's married, so that's a problem, but she might even be too evil for Josh."

"I think you've mentioned her," Josh says, his mouth twitching. "What was it you called her again?"

I bite my lip. "Aggressive?"

He smiles. "No, it was something else. I'm trying to think..."

"Don't try too hard," I reply. "We can't afford to have you fry a circuit board right before the backpacking trip or you'll need to be medevacked to Oahu."

We both laugh and for a second I forget there's anyone else in the car. I catch myself and turn back to Beth. "What's the deal with the backpacking trip?" I ask her.

"There are two distances. I signed all you kids up for the longer one. Jim and I will do the shorter. It's supposed to be one of the world's most scenic hikes."

Josh winces. "Mom, are you sure you want to backpack? Scenic usually means *altitude* and there's a big difference between hiking, and hiking with forty pounds of gear on your back."

"I'll be fine," she says, lips pinched.

He looks at her in the mirror. "How about if we drive over to the trail today to check it out?" he asks. "It's not the kind of thing you want to figure out when you're too far to get back easily."

They exchange another silent look and she concedes, unwillingly.

Six, who's been on his phone this entire time, looks up and for one unrealistic moment, I hope that he's stepping in to side with Josh about the backpacking trip. I'm not even sure *I'm* ready for this trip so there's no way Beth is. But he's only looking at me. "Babe, we got it," he says. "*Pitchfork* is doing a profile of us."

My eyes widen and when I smile at him, it isn't fake. A profile in *Pitchfork* could be huge for the band, just the push they need. Yet everyone in the car just looks politely blank, as if he's made the most mundane of announcements. As if he'd said *Babe, they serve piña coladas at the pool* or *Babe, let's make sure to get t-shirts today*.

"That's amazing," I reply, squeezing his hand. I turn to his parents. "*Pitchfork* is, like, huge."

"Well, it's no *Rolling Stone*," says Jim, and I could throttle him with my bare hands for trying to diminish Six's moment.

"*Rolling Stone* covers music but they're more general," I say. "*Pitchfork* is all music. It's the one people who are actually *into* music would read." My voice grows a little hard at the end, daring him to challenge me on this. He chooses not to, wisely.

"When's the interview?" I ask Six.

He pushes a hand through his hair and shoots me a worried glance. "They're talking about doing it sometime this week."

There's been an ongoing battle about who will be the *face* of the band—Six, the founder, or Brian, the lead singer. Six won't want to miss the interview and let Brian take over, especially as he has no respect for people like Brian who don't play an instrument, which is probably why his bullshit in Lanai bothered me as much as it did.

"You can call in," I say. "People do it all the time."

He nods, but his nostrils are flaring and he's still staring at his phone. I already know what he's thinking. I can see it in his face.

Don't do this to your mom, I think. Beth has been so eager to see him, to have this time with him.

"I could just fly back for the day," he suggests. "I'd be back the next night."

"But you've already missed half the trip," says Beth. "You would miss out on backpacking."

He laughs. "Sorry, Mom, but I wouldn't consider missing backpacking a big sacrifice."

His glance toward me is pleading. He wants me to back him up and I just won't do it.

"Going to LA would be a lot of effort for something you can

accomplish by Zoom," I say, a trifle coolly. "I promise you'll still be quoted."

He nods, discontent with my answer, and I have a feeling this isn't over.

Josh turns down a long road, passing a golf course, and we arrive at the St. Regis. Six calls Brian the second we're out of the car, arguing volubly, while I follow the Baileys inside.

The hotel isn't open-air the way the last two were, but it has the most magnificent view of all through the floor-to-ceiling windows along its back half: a coastline of green cliffs jutting out toward the deep blue sea. In all my travels, I've never seen anything like it.

I don't have to turn to know it's Josh standing beside me a moment later. "Every time we arrive at a hotel, I think it can't be topped," I say quietly.

He glances at me with something affectionate in his gaze, a way I've never seen him look at anyone else. "You're thinking of living off the land again, aren't you?"

I laugh. "I'm gonna see how backpacking goes before I commit."

He bites his lip. "Thanks for stepping in back there," he says. "In the car. My mom will be devastated if Joel leaves."

"I'll kill him with my bare hands if he leaves," I reply. "Probably not the kind of thing I should say aloud but my mom is good at her job. She'll make you look like an unreliable witness."

Beth approaches, waving keys. "Isn't it wonderful?" she asks.

"It's breathtaking," I tell her. "Thank you so much for doing all this. You've picked out the most amazing hotels and I'm so glad I got to see it all."

She smiles and wraps an arm around my shoulder. "I'm so glad you came. You have no idea how happy it makes me to have you here. Just wait 'til you see the views tomorrow."

Josh raises a brow at her. "That reminds me. We're going to check out the trail, aren't we?"

He gives me a grin over her head as she sighs loudly and starts toward the front doors. He's a good son. A good man. If his brother was just a little more like him, I might be able to make this work.

24

JOSH

My mother is almost impossible to irritate, and yet I've managed.

She doesn't want to look at the trail. She doesn't want to face her limitations. Clinging blindly to bad plans has worked for her thus far, if anyone would consider her marriage *working*. I've allowed her to do it. I've lived with her shitty choices and I've done what I can to keep her happy in spite of them.

But this is different. I read about this hike on the plane. Even if she isn't doing the dangerous part, it will still be steep and slippery, and while I want this trip to be everything she dreamed of, I can't let her get badly injured in a reckless last bid to see the world.

We arrive at the parking lot, and she's tired simply from the quarter-mile walk to the start of the trail. She marches forward anyway, into the dense woods, reminding me a little of stubborn Drew on our first hike.

I laugh quietly at the memory of her that day, so tired and thirsty because she refused to bring water.

My mother looks at me over her shoulder and her expres

sion softens. She's unable to stay mad at me or Joel for long, which is a big part of the problem. If she'd ever been able to stay mad at my brother, maybe he wouldn't have turned out to be such an asshole. "What's funny?" she asks, with a hint of a smile. "I know you're not already laughing at me."

"I was thinking about Drew, the day we hiked Pillboxes," I tell her. I'm still grinning. "She's so goddamn stubborn she wouldn't admit she was exhausted. She wouldn't even admit she needed water. All I had to do was tell her not to jump off one of the bunkers and she'd have done a swan dive just to prove me wrong."

My mother laughs. Already, not five minutes into this hike, her breath is labored. "I really love that girl," she says. "I hope your brother doesn't mess things up."

My chest is tight. My mother is too blind to Joel's faults to see just how terrible he is for Drew. "I suspect he already has."

My mother waves a dismissive hand. "They'll still end up together," she says. "Mark my words. She's good for him."

But he isn't good for *her*. I think of her in Lanai yesterday, saying *I'm not looking for that* when I suggested she should be able to lean on someone. Whatever happened to her growing up, being with him will only continue the cycle, and I want it to stop.

My mother continues to plow forward, though the path is muddy and it's going to be a beast to come back down, part of what makes this hike so treacherous.

Her pace is slowing. We have to step off the trail to let other people pass us. I can see in her eyes that she's mostly given up. I hate it, though it's for the best.

"I know it's hard," she says, "and I know you're very different people, but please make an effort with your brother. He's going to need you when I'm not here."

I close my eyes in frustration. He's the last person I want to help, he's the last person I want to support, but there is so little I can do for my mom, other than this. Other than being civil to my father when he doesn't even try to hide that he's cheating, or being pleasant to my brother when I want to punch him in the face. "I know, Mom," I tell her. "I'm doing my best."

We make it to the first lookout point. From here, there's a clear view of the cliffs stretching out for miles and miles, the waves crashing hundreds of feet below us. My mom looks at it and swallows. Her eyes fill with tears.

I wrap my arm around her. I knew the day I arrived in Honolulu that her cancer had spread. She was frail but also jaundiced, so it's probably in her liver. She wants us to have this one last trip together without the weight of what's coming. I'm trying to give it to her.

"It's a really good view," she whispers.

I swallow hard. "It is."

"Let's get a photo," she says, brushing away her tears. I hold the camera far enough to get the two of us and the coastline behind us. We both smile.

I hope I can look at this later on and convince myself we were happy.

Six and I sit out on the small beach overlooking Hanalei Bay and the cliffs of the Na Pali coast.

I want to kayak down this little river that winds toward Hanalei, but Six is scared to be away from his phone and more scared of losing it if we go in.

"I'm not letting Brian fuck me over," he says. "Because you know he'll try."

I can't help but think that if I were in his shoes, he'd be saying *Babe, chill.*

"Your mom was really upset about you missing the trip," I tell him while he waits for his email to refresh. He nods distractedly and I put down the cocktail menu. "Six, are you listening to me?" I demand. He glances up—alarmed, slightly irritated.

"Yeah, yeah," he says as if I'm nagging, "my mom was upset. I'm here now. I don't know what you want me to do."

Suddenly my patience with him evaporates. I'm not sure why, but this trip matters to Beth and it's as if we're all failing her, even me. She wants to bring her family together, she wants to see her boys settle down, she wants Jim to pay attention to

Six the way he does Josh, and it's like herding cats...the harder she works, the more they seem to wander off in different directions, evading her.

"I want you to stop being a jerk," I reply.

He meets my gaze at last. "*What*?"

"Six, take a look at your mother," I tell him, and suddenly my throat is clogged. "Do you know how goddamned lucky you are? All she wants in the entire world is to spend time with you and make you happy. That's *it*."

I have to stop because I really am going to cry and I'm not entirely sure why. I'm far too old to still be hoping for that from my own mother.

His brow furrows. For a moment he reminds me of Josh and I feel the oddest burst of affection for that little trough between his brows. Except Six *deserves* to worry a little. As far as I can tell he hasn't done nearly his share.

"Yeah," he says, "I know. What's your point?"

"My point is that you're taking her for granted," I reply. "My point is that she planned this entire trip for you and Josh, and you missed most of it, and now you're talking about leaving Kauai, and just once, you've got to put someone else first."

He rolls his eyes and snatches up the cocktail menu. "I'm still here, aren't I? It's like you *want* to be mad at me about something."

"No, I want you to stop even referencing the possibility of flying home for two days for this interview. Stop sitting there on your phone when she's talking to you. She had cancer. She got through it. Give her some indication you're glad she's still around."

His nostrils flare. He flags down the waitress. "You're making me sound like an asshole."

I rise from my chair. "I'm pretty sure you're making yourself sound like an asshole."

I wander down to the shore. The boulders and volcanic

rock make wading out tricky and require constant watchfulness, but it gives me something to focus on other than Six and Josh and the fact that this whole trip seems to be getting increasingly screwed up as it goes on. And the most screwed up part of all is that I only want to be around the wrong Bailey son.

I'm still out in the water when I see Beth and Josh walking down the long path to the beach, with him hovering a little over her, making sure she's okay on the steep bits. And for a moment my heart just swells.

I love everything about your face. My eyes travel over him as my mind spins quietly. *I love your nose and your stern brows and your full lower lip that rarely moves into a smile. I love it more for the fact that it* does *move for me. And I love the way your eyes light up when you see me, even when you are otherwise perfectly still.*

I love the way you take care of everyone, the way you always try to do the right thing.

Thank God you're not even a possibility.

Josh gets his mom set up on a lounge chair and comes to where I stand in the water. His eyes brush over me and then jerk back up to my face, as if he forgot himself for a moment.

"Thought I'd better make sure you don't need saving," he says.

I grin. "I never need saving. I'm in fantastic shape." His gaze darts, for a moment, to my hips and then away again. "How far did you and your mom go?"

He frowns. "We went up for about thirty minutes before she finally agreed it might be too much." There's a sort of sadness wrapped around him. I wish I knew how to cut through it. "It's gonna be a long day tomorrow, so, uh, choose what you wear carefully. I'm guessing if the whole trail is like what I saw, we won't reach the campsite 'til dinner."

I take a cautious step forward, trying to get past the rocks. Between the pulse of the waves and all the boulders, it feels like

I could topple right over. "Were you under the impression I was going to show up in a ballgown and heels? I'm not *Sloane*."

He gives a disgruntled laugh. "Glad you're still managing to take potshots when she's thousands of miles away. I just meant, like, don't wear some stupid lacy thong that'll ride up your ass the whole time."

I look at him over my shoulder. "Spend a lot of time thinking about my panties, do you?"

He blinks, shocked and guilty. *So* guilty, like a little boy caught with his hand in the cookie jar. He schools his expression. "Fine. When you're chafed, don't come crying to me."

"Did you really imagine that if I had chafing on my genitalia, I would come crying to you? *Oh, Josh, can you take a look at my vagina?*" I ask in a whispery baby voice. "*It hurts so bad.*"

"Jesus," he grunts, plowing forward to where the water is deeper. "Forget I brought it up."

"You don't need to worry about my panties!" I shout after him. "I'm not planning on wearing any."

He exhales then, and it's not weary or disdainful. He sounds like he just got the wind knocked out of him. I hope he's past the rocks, because he dives right in.

26

DREW

January 30th

I was nine when my mother announced she was leaving my father for Steven, her boss, who lived in New York City. She was full of promises about how much better our lives would be, but really it was her life she was concerned with.

I didn't want to leave New Jersey, or my bedroom, or my school. Most of all, I did not want to leave my father. "I'd give anything to stop her," he told me on my last night at home, "but there's nothing I can do."

My mother and Steven both had law degrees and money. They'd both been born in the US. There was no way my father could fight them. For the next two years, I heard my father say *I'd give anything* or *I'll do my best* and it broke my heart every time. Because I believed him, and nothing ever came of it.

The very last time I heard that phrase was the night I called to tell him my mother was removing his visitation rights. "I'll tell them I want to live with you," I pled in whispers, praying I wouldn't be overheard. "Talk to your lawyer."

"I'd give anything to make that possible, Lina," my father said. "I'll do my best."

I know now I should never have taken him at his word. I know now when someone says those things what they really mean is *I'm not even going to try*.

That's how I know that when Six says he's gonna do his best to come on the backpacking trip, it means he won't be coming at all.

Yes, he showed every sign of planning to come, frantically reorganizing both our packs while I was out of the room this morning, asking someone in the band to reschedule the *Pitchfork* interview. He even came all the way to the trail, but he didn't get out of the car when we did and I should have known then.

Josh was helping me with my backpack, which was too heavy for me. "Turn around," he said, grinning way too much as he placed it on my shoulders like I was a small child going to school for the first time.

"What are you trying not to laugh at?" I demanded.

"You're gonna go over like a turtle on its back with that thing on, and you'll never get back up," he said.

"Don't laugh too hard," I replied. "If I fall, I'm taking you with me."

Our eyes met. "Of course you are," he said softly.

That's when Six climbed out of the car and told us the *Pitchfork* interview was happening in thirty minutes. "I have to call in it for it, but I'll catch up," he said.

I stared at him. I thought I had no expectations of Six, but I realized then that I must, because he was still consistently managing to disappoint me. "*Catch up?* You don't even know where you're going."

"There's only one trail," Six said. "It might be a push, but I'll do my best."

As soon as those words left his mouth, I know unconsci

cally and beyond a doubt, that he and I were done. There was a
time when I loved how rebellious Six was. I lived vicariously
through his apathy. It was the middle finger I couldn't entirely
give anyone—my mother, the record label, Davis, my agent, my
publicist.

But today this was him giving *me* the middle finger.

He was definitely an express bus, just like I wanted. But he
was not heading anywhere I wanted to be.

I don't even glance at him as I turn toward the trail. I'll wait
until we're back in LA to end things, for Beth's sake, but this is
the moment in my heart when I leave him behind for good.

THERE ARE seven of us who meet at the trailhead, about a
quarter of a mile from the parking lot. The guide, Kai, a couple
from Belgium—Anna and Dietrich—and two women from
Seattle, Kathy and Samantha, who I assume are a couple
though I'm not quite sure. I tell them my name is Lina, but it's a
pretty earthy-looking group, the kind of people who might not
have recognized me even *with* platinum hair. What's also fright-
eningly clear is that, unlike us, they've done this before. Their
packs aren't rented and they have a thousand things hanging
off clasps—water bottles, dry shoes—which leaves me worried
Josh and I are grossly unprepared for this trip.

"Who's ready for some mud?" Kai asks and there are hoots
and hollers from the rest of the group. I don't holler. I'm from
the city. We don't really celebrate mud there so much. "You've
all signed a waiver so you know this, but I'm gonna say it again:
this is a difficult climb. Eleven of the hardest, most scenic miles
you will ever hike out, eleven scenic miles back. Most people do
this trail in four days. We'll make it in two."

There are more cheers. I glance at Josh, wondering what the
hell we've signed on for and what the hell Beth was thinking.

Sure, Josh and Six and I are in decent shape, but we're far from experienced climbers.

"My buddy Chris will be leading the easier trip a little after us with another guide, and you'll meet him at lunch. From there, he'll come with us for the part I know you're all looking forward to...Crawler's Ledge."

Crawler's Ledge? There's nothing about either of those words I like, and I like them together even less. The terrain is already wet and muddy. I look ahead to the deeply steep climb and wonder how much worse it's going to get.

"You'll be fine," Josh says, placing a light hand on my shoulder as we start up the trail. "I'm not going to let anything happen to you, Turtle."

"That's *not* my new nickname."

"Hard shell, soft interior," he says. "You've got to admit it works."

It works for us both. On the surface he's hard and unfriendly. His smiles are rare as dry earth in a rainforest. But beneath that exterior, he cares more than anyone I've ever met. I wonder if that hard shell of his is necessary just because he can't stand to care for even one more thing. I feel the same way.

We've barely begun before we are enfolded in jungle: deeply humid, densely green. The rocks and logs used to create steps up the steep cliff are muddy, requiring me to grab a branch here and there just to keep my balance. I try not to think about coming back down this hill, as slick as it is. Whenever I take a big step and feel my balance shift backward, Josh's hand is there, pressed lightly to my pack, making sure I don't go over.

We arrive, about thirty minutes in, at the first lookout point. I'm drenched in sweat, but the view makes it all worthwhile: cliffs to the north, the deepest blue waves crashing below.

"Whale," someone says, and then everyone crowds around us, trying to see. Josh tucks a finger into the waist of my shorts to make sure I don't go over the edge. I resented it so much that first day in Oahu when he suggested someone hold my hand so I didn't get lost. Now I sort of adore him for it.

I pull the water bottle from my bag and, thanks to the ice Josh dumped in there, the water is freezing cold and nothing has ever, ever been more delicious.

"Am I a genius?" he asks smug as ever, watching my apparent delight.

"I'll concede that you're slightly less dull than I originally thought."

A half smile turns up the corner of his mouth. "*Slightly less dull*," he says. "I'll have to add that to my Tinder profile."

"You're on Tinder?" I ask, and my stomach takes a ridiculous dive. Even if I wasn't already with his brother, even if he didn't live in Somalia, we are as ill-matched as any two people could be. Beginning with the fact that my education ended at the midpoint of his.

His eyes brush over my face. "Is there a reason I shouldn't be?"

I shrug. "I kind of figured you just used some service that provides you a replacement robot when the last one wears out. Stick up her ass, heavily focused on her manicure."

I turn, no longer interested in the stupid view. Cliffs, water, whatever. I've seen it.

"I'm not on Tinder," he says quietly from behind me. "I'd barely have time to date in Somalia even if it was possible."

And my shoulders settle, as if it should make a difference when it doesn't.

It can't.

~

WHEN WE REACH HANAKAPIAI BEACH, we are told to unbuckle our packs so we don't get swept away crossing the stream. I question the judgment of doing anything where getting *swept away* is a distinct possibility, but it's too late to back out of it now.

We go across, with Josh right at my back, his hand on my shoulder. It's equal parts annoying and sweet. We scramble up the other side of the creek bank, and Josh grins at me. He's grown happier, less burdened by the world, with every mile we set between ourselves and the start.

"You love this," I accuse.

He smiles wider. "I'm too tired to worry about anything right now," he suggests, buckling my pack for me.

I wish I knew what it would take to make him this free, this happy and unburdened, all the time. I swear, if it was within my power, I'd give it to him.

We follow Kai through a small valley, and then the *real* climbing begins. We ascend...and we continue to ascend. And then we ascend some more. There are no real views to speak of, and the sweat pouring down my face would obscure them anyway.

We stop at what we're told is the highest point on the trail—Space Rock, 700 feet above sea level. We have only completed three and a half miles out of eleven. My ice water is gone, my back hurts, and I sort of wish we'd signed on for the campsite at the halfway point.

After another mile, we descend into the Hanakoa Valley, where Beth and Jim would have stopped to camp for the night had they come. We cross one last stream and then I dump my backpack and collapse in the grass, stretching my arms overhead. "Go without me. I'll still be here when you get back tomorrow."

Josh lies beside me. "Nah, I'm good right here. What the hell was my mother thinking?" And then we both laugh, because there's literally no way Beth and Jim could have made it this far.

"I love your mom," I tell him.

"Yeah," he says after a moment, sounding wistful. "Me too. But I'm really starting to question her judgment."

Lunch is laid out. We've grabbed sandwiches and chips just as Chris arrives with the campers who'll be staying here tonight.

"You know who you sort of look like?" says one of them. "That singer." She turns to her husband. "What's her name? You know...*Naked*?" She does the shimmy from the video, the ridiculous, suggestive shimmy that is now practically synonymous with my name.

I hate my life sometimes.

"Drew Wilson," he says, tilting his head to peer at my face. "Holy shit, you do! I mean, she's always got the whorish makeup thing going on, but your eyes are exactly like hers."

Josh's nostrils flare in irritation. "Lina," he says, "come sit in the shade."

I follow him, grateful to get away. His jaw is locked tight as he takes a seat in the grass. "What's wrong?" I ask.

"Those two," he says, blowing out a breath. "I don't know how you stand that shit."

I laugh a little unhappily. "I'm a living parody," I tell him. "I'm used to it by now. And that wasn't even bad. That dude didn't know it was me. You wouldn't believe the number of people who *do* know and still say it."

"I don't understand," he replies. "Davis has you singing shit you hate. You don't get to write your own music anymore and you have nothing to yourself. Like...what could possibly be the benefit of continuing to do it?"

I reach for a few blades of grass beside my hand and give them a hard tug. They break off but don't pull from the root. "Everyone says I'm like my dad," I tell him, with a hitch of my shoulder. "And my dad failed. My dad died this pathetic...joke.

It's not how I want my story to end, and now I can't go backward. I either keep succeeding or I'm a pathetic joke."

"I feel like there might be a third option in there, somewhere," he says.

"That's what everyone who dies a pathetic joke tells themselves."

Kai crosses the field and crouches before us. "We've still got six miles left. I can't keep waiting for your brother," he tells Josh, who then glances at me.

It occurs to me only now that Six has our tent, which means I'll be sharing with Josh tonight. It's not as if it's a big deal, but it still makes me nervous.

"It's okay," I tell them.

"You sure?" Josh asks.

I glance at him. "We both knew he wasn't coming."

He looks surprised. As if he knew, but he didn't think I did. Does he truly believe that all this time I was duped by Six? That I was too dumb to see what he was? The truth is I expected little and I got even less.

Kai gathers us a minute later and we begin to climb again. All too soon the trail narrows. I now understand why we had to sign mountains of liability waivers last night. We are edging right along the cliff, and stepping even six inches to the right would send me hurtling to my death.

"You've got to be kidding me," Josh says.

I turn to glance at him and he growls at me.

"Face forward," he barks. "And please keep your eyes on the fucking trail."

For the better part of two hours, we fear for our lives. As I cling to the side of the mountain while a gust of wind sweeps by, I wonder who the hell ever decided to try this in the first place and why idiots like us *continue* to try it.

We descend to our final destination, Kalalau Beach, just before sunset. As exhausted and sore and filthy as I am, I don't think I've ever been so ecstatic in my life. *Everyone* is ecstatic. Josh grins down at me, happier and freer than I've ever seen him look.

There is cheering and jumping and after we've dumped our shit and kicked off our boots, the tents are put up as quickly as possible and people start running to the water. I look at Josh and he looks at me and then we both run too, stripping our shirts off in the sand behind us as we go.

The water in January is warmer than LA's in the height of summer, a pleasure to dive into, and when I emerge, Josh is beside me, water beading off his lovely chest and his perfect arms and suddenly this backpacking trip has gone from being the stupidest thing I've ever signed on for to the smartest.

We are too tired, too exultant, for this to be weird anymore. He's shirtless and I'm stripped down to my jogging bra and shorts and we splash each other like children—bad children who ignore the dying light, the chilly breeze, and even the sharks that probably feed at dusk somewhere nearby.

By the time Chris shouts that dinner is ready, the air has grown cool. "Which of us gets the tent first?" I ask.

Josh's eyes light up. "I'll race you."

"That hardly seems fair. You're a foot taller. A gentleman would—"

"I'll give you a ten second head start. Final offer."

I take off with a screech. Even with the head start, I don't have a chance of beating him and I know it and it doesn't matter. I just want more of these moments with him, when he's so happy and so free. I want to keep them coming as long as I possibly can.

He catches me easily but then slows at the end to let me hit the boulder in front of our tent just before he does.

"I won!" I shout, throwing my arms in the air, jumping around in the grass and very intentionally ignoring the fact that he *let* me win. "Vic-tor-y! Vic-tor-y!"

"You're such a dick," he says with a laugh, and I have no idea why I do it, but my leg swings up to deliver another roundhouse kick, just like it did the first morning we ran together.

And he catches it and flips me just the same way. Except this time, when my back lands in the grass, he's above me, his hand bracing my fall, his eyes locked with mine. He's shirtless, our shorts cling to us, and I can feel *all* of him, warm and hard and hungry. I can picture how this might unfold if we were other people, in another place—how his hand might slide from the back of my neck down to my waist. How it might move from there to slip inside the seam of my shorts. How he'd lower himself until we were pressed tight against each other.

My gaze dips to his mouth, his lovely soft mouth I'd give anything to feel against my own.

It's only a second, but infinity rests within it. And I see exactly what we could have been. I see what he wants, what I want, and how terrifying it would be if it was at all possible. He would be more. He would be the long journey into the unknown. And I'm pretty sure, with him, I could be convinced to try.

27

JOSH

That night, we sit around the fire eating the food Chris made. We all laugh too easily, exhausted and slap happy. Drew and I have already set up our sleeping pads a respectful distance apart, and there isn't anything to discuss, really, but I am painfully, intensely aware of the fact that I'm going to be sleeping near her tonight.

My brother is an idiot. If she were mine, I wouldn't have let her come on this trip alone and I sure as hell wouldn't be letting her share a tent with another guy. Maybe Joel assumes I'm safe, but I'm a lot less safe than he thinks.

We are all yawning once dinner is over. She is bundled up in sweats but she inches closer and closer to the fire as the wind picks up. Chris and Kai take turns playing the ukulele, but eventually even they are bothered by the gusts of wind whipping off the water. *Rain*, one of them mouths to the other, and we all head to our tents.

"You want to change?" I ask, not meeting her eye. I'm doing my level best not to think of her naked inside our tent at any point. "I can wait outside."

She shakes her head. "I'm too cold. I'm sleeping like this. I just need to brush my teeth."

We both climb in and I grab my toothbrush while she searches her backpack.

And then I hear her quiet, whispered oath. "Shit," she says. "Shit."

I turn. The contents of her backpack are spread all over the tent. For some reason she's brought two sleeping bags and a pair of shoes that can't possibly be hers. "You okay?"

"No," she whispers. She buries her head in her hands, taking slow measured breaths, as if willing herself to calm. "Six moved our stuff. He put his sleeping bag in my pack, and he took my toiletry kit. My inhaler was in there."

My stomach drops. We are eleven miles from civilization. No one has a cell signal. She's already thought these things through, and right now she's trying not to panic.

"It's okay," I tell her. I want to kill my brother, revive him, then kill him again but my voice is firm and calm. "You might not even need it."

"What happens if I do?" She sounds breathless even as she asks the question.

I'm already planning, thinking. A part of me wants to get her out of here tonight. If we left the packs I could carry her, but that path along the cliff was treacherous on a sunny day. God only knows what would happen at night, especially if it's storming.

"They must have a way to radio for help," I tell her. It's *probably* true.

She laughs, but it comes out sounding a bit more like a sob. "What good will that do? How long can I go without oxygen?"

My eyes squeeze shut. Fucking Joel. Fucking inconsiderate, useless, narcissistic Joel. How could he have done this? I want to rage at someone, but the only thing that matters right now is keeping her calm. If I can convince her she's going to be fine, she might actually *be* fine.

I want her upright until her breathing is stable, so I move behind her and pull her against my chest.

"Here is our absolute worst-case scenario," I tell her. My voice is measured, certain, almost bored. My heart is ticking like a bomb. "If you have an asthma attack and we can't get it to stop, we call for help. If help is taking too long, I do an emergency tracheotomy. It's not the ideal situation, but I have what I need. I'd just be placing a small hole in your trachea, and I'd use a hand vent to push you oxygen until help arrived."

She laughs and sobs at once. "Having you perform makeshift surgery on me on the beach is a pretty bad worst-case scenario."

"Nah," I reply. "Believe me, I've dealt with worse."

And I have, but it would terrify me because it's *her*. I couldn't live with myself afterward if something went wrong.

"I'd go with you in the helicopter," I continue, "even if we have to go to Oahu because—I don't know if you're aware of this—medical care on the island isn't great."

She laughs, and this time I don't hear any tears. She's breathing again. I push our sleeping pads together and spread my open sleeping bag over them like a sheet.

"Come here," I tell her, lying down and pulling her against my chest. She does, her small hand grasping the fabric of my shirt unconsciously, as if for comfort, while her body tucks perfectly into my side. She rests her head on my chest, just below my shoulder. I pull one of the other sleeping bags over us both.

"And then, once we're back in Oahu and I've secured you a cappuccino and some Sour Patch Kids, I will ask you why the hell you're dating my brother and you'll explain it to me. I'm assuming there must be sorcery involved, as there's no other logical explanation."

The rain pelts the tent and she nestles closer. "Assuming I operate logically was your first error."

Not checking to make sure she had her inhaler was my first error. Maybe she still has lingering faith in my brother, but I have none. I should have known he'd do something like this. I reach up and click the lantern off.

"Thank you," she says quietly.

My hand moves to her hip. "I'm not molesting you," I tell her. "But I can't sleep with my arm straight at my side."

"That surprises me," she says. "Not what I pictured."

"I didn't realize you pictured me sleeping."

"It was only when I wanted to creep myself out. Mostly, I saw you posed like a corpse."

I smile in the darkness. "So wishful thinking, then?"

She laughs. "Precisely."

Sloane was wrong about her. Maybe my feelings for her are messy, but *she* isn't. She's a tiny little fighter, resilient and perfect just as she is.

It doesn't take long, with my breath against her hair and rain lashing the tent, for her to fall asleep. But I lie awake for a long time.

I will never forgive my brother for this. I'm going to stay calm tomorrow, until I get her home, and I'll probably put a good face on things for my mother's sake. But I'm never going to fucking let this go.

28

DREW

January 31st

There's a warm, hard body snuggled up against my back and an erection the size of the Washington Monument pressed against my ass.

It wakes me. Because I know what it feels like to be nestled against Six, and that is not Six. Jesus Christ, that's not Six.

There is obviously no longer a safe distance between us, and Josh's arm is tight around me, his hand pressed flat to my stomach, his breathing still slow and even in sleep. I never would have assumed he was a cuddler. I *would* have assumed he had a sizable appendage if I'd thought about it, simply because, well, he's a big guy.

Who am I kidding? I've thought about it.

But how do I proceed now? I don't want to wake him because then we both have to deal with the awkwardness of this. How do you make an erection die? Other than talking about my feelings, nothing comes to mind.

I know when he wakes because for half a second he curls

closer, and then I hear him say "shit" far too close to my ear and feel him roll away.

I suppose I could pretend to be asleep but that's really not me. "Happy to see me this morning?" I ask instead.

"Don't get too flattered," he says moodily. "I just need to pee."

"I wasn't flattered. I assumed it was one of your robotic parts malfunctioning. Though I find the idea of a malfunctioning sex robot weirdly titillating."

"Drew," he says between his teeth, "that really isn't helping."

I like the idea of Josh with a raging erection he can't get rid of slightly too much, but he was nice to me last night so I decide to be a decent human being for once. "What would help change the mood?"

"You seem to enjoy talking about death," he says. "That should do it."

"Hmmm," I say, trying to think of something death related. "I really only enjoyed discussing Sloane's death, to be honest, but let me think. Oh, got it. When was your first funeral?"

"My grandmother," he says. "When I was ten. She didn't look real. Yours?"

"My dad, when I was eleven." I stare at the top of the tent, at the beads of water all over its surface. "It was a closed casket. I think that's part of what made it so hard to accept."

He glances at me over his shoulder. "Why was it a closed casket?"

"You and your sexy questions," I say, poking him. *He's such a doctor.* "Suicide, so it was too messy. Brains *everywhere*, apparently. Is this still turning you on? Because that wouldn't surprise me about you."

He gives a short, low laugh. "No."

"So anyway, I convinced myself he wasn't really in there. For that first year I kept thinking he was going to come back for me, and I pictured him, like, climbing through my window, or pulling up in front of our apartment in his Jeep and laying on the horn. And then on the anniversary of his death, I woke up and I finally realized nothing was going to change."

I had been shocked, and I was also old enough to know how stupid it was that I was shocked. And when my mother said *What's wrong with you?* in that tone she had, as if she was already mad at me before I'd answered, I didn't dare tell her why.

He's rolled toward me over the course of this fun trip down memory lane. "Jesus," he says. "I'm sorry."

"It was fifteen years ago. I'm over it. How's your dick?"

"It's great," he says with a quarter smile. "Thanks for asking."

I wasn't sad, but something about the sympathy in his eyes makes ancient grief stir and I have to force it back into its little box. "You'd better go pee before I pull this sleeping bag off. I don't want you getting excited again."

"Yeah, you'll be pretty irresistible in three pairs of sweats. And by the way, just because something happened a long time ago doesn't mean you aren't still allowed to be sad about it."

I swallow hard. It would be stupid to be sad about something that happened fifteen years ago. Especially when there's plenty to be sad about right now.

He lifts himself from the floor in one swift move and opens the tent to go pee. I follow him out but my exit is way less graceful, my muscles screaming in protest from overuse.

"Shit," we say at the exact same time as we step outside. The sky is a worrisome gray, the cliffs are shrouded in fog. Everything, absolutely everything, is soaking wet. Chris and Kai are on a walkie talkie with someone. They both look troubled as they explain the situation to us a moment later: the trail will be treacherous, but we only have enough food for today, and if it rains tomorrow, we're screwed.

They leave it up to us, and as a group we vote to head back.

No one wants to potentially be stuck here for several days if the weather doesn't improve. We agree to skip breakfast just in case the trail's washed out and we have to return.

The rain is merely a light drizzle, but by the time we've packed everything and have the tent put away, I'm soaked through my rain jacket and Josh is so stressed about it all that he's stressing *me* out.

"I don't like this," he says. "Let's leave your pack. I'll dump my sleeping bag and the tent here and you can shove anything you want to keep in mine."

I stare at him in shock for a moment, and slowly my chest starts to warm. He's not worried about the trail and he's not worried about himself. He's just worried about me. "I'll be fine," I tell him. "Besides, if we get stuck up there, we might *need* the tent and the sleeping bags."

I can see him trying to find an alternative, but he knows I'm right. "Promise me you'll be careful," he says, his jaw locked tight. "Small steps. I'm gonna be right behind you, just..." He blows out a breath and pushes a hand through his hair. "Just promise."

I can't think of a time in my life where anyone has cared this much about my well-being, even when I was an age where they still should have. I have to swallow hard as I nod. "I promise."

We begin. The slope is muddy and slick. Our progress is painfully slow, and as we get higher we discover the narrow path is almost entirely washed out.

"Jesus Christ," Josh hisses behind me. "Slow down."

It's in my nature to snap at even the mildest criticism, except I know he's not criticizing me. He's simply panicking on my behalf. I slow down.

We make little progress, and even though we skipped breakfast and don't dawdle, it takes us far too long to finally hit Crawler's Ledge. I cling to the side, using vines and trees and anything else I can grab. Adrenaline has my hands shaking, w heart thudding so loud in my chest it seems audible, and when I hear a suspicious noise behind me, I turn, panicked I might find him falling. "Face forward," he barks, his voice sharp. "Don't worry about me."

It takes us hours to inch over the narrow paths that edge the side of the cliff. The ground is slick, the winds are occasionally strong, and the skies open sporadically, spitting just enough rain to make my chest seize up. I know if I start to slip, Josh will try to save me. It's terrifying, more than anything else, because the odds are that I'd just pull him over the side with me.

It's late afternoon by the time we begin our descent into the Hanakoa Valley, yesterday's lunch stop. The trail is slick and muddy, but at least I don't have to worry I'll look back to discover he's gone over the edge.

"What's the first thing you'll do when you get to the hotel?" I ask him, as if we are soldiers who've long been at war.

"Eat," he says. "I don't care how filthy I am, I want the biggest steak you've ever seen in your life. And a potato. And maybe another steak."

I laugh. "I just want a shower. God, I want a hot shower so bad."

"And then what?"

"Another shower."

Thirty minutes into our slippery descent we all hear it: the sound of rushing water. Kai's shoulders sag. "That creek from yesterday?" he says. "It's now a raging river."

When we reach the valley, we discover the campers who stayed down here last night are gone. Kai tells us the guide who helped them with dinner last night had the foresight to move them across the river before the bad weather started. But we have no such luck, and are forced to set up our tents inside a covered shelter near the creek's edge. It's so tight that we're practically on top of each other—I could reach outside of our tent and right into someone else's—but it's better than trying to set up in the rain, and I don't care where we sleep as long as I'm dry.

Josh lets me change first. I groan aloud as I remove layer upon layer of wet clothes.

"Are you okay?" Josh asks from outside the tent.

"So good," I moan, peeling off my sports bra and my socks at last. It's cold today and I'm in here butt naked and it's still so much better than being covered in soggy fabric. "Ecstatic. Most importantly, I'm almost dry."

He grunts. "I've never heard someone make dry clothes sound so sexual."

I use a spare t-shirt to dry off. "It's *better* than sex, believe me."

He gives a low laugh of disbelief. "Then you've been sleeping with the wrong people," he says, and I freeze in the middle of drying myself off, my stomach suddenly twisting with want. I picture him in here with me, pressing me flat to the floor, caging me in with his large body, those perfect arms braced on either side of me. And that's probably nothing I should be picturing when we're spending another night together, alone.

Once we've both changed, we hang our wet things at the other end of the shelter with everyone else's. We eat the food we should have had for lunch, and then, though it's barely dark, we retire. There's not much else to do and it's not like it was going to be a late night anyway—I think everyone is as physically and emotionally drained as I am from the day we've had.

Anna stops by each tent, delivering pieces of chocolate. I dig into a side pocket and discover that Six stashed enough mini-bottles of booze to share with the group, which certainly wouldn't help my reputation if anyone knew who I was.

Chris plays a few songs on the ukulele and then reaches out

through the tent flaps to the couple beside him. "Pass it along until it reaches someone who can play it," he says.

Dietrich takes a turn and gives up, passing it to us. I start to hand it over to Kathy and Samantha, but Josh stops me.

"Play something," he demands.

"What makes you think I can play the ukulele?"

"If you can play piano and guitar, I guarantee you can do this too."

"It's different," I tell him. "It's tuned differently."

He leans back with his hands behind his head. "I wouldn't start pissing off the only guy here who can keep you warm tonight."

"I suspect Chris and Kai wouldn't mind keeping me warm," I suggest, and I laugh at his quiet growl before settling the ukulele in my lap.

I try a few chords to get a feel for it. Each string is tuned about a quarter note higher than a guitar, but otherwise, it isn't so different. I start slowly with *Landslide* by Fleetwood Mac, which my father taught me to play long ago, and though I refuse to sing in case I give myself away, Kathy starts singing and soon everyone joins in.

They clap when the song's over. "Holy shit, Lina," says Kai. "Why didn't you say something? Now I feel like an asshole."

I play Ryan Adam's version of *Wildest Dreams*, and then let it morph to the song I've been working on.

"I like that," says Samantha. "Who is it?"

"No one," I reply. "Just this Russian girl I knew back home."

I try to hand the ukulele over, but no one is willing to follow me. "Keep playing, Lina!" they shout.

"Sorry," I call back. "I'm too cold."

"Liar," says Kathy. "You just want to snuggle with your hot boyfriend."

I laugh and Josh does too.

"Come here," Josh says quietly. "Come snuggle with your

hot boyfriend." He's joking but I thrill at the idea anyway. I lie down with my back to his chest and once I've stretched out, he takes my sleeping bag and the extra one and pulls them over the top of us both.

He angles himself so his crotch is not against me, but the heat of his chest is plenty, and after another hesitant moment, his hand—broad, possessive—lands on my waist and slides to my hip.

The shelter grows quiet as tent flaps finally close for the night. I can feel his breath against the top of my head.

"Tell me something, Josh," I whisper. "Tell me something no one else knows."

He presses his face to the top of my head and holds it there for a moment, as if he's saying a prayer.

"I was jealous," he says quietly.

"What?" I roll toward him, not understanding.

He meets my gaze for only a moment, then his eyes fall closed. "The night we met? The shit I said about you stealing the silver? I was just pissed off and jealous, and I didn't think *he* should get to wind up with someone like you. But instead of saying it all, I made it sound like my problem was with you. And I'm so unbelievably sorry you heard that."

I roll over again and press my back to his chest. I wish his hand, now resting lightly on my hip, would slide up along my rib cage. That he'd pull me tight against him, the way we woke this morning, and press his mouth to my neck. I wish I could hear the sound of his breathing grow heavy as I reached back to grasp him.

I picture him rolling me to my back, his hands exploring my body, tugging my shorts down. Slowly pressing inside me.

I squirm. It's such a bad idea to let my brain venture down this path. He shifts onto his back then and I follow, rolling into the curve of his arm to face him.

My hand falls to his stomach and brushes something else

instead. He hisses through his teeth and turns away, rolling onto his stomach.

"Sorry," I whisper. "I didn't mean to..."

"I know," he grunts. There is silence. He can't blame it on needing to pee. "It's been a really long time," he finally says.

"Yeah, me too," I tell him.

I hear his disgruntled laugh. "It's been a little longer than one night for me."

"I'm not sleeping with your brother," I reply, my voice barely a whisper. "It was one of the conditions I set out before I'd agree to come on this trip."

He makes that noise he does occasionally, as if all the air's been knocked out of him.

He remains on his stomach but turns his head to face me. "Haven't you been dating him for, like, a year or two? Why would you suddenly refuse to sleep with him?" His voice is as low and careful as mine.

"We were seeing each other casually before and I ended things last August," I tell him. "He asked me to give him a chance and I agreed, but I didn't want...sex confuses things."

"I'd probably be better off not knowing that," he groans, turning his face into his makeshift pillow.

And I understand that. I'd be better off too.

I'm exhausted, but I remain awake for a long time after that, wishing I was still just Ilina Andreyev, living in some shitty apartment I can barely afford, and curled under a blanket with a doctor named Josh. Whose brother I'd never met.

29

JOSH

February 1st

I wake in the morning, hard as nails.

It's not entirely a surprise, as that's how I spent most of the previous night.

It doesn't help that I'm currently pressed—insistent and throbbing—against Drew's ass. I roll away from her, willing it to retreat, and she wakes.

"Is it just me or did the temperature drop about forty degrees?" she asks, yawning.

I'm pretty sure it did—another reason I was up most of the night. Cold weather and significant temperature changes can trigger asthma. I spent the night alternating between checking her breathing and trying to will my erection away. I want to ask her about it even now, but I'm worried I'll trigger a panic attack if she senses I'm concerned. My fury at Joel has only grown over the course of this trip.

She rolls over, clinging to my back for warmth. I can feel her nipples even through her *sweatshirt*.

Fuck my life.

"You talk in your sleep," I tell her.

"You're making that up," she says, but when I don't argue, she concedes with a sigh. "What did I say?"

"You were talking about how hot I am." I can feel her cheek curving against my spine as she smiles. "Fine. I might have misinterpreted that part. No seriously, you just kept repeating numbers."

"That lines up," she says. "I'm extremely good at math, having made it all the way through the eleventh grade."

I laugh. "It was less math and more like...you were ordering Chinese food. You kept repeating the same numbers again and again saying 'the one-ninety-nine' and 'the eight-eight'. Do you remember what it was?"

She stiffens and rolls away. "No."

There are no jokes about Chinese food or implications that they were sexual positions.

That's how I know she's lying to me.

THE RIVER IS DEEMED passable when everyone wakes. We pack up our stuff and plunge in, tethered to one another. The water is surprisingly cold, and I place a hand on Drew's shoulder—in part because the stream is still rushing fast enough to sweep someone to sea, in part because it allows me to silently assess her breathing once more. She still seems fine, thank God.

When we reach the other side, everyone is soaking wet and filthy but buoyant, thrilled to have made it. There are cheers and laughter and it's a relief, but I don't feel all that celebratory. When Drew and I say goodbye at the airport tomorrow, that will be it...unless she actually stays with my brother, which would be even worse.

The commentary grows bawdy as we descend toward Hanakapiai Beach and our final river crossing.

Dietrich, Anna's husband, says something to Kathy and Samantha about noises coming from their tent and says he was tempted to watch.

"We heard you in your tent last night too, Dietrich!" shouts Kathy in reply. "Sounded like you needed to be watching *someone* because you were definitely doing it wrong."

There is laughter and then Kai says, "If we're watching people, my vote is for Josh and Lina because how does that work? He's, like, twice her size."

"I bet they make it work," says Kathy with a throaty laugh.

I shut my eyes momentarily. God help me, but I've spent a lot of time thinking about how we'd make it work. Drew buries her face in her hands, simultaneously amused and embarrassed. "We're both virgins, actually," she announces.

"Josh, dude, tell me she's full of shit," begs Kai, sounding personally wounded by the possibility.

"She's full of shit," I mutter. There's literally no way that would be true if she and I were a couple.

We cross the last stream, make our final climb, and then descend at last. At the end of the trail, the women hug and Kathy pulls Drew aside and asks for an autograph.

"You don't look *that* different with darker hair," she says, winking at me.

We head to the parking lot. Even from a distance, I can see Joel there, sitting on the hood of the Jeep. He hops down and starts to approach with a bouquet in one hand, a bottle of tequila in the other—and a shit-eating grin on his face like he's already sure he'll be forgiven.

That grin is what has me walking faster. Drew grumbles behind me, accusing me of trying to compete with her, but that's not what this is.

Joel steps forward, still smiling, holding out the bottle of tequila, which I suppose is some kind of *Thanks for taking care of my girlfriend* gift.

My fist swings out before I've even thought it through. He bends over, airless and gasping, and I hit him again.

"What the fuck, dude?" he shouts, but I'm not done. I throw him against the Jeep, and it all spills out. All the tension I've held inside me for two days has corroded my patience with him down to nothing.

"You had her fucking inhaler!" I shout. "She could have *died* because you couldn't be troubled to show up!"

"I didn't know!" shouts Joel. I have no idea if he's telling the truth. It hardly matters. He should have checked. He should have killed himself not to abandon her.

"Josh," Drew says behind me, soft and shocked.

I let him go and he walks straight to Drew, pulling her against his chest. She is stiff in his arms.

"I'm so sorry," he says. "I had no idea. Are you okay?"

"I'm fine," she says, stepping away from him. "We should get going. I want to shower before we head to the airport."

"I'm really sorry," Joel says again. "I meant to meet y'all at the stop, but the interview ran long."

His hand goes to the small of her back, as if she didn't need any assistance along one of the world's deadliest trails but needs assistance *now*, across ten feet of flat parking lot. He picks up the flowers he dropped when I grabbed him and hands them to her. "These are for you."

"Jesus fucking Christ," I mutter, reaching over to remove her backpack.

Her eyes meet mine. Her smile is apologetic. I hope to God it doesn't mean she's letting this all go.

PART IV

OAHU

"Say what you will about the other islands, there's no doubt
Oahu's medical care is second to none."
Oahu: The Adventure of a Lifetime

30

DREW

I've lost count of the number of times Six has tried to hug me between leaving the trail and boarding this plane. He's constitutionally incapable of believing he isn't forgiven. I might have been able to put up with it all if I hadn't seen my toiletry kit dumped out on the bathroom counter, my inhaler clearly visible.

I cried then, but my tears weren't over him. I've always known what he is and what he is not, and any hope we had of a relationship died days ago. I cried because of *me*, because I'm fucked up enough to have put up with it all. And because somewhere in the world, Josh will continue to exist without me—big, beautiful, endlessly protective—and I'm the piece of shit who will never deserve him.

"What would you like to do tonight?" Six asks, tucking a strand of hair back from my face. I want to jerk away from him. I want to ask the airline attendant for a different seat. It's only for Beth's sake that I don't, but I'm not sure how to keep up this charade through the final night of the trip.

"I think your parents made a reservation for dinner," I reply. "And they want to do that sunset thing at the hotel."

He groans. "Jesus, *again*?" As if the sunset is like Mount Rushmore, something you only need to see once. "We can do our own thing."

"That would be kind of shitty to your parents," I reply. "They probably want everyone together on the last night."

He snorts. "Right. They want everyone together so my father can sit there and talk only to Josh? Hard pass."

That chip he has on his shoulder, I wonder if he even means what he says anymore, or if it's just a convenient way to blame someone else for his failings. "I'm staying with your parents," I reply. "You can do what you want."

And then my gaze moves past him to Josh, sitting alone across the aisle from us. He's got his laptop out, feverishly typing.

He's just...lovely. How did I never notice that flush to his cheeks, the way his tongue taps his lip when he's deep in thought?

Or those hands. Jesus. Those big hands, calloused from doing God knows what and the tendons in his forearms that move as he types.

Ah, except you did notice, I think. *You always noticed and you hated yourself for it while pretending it was him you hated instead.*

We arrive in Oahu, grab our bags and walk out to the van waiting to take us to the hotel. Six, chatting amiably with our driver, starts to take the front seat.

"For the thousandth time," Josh says between his teeth, "she gets carsick."

This is what it's like, I think, *when someone actually cares about you. They remember you get carsick. They worry about your inhaler.*

He catches my gaze and for a moment our eyes lock, and it's like that moment on Kalalau Beach all over again. When I saw everything he was and he saw me back.

And tomorrow, it all comes to an end.

WE CHECK into the same rooms we had before. Six tries to pull me in for yet another hug and I push him away. "Please just stop," I tell him and he stomps out of the room, irritated with me.

I open my suitcase but most of my nice clothes are looking rumpled and worse for wear. On a whim, I call downstairs and get them to deliver that white dress Josh and I saw in the window. For just this one night, I want to be that other girl, the one I might have been if my entire life had been different.

Once I've showered, I don the crisp white cotton dress—a sleeveless V-neck with an empire waist, draping loosely from my rib cage to my ankles. There's a hint of cleavage, but it's more girlish than sexy, and in the mirror I see a woman Josh would take to a work party, would come home to after a long day. A woman who isn't a disaster, who's happy with a simple life instead of a girl who's unhappy with her complex one.

For a moment, I want to be her so bad I can taste it.

I grab my purse and room key and walk out the door at the same moment Josh does.

He comes to a stop, his eyes moving over me, head to foot. He pushes his damp hair off his forehead and releases a small breath.

"Is that the dress from the window?" he asks. His voice is like velvet.

"Yeah," I say. I feel stupid now, as if I reached too far to be something I'm not. I shrug. "All my clothes were dirty and—"

"I like it," he says. He coughs, looks sheepish suddenly. "I mean...you look nice."

My cheeks heat like a preteen on her first date.

He looks past me. "Where's Joel?" His brows pull together in consternation.

I exhale heavily. "He stormed out of the room a while ago. I honestly have no idea where he went."

Josh's nostrils flare and his mouth opens, but then—his jaw grinding with the effort—he stops himself from saying whatever he was about to and gestures toward the elevator. We walk side by side, the soft fabric of my dress swishing against his shorts. He holds the elevator door for me and pushes the buttons inside.

"So what happens when you get back to LA?" he asks.

My gaze flickers to his, uncertain if he means in general or with his brother specifically. "I'm only there through the weekend. And then I'm on to New York to pack up and leave for my apology interviews before I complete the tour."

"I don't know why you're going along with that," he says.

"I'm okay with people believing what they want," I reply. "As long as it isn't the truth."

Telling the world I get panic attacks is like inviting them to research my past, beyond all the half-truths I've told. They'd dig and dig until they discovered where it all began—my mother's affair, my father's death. It was hard enough to live through once. I don't need to relive it in every interview I give for the rest of my life.

We reach the bar just as the sun sinks behind the horizon. The crowd is already starting to disperse.

Beth, Jim and Six are all sitting together looking a little miserable, but Beth lights up as Josh pulls a chair out for me.

"Don't you look lovely," she says, so earnestly and with so much affection it leaves me feeling close to tears.

I smile at her, hiding the lump in my throat. Beth is so much better to me than any member of my family is, and I'm desperately sad it's about to come to an end.

"Thank you," I manage to say. It's such a nice moment, and I get the feeling that Six—leaning back in his chair, swishing ...

way he does when he's drunk or about to be an asshole—is about to ruin it.

"You look like a preschool teacher," he says.

Josh, behind me, stiffens. "Watch your fucking mouth," he says, pressing me into the seat with his hand on my shoulder, his eyes never leaving Six's face.

"What?" Six asks with a smirk. "It wasn't an insult. I like preschool teachers just fine."

Josh remains behind my chair. "Get up," he tells Six.

"Josh," his mother says gently. "Just take a seat, honey. He's had too much to drink and—"

Six's chair scrapes the cement as he pushes backward. "I'm going out," he announces, looking at me. "You coming?" It's more a statement than a question. He *assumes* I'm coming, and he's set this up so no one can win. If I leave with him, Beth will be upset. If I stay, she'll worry that we're fighting. I can't believe he's doing this to me *or* her.

"It's our last night here," I reply, remaining in my seat. "I think we should stay."

His mouth presses flat. "Fine. Have fun." And then he's gone. Beth's eyes close and her shoulders sag.

Josh exhales. "I'm sorry, Mom."

She waves him off. "I just wish the two of you got along. The day will come when you only have each other."

She chokes on those last words and Jim takes her hand. "It's been a stressful few days," he says. "Let's just head to the room."

"No," Beth argues, swallowing, "Drew was right. It's our last night."

But she looks sad and exhausted and it's clear she's pushed herself too hard. "We have a very long day of travel together tomorrow," I tell her. "Don't stay on my account. I doubt I'll be up that long myself."

Beth allows herself to be led upstairs, and then it's only me and Josh. He once said I was the glue holding them together, but it hardly feels that way. If I'd just left when Sloane did, maybe the four of them would be sitting at this table still. Josh sinks into the seat across from mine and kicks my foot.

"None of this is your fault," he says quietly.

"It feels like it is."

"I think you've just gotten very used to being blamed," he says. "My brother started this by being a callous, spoiled little shit, and the only problem is that he continued to be one."

"But your mom—"

"Wants the world for her boys. Every mother probably does. It's not your fault she can't give it to them." He gives me a small smile. "We basically started this trip together alone. Might as well end it this way too."

I smile against my will. "You want to hear something unsettling?" I ask, desperate to lighten the mood. "Your parents are the only ones on this trip who had sex."

"That," he replies "was *so* unnecessary." And then he laughs, and as badly as this night has gone, I'm glad it's turned out this way too.

We order drinks and food and it's easy and hard at the same time. Being near him is like seeing exactly how happy you could be if you'd been born into someone else's life. "Are you over there thinking deep thoughts?" he asks.

I smile. "I'm not smart enough for deep thoughts, only shallow ones."

He shakes his head as he refills my wine glass. "That's not true. And I don't think I've ever met someone who hides as much as you do either."

"Hides?" I ask. I pick up the wine glass and hold it to my chest. "I'm an open book."

"Oh yeah?" he asks. "Then how'd you get that scar on your nose?"

"Taking down Bin Laden," I reply, pushing my hair back. "I was a Navy SEAL before I went into music."

He smiles. "That's impressive. Especially since you'd have been, like, twelve."

I shrug. "As you should know by now, I'm incredibly fit."

He laughs and lets it go, thank God. Maybe I'm not an open book, but that's how it is when you know every answer will only lead to more questions.

He excuses himself and walks up to the stage, to the guy playing guitar there. It seems bizarrely outgoing for Josh. I'm not sure I've ever seen him *willingly* speak to anyone aside from his family.

I raise a brow when he returns. "What was that about?"

"He wanted to know where you got the scar on your nose," he replies. "I told him you were in a fight club and couldn't discuss it."

I grin. "The first rule of fight club..."

"Is don't talk about fight club," he concludes.

The guy on the stage taps on the microphone to get everyone's attention. I turn toward him and he's looking straight at me. "I understand we have a guitar player in the house," he says into the mic. "Lina, come on up here."

I blink, looking at the smattering of people still sitting here, before I turn to stare at Josh.

"Dude, what the *fuck*?" I whisper.

"You were able to astonish everyone last night playing an instrument you'd never actually played before. And you sing in front of thousands of people. How could *this* be a big deal?"

I swallow. "That's different."

"Because it doesn't matter," he says, rising to his feet and reaching out a hand to me. "Maybe it's time you tried doing something that does. Play your new song. Play the old songs you wrote. Just promise me you won't play *Naked*."

I laugh. "God, you're the worst."

He just grins. "That song is such a trainwreck."

I'm still laughing, still terrified, as I make my way up to the stage. Which isn't even a stage, really, just a two-foot-high plat-form big enough for four people at most.

A guitar is placed in my hands and I mess around tuning it simply to drown out the noise in my head. I'm tempted to simply play something old, something from the 70s that my father taught me. Fleetwood Mac, maybe, or The Eagles. It's an older crowd. They'd like it and I could slink away.

But Josh is right. This is a chance to be that other version of myself, the real one I've spent so many years hiding, so I start with one of the songs I used to play, an original I submitted which led to my first record deal but never made it onto the album. *Not sexy enough*, Davis said. I should have known right there we had painfully different visions for my career, not that it would have mattered. I was hungry and desperate back then. I'd have sung anything if it led to a record deal. I was tired of being broke, yes, but mostly I wanted something to throw in my mother's face after the years she spent telling me I was wasting my life.

I've played it so often that it comes now with no thought, but there are goosebumps on my arms. When the words are your own, it's like standing naked in front of the world with no idea if they'll cheer or boo at the end.

I play the final notes, and the applause comes fast and loud and sharp. It's the sort of applause that comes when you've surprised people, in a good way. I remember this feeling from when I was a teenager, and the quiet hope that accompanied it: that maybe I was slightly less useless than I'd been led to believe, than I'd allowed myself to believe.

Before the applause starts to die down, I turn and try to hand the guitar back to the musician, but he waves me off. "You play way better than I do," he says.

I hesitate, but then I glance at Josh and he smiles at me, and that's all it takes. I sling the guitar strap over my shoulder and face the crowd again.

I play two more of the early songs, and then, with a deep breath, I strum the first few chords of the new song, trying to get a feel for it again.

I've played around with it, of course, but I've never performed it before and the two things are night and day. I've always kept the vocals simple and spare, whispered almost, because I've been singing them in hotel rooms, terrified of being overheard. "Umm, this is something I've been working on, but it's a little rough," I warn the crowd. "Bear with me here."

My heart beats hard. It's not simply that it's mine. It's that this song is more earnest and heartfelt than anything I've ever sung. It's about knowing exactly the life you'd choose if you could step out of the one you were in, and it reveals more about me than I'd like to share.

I begin tentatively, still considering ditching out even as I begin to sing. But toward the end of the first verse, it suddenly starts to feel right. As if I'm exactly where I'm supposed to be, doing exactly what I'm supposed to be doing, and it can't go wrong because...I love this song. I love it more than I've ever loved anything, and in a way, it doesn't even matter if anyone else feels the same.

The crowd is on the edge of their seats. I can feel the excitement in the air. Those baby fine hairs on the back of my arms stand on end as if electrified as I head toward the chorus. And then I look at Josh and realize something: I wrote these words about him. I thought I was writing it about my career, about how I'd choose a different life. But no, it was simply him. He's what I would choose.

The song is still brief, since I've only got two verses. It ends quickly and then people are jumping to their feet, clapping for me, and it means more than any standing ovation in a sold-out arena ever has because they're actually clapping for *me*. For

Ilina Andreyev, the nobody daughter of a fuck-up who is falling for the wrong guy.

"That was amazing," says a woman, gripping my arms as I walk off the stage to get back to Josh. "Don't let all that talent go to waste."

I smile at her but I'm shaking, so high from the experience I feel like I can barely put one foot in front of the other. I stumble forward, past all the back pats and the shoulder slaps and fall against Josh, standing near our table, like he's home base, like nothing can hurt me if he's near.

His arms wrap around me. "You were perfect, Ilina Andreyev," he says quietly.

I could argue that it could have been better, that I went into the first verse too late, but I don't. In an imperfect life, it—and this moment—are as close to perfect as I've ever come.

We walk back to our wing slowly. The breeze rustles through the palms, the crickets chirp. I wish we were running in the morning but our flight leaves too early.

"So what are you gonna do?" he asks as we walk into the elevator.

I blink up at him, unable to imagine any question he isn't the center of. *Am I going to tell him how I feel? Am I going to think about him every single day after we leave here?* "Do?" I repeat.

"With the song," he says, and something inside me deflates. But really, what did I think he might ask me? "Are you going to push to add it to the new album?"

I give him a sad smile. In order for that to happen, I'd have to fight for it, and then it would get turned into overproduced garbage, and I'd have to share the writing credit with four assholes the record label brings in to 'help' and it's *my* song. Plus, it would never be a single. It would be the song everyone skips past to get to the next *Naked*. "Nah. It would never work."

"I don't get you," he says. "You aren't happy with the way things are going. Your manager is a dick. You've been pushed into singing shit you hate, and you just keep signing up for more of it. Why not just step off the bus and get on a new one, going somewhere you want to be?"

I blink up at him. He's co-opted my theory about love, but I guess it works here as well as there. "Because I know where this bus goes. *That* one could lead me to a super bad section of town and dump me there."

We've reached my door. It strikes me this may be our last moment alone, and I want to say something big to him, but the words just don't come. "Thanks for making me get out there tonight," I tell him instead. "I'm glad I did it."

His eyes hold mine and he bites his lip. "Drew," he says. He pushes a hand through his hair. "I—"

Just then my door opens and Six stands there, looking between the two of us. "What's going on?" he asks. The question is mild, containing only the barest hint of suspicion. It's simply guilt that has me feeling like I was just caught at something.

"Nothing," I say. My eyes dart to Josh's. "Good night," I whisper as I walk past Six into the room. My steps drag. There is something so deeply wrong with the fact that I'm *here* rather than with Josh right now.

Six shuts the door and attempts to hug me. "Don't," I snap. "You were awful to me and your mother left in tears. A hug might fix this with her, but it fixes nothing with me."

I storm away to get ready for bed, and it's only after I slide between the sheets that he joins me again, wrapping an arm around my waist. All I can think of is Josh's arm, Josh's broad chest pressed to my back. I take small breaths through my nose, desperate to get through this last night and get back home.

"Drew," Six whispers. "I'm sorry, okay? I messed up. I know I messed up. I was an asshole. But you're what I want. You've always been what I wanted and I just didn't...I wasn't ready, okay? I wasn't ready and now I am. It's going to be different from now on."

"It's late," I reply. He's drunk and I don't want this to turn into a fight and I definitely don't want to find myself going to the front desk and asking for my own room. "Can we discuss this tomorrow?"

He pulls me closer. I have to force myself to stay in place. "Yes, baby," he says. "Anything you want. From here on, you make the rules."

It's not until he's asleep that I grab my pillow and head to the couch. Six makes a mess of everything, but I do too. Which of us really wreaked more havoc on this trip? Which of us was the reason Sloane left, which of us is the reason Beth never managed to bring her boys together?

Maybe we're a perfect match after all. We both ruin everything we touch.

31

DREW

February 2nd

The sun has just come up when we assemble in front of the hotel to head to the airport. Six is careful with me, sweet and solicitous.

He opens the van's front door. "She gets carsick," he tells the driver, pressing his lips to my forehead. "She needs to ride up here with you."

I climb into the front seat, feeling like I could easily burst into tears at any moment. Inside me, there's a wire pulled taut, and my throat aches with the effort it takes to keep it from snapping. I stare out the window saying goodbye to this island, wishing I could replay a thousand moments I've had these past days—and every single one of them was with Josh.

He's in the back right now, with his father grilling him about his schedule these next few weeks. The idea that Josh and I will be on the same coast and not see each other seems impossible to me, but what would I even say? *Hey, I'm ending this with your brother. Want to get a drink before you leave for a year?*

Even if I could somehow come up with the right words—and there is really no clean, acceptable way to hit on your ex's brother—it would be futile anyhow. He's leaving, he could never tell his family, and I can barely picture the amount of blame that would be bandied about if people knew I'd ditched Six for his brother. We view men like wayward little boys, but we judge women the way we do ourselves: as harshly as possible. It's hard enough handling the judgment I get over things I *haven't* done.

We arrive. The luggage is dealt with and then we go to the first-class lounge to wait. Six goes to the bar for a drink and I take a seat next to Beth. "You look tired, hon," she says, running a hand over my hair. "I figured you'd sleep like a baby last night."

I blink tears away. What might it have been like to be raised by someone like Beth, someone who watches out for you, worries about you? To simply have a bad day or a bad night's sleep and have someone concerned rather than accusing you of "sulking" or "theatrics".

"I'm fine," I tell her. "I've had such an amazing trip. I really can't thank you enough for including me." By which I mean *Thank you so much for making me feel like you wanted me here, for not ever making me feel like a burden. Thank you for letting me see what that's like.*

She wraps an arm around my shoulders and rests her head against mine. "Hawaii with my boys was always a dream of mine," she says. "But you made it better."

Six returns with gin and tonics for us both. Beth releases me and his arm replaces hers. Josh's gaze narrows, and remains on us as Six's mouth presses to the side of my head. Six is talking about what we'll do this week in LA and I want to sink in my seat. I know I won't be seeing him once we're home, but I put up with it all for Beth's sake until I can't stand it.

"I'll be back in a minute," I announce, and I walk out of the lounge and into the shops, trying to talk myself out of crying as I look around. Nothing in my life is different than it was when I arrived in Hawaii twelve days ago, but everything that mattered before just feels meaningless now. I buy something for Tali, and then stop to watch as people swarm at a gate to board their flight. A man wraps his arm around his wife's waist, shoots a warning glare at the people encroaching from behind. She leans into him, as if he'll always be there. The day is probably going to come when she leans and he lets her fall, but I feel very alone watching them anyway.

I slowly walk back to the first-class lounge and just as it comes into view, a figure pushes away from the wall. Josh, his lovely brow furrowed, watching me.

"My flight is boarding," he says. "But I wanted to say goodbye."

"I don't understand," I whisper. I sound as if I've been punched. Even if we weren't going to be sitting together, I thought I had at least six more hours to look over at him. "You're not coming to LA?"

His shake of the head is so small it's barely noticeable. He holds my gaze as if he knows I'm upset, knows *why* I'm upset. "I have to give a talk at Stanford tomorrow. I'm flying straight to San Francisco."

"Oh." I feel frozen, trying to ward off the wave of grief as it hits.

The speaker overhead announces the final boarding call.

He steps closer. Close enough that I can feel his breath against my face. "Tell me something real," he says.

I try to smile but it's twisted by sadness. I wish I could give him the entire world. I wish there was anything he wanted that my money could buy. But all he wants is a tiny bit of the truth from me, maybe because he knows it's the hardest thing for me to give.

"When I was eleven, my dad got drunk and threw a bottle at

my face," I tell him. My dad was the only person who seemed to like me back then, but even he didn't like me quite enough. "He lost visitation and that was the last time I saw him. That's how I got the scar."

What a sad, awkward little gift to give him. My way of saying *I trust you, Josh, and I don't trust anyone else*. I turn to walk away so he won't see me cry, and have taken exactly one step when he says my name and reaches for me.

And that's all it takes: he closes the distance, pulling me against him, and his hands are cradling my jaw and his mouth is on mine as if it's always wanted to be there. For one long, breathless moment, nothing exists but him and the way he is kissing me.

"I would give anything for things to have been different," he says. And then he walks away, disappearing into the crowd of people boarding their flight.

I want to reach up to feel my lips, to assure myself the kiss really happened.

I want to run after him.

Instead, I return to the lounge on unsteady legs, feeling like something inside me just died.

Beth, Jim and Six all sit there, scrolling through their phones. We've traveled together for two weeks straight but Josh was the part that made me happy. Josh was the part that felt like home.

When our flight boards, Six grabs his blanket and spreads it over the two of us. Beneath it, he reaches for my hand. I suspect I've got about thirty seconds before he tries to move it to his dick. And I can't do this, not for another moment.

"Hey," he says. "I know we still need to talk."

I pull my hand away and reach for the headphones. "No, we don't. Whatever this was, it is definitely over."

I honestly can't believe I ever dated him in the first place.

PART V

HOME

"It's almost too broad a topic for just one book."
From *Mainland US: Adequate Medical Care and Lots to See*

32

DREW

I wake to sun streaming through the floor-to-ceiling windows of the cottage I'm renting at the Chateau Marmont. I have fifteen missed calls from Davis. Not a single one from Josh.

I shuffle out of bed only to draw the drapes closed, and then I return, flopping face down on the mattress.

I'm not sure how to go back to my regular life. I'm not sure what made my feet move before. I *thought* I knew. I thought I wanted to be vindicated, that I wanted to make more money than my stepfather, have more fame and clout than the whole family put together, and possibly use it to ruin my stepfather's firm. But now it just seems...petty. Now it just seems like I've been fueling myself with rage because I had nothing else to drag me out of bed in the morning.

I get up long enough to order an Hermès scarf for Beth. I have it hand delivered along with a note thanking her for the trip and telling her how much I enjoyed spending time with her. I apologize, too, for the way things worked out with Six. It must have been pretty clear it was over on the way home, but there is a small part of me that wants to make sure she knows, that wants to make sure *Josh* knows, though it will change absolutely nothing. How could it? I can't jump from one brother to the next, and Josh cares too much about his mom to throw that kind of grenade into the middle of the family, even if he was staying here—which he is not.

Eventually, I accept the calls from Davis, as it's only a matter of time before he shows up at my door—he knows this is the only place I stay in LA—and the next morning I find myself walking into my publicist's conference room for a strategy meeting I don't want to be at.

I hate my publicist's big, soulless office complex, all gray cement block and glass. The first-floor room looks as if it could survive a bomb blast, though I wouldn't want it to. Same goes for the expressionless people sitting around the table.

"What the hell did you do to your hair?" Davis demands, as if the room isn't full of officious strangers in suits, listening avidly.

Two weeks ago, I'd have felt like I needed to apologize, as if it was someone else's hair I cut without permission. Now I'm just irritated. "It's called a haircut, Davis. Are you unfamiliar with the term? Have one of your suited minions look it up for you."

Stephanie, the publicist, frowns at me and puts a hand on his shoulder. She often winds up playing peacemaker, but he's the one she will defer to in the end. "Settle down. Maybe this is good. We're showing the new, more serious side of her. It can be like she's turned over a new leaf."

Davis slumps in his chair. "No one will want to fuck the more serious side of her, however."

I imagine Josh hearing this—I suspect he'd be out of his chair. What did he say to that surf instructor? *Come repeat that on shore, asshole.* I'd love to hear him say that to Davis.

"I looked like this when you met me," I remind him, taking a seat at the far end of the table. They both blink, if is M forgotten I had a voice at all. "You thought I was pretty enough *then*."

"But were you famous then?" he asks. "No, you were not."

"I still think we should say she went to rehab," Stephanie tells him. "No one is going to believe there weren't illegal substances involved."

Davis shakes his head. "There are too many photos of her in Hawaii. Let's just stipulate that it isn't discussed in interviews and release a statement *implying* she was at rehab without stating it outright. Just refer to *some much-needed time away*. Everyone will assume it's rehab, she apologizes, people move on."

I sit back, listening to them discuss me as if I'm not in the room. As if I'm an entity rather than a person. How long has it been like this and why did I allow it? I suppose because when it started, I just felt lucky and I didn't want to jinx it. And what's different today is that I no longer feel lucky. I don't care quite so much if I jinx it.

"I'm not apologizing," I say flatly. "And I'm not letting anyone imply I'm on drugs."

They look at me again, surprised, irritated. *The sex doll speaks and thinks she has a right to make demands*, their faces say.

"Please let us do our jobs," Stephanie says. "We're trying to get you out of a mess you've created."

I stand up and they both look surprised. Again.

"What are you doing?" asks Davis.

"It's called walking out," I reply. "And if this press tour doesn't go the way I like, prepare to see a lot more of it."

The room is utterly silent as I make my way to the door. I want to feel empowered, but instead the world just feels very large, too full and too empty all at once. The problem with burning bridges is that you need to have someplace else to go.

I'T's Tali I call in desperation.

She meets me at a sunny patio café in Huntington Beach, halfway between Laguna and LA. The sight of her temporarily makes me forget all my woes.

"Holy shit," I say, staring at her stomach. She didn't look so pregnant the last time I saw her, but now... "You can't possibly have two more months left."

She laughs and sinks into the chair across from me like a pregnant woman would, hand on her stomach as if she's not sure the baby knows to come with her. "It's bizarre, I know."

"What if this kid is Hayes's size?" I ask. "Your vagina will be permanently ruined."

She raises a brow. "It's as if you consulted a list of the worst possible things to say to a pregnant woman and are running through them as fast as possible."

"Sorry," I say meekly. "No filter."

She laughs. "You and Hayes both. He asked my doctor if we could just go ahead and schedule this as a C-section 'to ensure everything remains the appropriate size'. So enough about me and my vagina...which Bailey brother are you with today?"

I roll my eyes. I texted her about the Kalalau Trail, but she doesn't know everything that came afterward, and there's really no reason to tell her. Nothing will come of it. "Neither of them."

"Well," she says with a sigh. "I guess it could be worse."

"Josh kissed me," I blurt. *So much for keeping it to myself.* "At the airport."

She is wide-eyed with delight. "That's so—"

"Don't say it."

She says it anyway. "Romantic."

I lean back in my seat and pull my hair out of its messy bun. "You think *everything* is romantic."

"Believe me, there was never a single thing you told me about Six that I'd have claimed was romantic. And I mean. "

She pulls out her phone. I have no idea how she has pictures of Josh at the ready, but she does. "Look at this guy."

He isn't smiling in the picture. He isn't even posing in the picture. He's standing there in scrubs talking to someone, looking distracted and pissy and perfect and I just...miss him. That's all there is to it. I miss him so much that it makes everything else pale by contrast. I've avoided looking Josh up online for this very reason—because I knew it would hurt, and because I knew there'd be this swirl of longing in my chest and I'd have nowhere to go with it.

"I don't know what to do," I whisper.

"Does he know you're not with his brother?" she asks. "That might help."

I nod. "I told Beth and I'm sure she's told Josh," I reply. "He's the person she seems to lean on the most."

I want Tali to give me an excuse for why I haven't heard from him, but there's nothing. All I see in her eyes is sympathy right now, as if this is a story that's already come to a close.

WHEN I GET BACK to the hotel, I climb into bed and stay there. I don't run. I don't worry about what I'm eating. My hygiene is questionable at best, but I figure it's my last hurrah: once the tour begins, it'll be upkeep and starvation 24/7. It always is.

I'm still in bed on Sunday, the day before I leave, when my cell rings. The moment I see Beth's name the fog hanging over me vanishes. I sit up, yanking my eye mask off the top of my head. I can't stop the small thrill in my chest, though she's probably just calling about the scarf or to discuss the breakup.

"Drew!" she cries, "I'm so happy I caught you. You weren't asleep, were you?"

I force a laugh. "Of course not," I reply. "It's..." I look at the clock. "After one."

"We're having lunch at the Chateau and I just heard someone say you're staying here in the hotel. Are you around? Can you pop by to say hello?"

I want to ask who's coming as I agree, but I don't.

Instead, I literally run into the shower, yelping at the cold water as I start to scrub, already scolding myself. "Josh won't be there," I announce to the shower walls. "And you're an idiot getting your hopes up about nothing."

What would I even say if he was there? It's not as if I can tell him in front of his parents that nothing but him has mattered to me since that moment in the airport, and probably long before that. I won't be able to say anything at all. And if it mattered to him that I wasn't with his brother he'd have said something by now.

I scrape my wet hair back from my face and pull it up into a bun, dab on a bit of lip gloss and mascara and pull a silk tank and skirt out of my closet, the kind of thing a publicist might wear but *Drew Wilson* would not.

I approve of the girl I see in the mirror. She looks exotic, French. Audrey Hepburn with lighter hair and a decent tan. I want Josh to be there so badly I can taste it. I want him to be there so badly I'm not sure I'll be able to stand my disappointment if he isn't.

I walk from my room to the restaurant's patio which sits under the graceful arch of palms, diluting the sun overhead. Planters divide the space but I notice heads turning as I approach. My new hair is still a miracle, however...people suspect I'm *someone*, but until they can put a name with my face, I get to remain anonymous. And I want anonymity more than anything right now, because in a moment I will either appear thrilled or devastated and there is no middle ground.

I'm about to approach the hostess when I see him.

Josh.

In khakis and a button-down, sleeves rolled up looking

impossibly beautiful. I remember ridiculing him for wearing that exact outfit when I arrived in Honolulu. Now I'm thinking I've never seen anything hotter in my life. It's as if he is suddenly the prototype upon which my tastes are created— if he decided to start wearing tank tops and Speedos, as unlikely as that is, I'd probably decide that also was my favorite outfit.

His eyes lock on mine, and there's a hard stab of want in my abdomen at the sight of him.

"I see them," I tell the hostess, my voice admirably calm and adult.

I make my way toward the table with the strangest mix of euphoria and fear swimming in my stomach, like nothing I've ever felt, even walking on stage. I worry it's all written on my face.

The Baileys rise as I approach. I hug Beth, and even Jim, and then I turn to face Josh. How did I forget how tall he is? Even in my small heels he looks like a giant above me.

He steps forward. I wouldn't say he looks happy to see me. It's more as if I'm something he unwillingly can't look away from. His arms wrap around me all too briefly.

"How have you been?" he asks. His voice is cool with disinterest.

I feel like I've been punched and I'm mad at myself for expecting anything from him in the first place.

"Good," I lie. My throat sounds like it's full of gravel. "Really good. I leave for New York tomorrow."

He nods and pulls out a chair for me beside him. Only remnants of their lunch remain. I wish I'd skipped the shower so I had more time with him. I also wish I hadn't come at all.

Beth starts telling me all about how he's testifying to Congress later in the week. "You'll have to watch him on C-SPAN if you get a chance," she urges, pride shining in her eyes.

I glance quietly running a hand over his face. "Mom,

you've got to stop telling people to watch C-SPAN. Especially people who are appearing on primetime the same day."

He knows my schedule. I want it to mean something. *God*, I want it to mean something, but he's barely even looking at me.

"I'm just proud of you, honey," Beth says to him, leaning back so the waitress can clear her plate. "Besides, Drew's practically family." She squeezes my hand. "Thank you so much for the scarf and the sweet note. I'm sorry things didn't work out with Joel, but you're both young still. Anything can happen."

Josh's gaze jerks to mine. That wariness in his eyes is now shock and—something else.

He didn't know. I have no idea if that changes anything, but based on the way he's looking at me now, it might.

Jim pays the bill while Beth asks about my plans and then suddenly we are all standing and my chance to change something between us is pretty much gone.

"Josh, honey, I want to go to the gift shop," she says. "Can you get the car? We'll meet you in front."

He nods, never taking his eyes off me.

I hug his parents goodbye and then it's just the two of us.

"So," I say nervously. The moment is too much. I stare at his shirt, focus on the texture of it. It would feel like fine grit sandpaper under my fingers, his chest hard beneath it.

"Let's walk," he says with the sort of decisiveness that makes my knees weak. I let myself be led from the restaurant. "Where's your room?"

I point toward the cottages weakly and we move, his hand on the small of my back as if we are a couple. I fumble with the key. The cottages at the Chateau are weirdly old-fashioned and still look like the sort of place where some 1950s starlet might drink herself to death in a satin robe. I wish now I'd stayed someplace modern, someplace for the well-adjusted.

When the door opens, he follows me inside and doesn't look at the room at all. He's only looking at me. I want to memorize his skin, his lovely mouth, his deep-set eyes. I search his face, wondering why he's here, looking for an answer so I won't have to ask.

He takes a step forward. I take one too. It feels as if we are magnetized, as if I can't stop moving his way until we are pressed together, skin to skin.

"Why didn't you tell me you broke up with Joel?" he asks.

"Would it have mattered?"

He pushes his hands into my hair, gripping my face in a way that shocks me, leaves me breathless. "That cannot be a serious question."

And then he kisses me. Not the way he kissed me in the airport. This time, he kisses me as if we've been kept apart by war and deserts and decades and he kept praying, the entire time, we'd somehow find each other.

He lifts me onto the small table behind me. His hands are on my bare thighs and our mouths are frantic. I groan and he pulls back.

"Drew," he whispers, his eyes closed. He's about to say goodbye and I won't allow it.

"Stay," I command.

His mouth lingers over mine, his palms stretch over my skin —my thighs, my ass, and higher—as if he's trying to touch as much of me as he can. "I have to take my parents home. My dad doesn't drive in the city."

And, of course, he can't tell them why he'd like to remain.

My hands slide up his shirt, clinging.

"Can you come back?" I ask.

There's a hint of a smile in the curve of his lips. "Yeah," he says. "I'm definitely coming back."

~

Two hours later, I hear his knock on the door.

In the time since he left, I've picked up the room and made the bed, all evidence of my depressive state hidden. I have showered again, shaved every inch of skin, moisturized, chosen better lingerie, and then put the same outfit on so he won't know I did it.

I am unreasonably nervous and far too sober. I wish I'd had a drink. I wish I'd had *ten* drinks.

He's in shorts and a t-shirt. It's my new favorite outfit. He bites down on his smile, his eyes curving into quarter moons, a flash of the dimple in his cheek. I want him more than I've ever wanted anyone and it feels like I'll never be brave enough for it at the same time.

"Do you want a drink?" I ask him. "I need a drink."

I reach for the champagne bottle on ice, provided by God knows who and God knows why. He takes it from my hand.

"I don't need a drink." He pops the cork with practiced ease, which surprises me. I didn't picture him having a lot of experience with champagne. "Should it bother me that you need one the second I walk in the room?"

I hop on the counter and hold out a champagne flute as if I'm still the casual girl who doesn't care about anything all that much. And then his gaze levels me, forces honest words from my mouth. "I'm nervous. You make me nervous."

His upper lip quirks up for half a second as he pours, quietly pleased. "You just spent several days risking life and limb trudging through mud with me. You've shared a tent with me. How could I be making you nervous *now*?"

"I wasn't about to sleep with you any of those times."

His eyes darken in a way that makes me shiver. Feral, dangerous, *certain* eyes. "And you're about to now?"

"We could play Monopoly if you prefer."

"Monopoly is a stupid fucking game," he says, stepping between my legs. He's decided something. I shiver again.

"Sounds like someone's not very good at M̶o̶n̶o̶p̶o̶l̶y̶"

He pulls the champagne flute from my hand. "I could kick your ass at Monopoly. Grab St. James Place and you've won the game."

He pulls my hips to his, his gaze trailing over my face before he leans down and kisses me. A light kiss made of whispers. A brush, a graze, his breath offering nearly as much pressure as his mouth.

"I haven't really done this before," I whisper. "Been present for it, I mean. I'm always drunk or high or half-asleep or just... zoning out."

He stops for a moment and studies me. "Why?"

I shrug. I know it makes no sense. Half my songs are about sex and the truth is I find it terrifying. "It was too...intimate. And I've always tried to bypass that feeling, but I don't want it to be that way with you."

He pushes the hair away from my face. "I want the real you, bad or good. Don't pretend things are fine if they're not, okay?"

I nod and pull him back to me. When he kisses me again, my nerves disappear, because he's so damned good at this. I've been kissed a thousand times by men who treated it like an annoying pitstop before the journey could begin. Josh kisses like this is the journey right here, as if this alone is enough.

It feels as if I'm made of warm air and little else. As if, without the weight of his hands, I might float away entirely or melt into a puddle at his feet.

His hands slide up to the silk tank and run beneath it, gliding over my skin, calloused thumbs grazing my rib cage, the underside of my breasts. Just the barest brush of his thumb but I feel it everywhere.

A man has never made me gasp simply by touching my breasts, but I'm not sure I've ever been seduced in precisely this way before either. As if I'm something precious and fragile, something to be savored.

"You okay?" he asks. He is hard as steel now, wedged between us, pressing against me.

"It was a good gasp," I reply breathlessly.

His fingers slide to my back and undo my strapless bra, removing it from beneath the shirt with practiced ease.

He pulls his head back just enough to glance down. My nipples poke the confines of the silk aggressively now, rubbing against the smooth fabric with every breath I take.

He shakes his head. "You tortured me on that goddamned trip." Over the tank, he runs a palm over one nipple before brushing it with his thumb, flicking it with his forefinger. I arch into his touch and my thighs tighten around him in response. I feel it everywhere. "I tried so fucking hard not to look," he groans. He bends to take one of my nipples between his teeth, tank and all. There's something strangely erotic in his refusal to undress me, in the feel of the now-wet silk against sensitive skin.

My legs lock around his waist, trying to pull him closer. I rock my hips, desperate for friction. If it takes him ten seconds to get inside me, that will be ten seconds too long. I reach for the button on his shorts.

His mouth is still on my breast. He raises a brow, stays my hand. "In a rush?"

"I'm ready," I tell him in lieu of the much cruder words I might normally use. I have no idea why I'm suddenly so timid. Maybe it's simply that I don't want to be *Drew Wilson* today. I don't want to be the brazen pop star who sings about sex without a hint of embarrassment. With Josh, I just want to be me, the real me. And that person is uncertain and even a little scared by this whole thing.

His hand slides up my thigh and presses between my legs. I see it in his face the moment he notes that my thong is soaked. It's like an electric charge.

"So you are," he says, removing his hand. He lifts me up and starts moving us toward the bedroom. "But I have thought about this for an extremely long time, and I want to savor it."

I snort, wrapping my legs around his waist. He carries me as if I weigh nothing at all. "You didn't even like me until a week ago."

"Wrong," he says, laying me on the bed. "And I'd have given up everything I own for *this* even if I didn't like you."

"That would be more flattering if you owned anything."

He laughs, kneeling between my legs to remove my tank at last, his eyes traveling over the exposed skin. I've never seen someone observe me the way he is now, like I'm some lost artifact no one thought was real.

"I'm feeling a little naked here," I tell him. "And if you turn that into a joke about the fucking song, I will kill you. I'll probably kill you and then have sex with your corpse, if that's anatomically possible, but the part where you die is the certainty."

He gives a low laugh and then starts to unbutton his shirt, tossing it behind him when he's done. "Better?" he asks.

All I can do is nod my approval, my eyes glued to his perfect chest. I've seen him without a shirt, of course, many times. But never like this...never above me, so much larger, so...mine. It's too much and not enough all at once. I'll never be able to get my fill of him. "Come here," I say, reaching up. His bare chest presses to mine. Skin to skin. The sensation is heady and intoxicating. I wish I could keep him like this forever, but this is probably only happening because I can't. That's what makes him safe.

His mouth moves to my neck as his hand slides inside my panties at last. I can't hold in the moan that escapes me.

"Jesus," he whispers, his strong fingers slipping in me and over me and making conscious thought difficult. He tugs the panties down my thighs and I kick them off as I reach for him. The button on his shorts releases easily, and I slide his boxers down just enough to see that tattoo I once glimpsed—a snake climbing a pole, inside this weird star.

"I wondered what was here," I tell him, my voice throaty with desire.

He glances down at my fingers, pressing against it. His nostrils flare as if even this much contact is too much. "It's the Star of Life," he says. "Symbol of emergency medicine. I lost a bet and that's what my friends picked."

They chose well. "What will I find if I keep exploring?" I ask, and my hand ventures further into his boxers until I grip him, hot and firm in my hand.

He stills for a moment, his eyelids fluttering closed. "Fuck," he groans as my hand wraps around him. "Drew...it's been a really long time." He sounds like he's choking.

"Good," I whisper. "Then you'll be able to go more than once."

He gives a pained laugh as my palm slides over him. He's thick in my hand, long and smooth as I stroke him from base to tip. His hand wraps around my wrist to stop me. "I don't think that's anything you'll have to worry about."

I lose my grip on him as he moves back and climbs off the mattress. He kicks off his shorts and boxers, then removes a condom from his wallet. The bed sinks beneath me as he kneels between my legs to roll it on. I'm feverish, slightly dazed, by the sight of him between my thighs. He is perfect *everywhere*.

And as exposed as I am right now with my legs wide, the way he looks at me—hungry, fierce—makes me feel sexy and powerful rather than vulnerable.

He leans over and places a kiss on my stomach, then between my breasts, and braces himself above me, pressing between my legs, watching my face earnestly, as if this matters. It feels almost too intimate. When he starts to thrust inside me, I close my eyes.

"Don't," he says. "I want you to see exactly who you're with."

"I do," I whisper, and he pushes in. Slowly. I feel every inch of him as he continues until he's fully inside me—so thick and perfect that the pleasure overwhelms me. My eyes want to shut, but I'm glad they don't, because it means I get to see his reaction too: his long lashes dipping for a moment, the soft, inaudible "*god*" he murmurs as he slides in the rest of the way.

I get to watch him suck in air between his teeth as he pulls back, and, finally, his own eyes shutting when he fills me again. His mouth dips to my neck then, presses to my skin. "Now you're the one who isn't looking," I say breathlessly as he pulls out.

"There was never a moment's doubt who I was with," he replies.

Ah. I love that. I love that I know it's true, I love that it sounds like something he'd rather not have admitted in the first place, that he isn't saying it in some attempt to charm me but simply because he doesn't want to lie.

It's a tight fit, the two of us. If I wasn't so wet, it would be *too* tight, but instead it's delicious, that friction.

There's an exquisite ache in my center and it's growing. I want to do this all night, moving as slowly as possible toward the moment when it all breaks open, but I'm already too far gone.

I wrap my legs around him, pulling myself closer, and it's as if that ache in my center has taken on a life of its own. "Faster," I beg.

He winces. "Jesus, I'm gonna come so hard."

But he complies, drawing back and slamming into me. I see stars. Again and again he does it, faster and deeper with every stroke. I cling to him, desperately holding on. And then I can no longer keep my eyes open and light explodes behind my eyelids. I come, gasping his name, my head falling backward, only vaguely aware of him thrusting hard and then holding

He falls by my side, wincing as he pulls out and ties off the condom. And then he tugs me against him.

"I've wanted that for so long that if you'd asked me an hour ago, I'd have told you it couldn't possibly live up to my expectations," he says. "Yet it was better."

I peer up at him. "I have to assume you didn't want it for *that* long," I reply. "You're still the guy whose primary concern a few weeks ago was where I would vomit."

He laughs. "I've wanted you since the first night I saw you," he says. "Last summer, at the party."

"You acted like you hated me at that party."

His mouth curves up just a hint. An almost smile that is rueful and apologetic at the same time. "Sometimes," he says, pulling the sheets over us both, "it's easier to hate something than admit you're just pissed off you'll never have it."

And with that said, we're both remembering *why* he thought he could never have it. Does he feel guilty? Because I do, even if Six did pretty much everything wrong.

"Where do your parents think you are?" I ask.

He runs a hand through his hair. "I said I was out with friends," he says. "I hate keeping secrets but my mom can never know about this. She still has it in her head that Joel and I will be close one day. I think, mostly, she wants him to have someone to lean on when they're gone. She'd be devastated if she knew."

I force myself to smile. There's no reason what he's saying should hurt. I guess a part of me wonders if it's *entirely* for Beth's sake that he wants to keep it a secret. I'm hardly the sort of girl his buddies from med school seek out.

"I won't say anything," I tell him. "Jumping from one brother to the next wouldn't do my public image a lot of good anyway."

This really can't go anywhere, but it only occurs to me now that I'll probably never see him again after he leaves my room

He lives in some awful, war-torn country and has no plans to leave and if he *did* plan to leave, he'd have to lie to everyone he knows to make anything between us happen.

He raises himself on his forearm, pushing the hair away from my face. "I really like you, Drew. If I wasn't already leaving...I'm not sure I'd be able to stay away."

If he wasn't already leaving, I'm not sure I'd have let this happen in the first place. But that's a little too much truth for this moment, and the clock is ticking.

So instead, I pull him toward me and try to forget this ever has to end.

33

JOSH

It's hard to believe I looked forward to this meeting in DC a few weeks ago. Yes, I knew even then it would be tedious, full of politicians attempting to sound earnest, like they really care about the state of Somalian refugee camps when they can barely care long enough to listen to me speak. But I was excited by the possibilities it offered. With more funding, we could improve security enough to get a decent medical team in place, if nothing else.

Right now, though, even that possibility pales beside the memory of Drew stretched out in bed Monday morning, naked beneath a thin sheet.

What would she say if I told her I needed to see her again before I leave? She'd probably panic.

We've exchanged a few texts since I left her cottage four days ago. Casual, funny texts when what I want to do is write her every minute of every day. I want to tell her that I can't get Sunday night out of my head and that I felt obsessed with her *before* then, and now it's like I'm never going to get a full breath again if I don't manage to see her.

The morning session ends and afterward is the

bullshit lunch in the Senate dining room, where phones are forbidden and the menu looks like something from 1940—every dish involving meat and gravy.

"I heard a rumor," says the senator beside me, "that your brother plays guitar for Breaking Milk."

Heads lift, and suddenly I'm an object of interest at the table.

I sigh. What's wrong with our society when my idiot brother is fascinating but the plight of starving children and amputees without appropriate medical equipment is too boring to maintain interest? "Yeah," I reply, cutting into my pot roast. "He is."

"Ohmygod," says the staffer across the table. She's in her late twenties and seemed like a reasonable person until now, with her eyes wide and her mouth hanging open. "He was just in Hawaii. Were you with him?"

I attempt to smile, but I imagine it looks more like a flinch. "Yeah, family trip."

"So you know Drew Wilson?" she asks, and suddenly the whole table is listening. My jaw grinds. I resent the fact that Drew's name is linked with my brother's at all. It never should have been for even a moment.

"We've met," I say guardedly.

"Are they engaged?" she asks. "I heard they got engaged in Hawaii."

My laughter is so angry it fools no one. "No," I reply, cutting myself off before I can say more, before I can say *She dumped him and he'll never lay his hands on her again*.

Except...is that even true? They travel in the same circles. Will they run into each other at a party? Will she forget all the reasons she wasn't interested in him anymore? Once upon a time, the idea of the two of them together irked me. Now it makes me want to put my fist through a wall.

I rise, placing my napkin on the chair, and excuse myself.

The second I'm in the hall I pull out my phone. I don't know what I can possibly say or what I hope to accomplish. *Swear to me you'll never get back together with Joel* would sound completely jealous and psychotic—which is pretty much how I feel. I open my texts, and the most recent one is from her.

Drew: I just saw you on TV.

And in the midst of all my stupidity and jealousy, I smile. And realize how much I miss her. How that one night with her in LA wasn't nearly enough.

Me: I didn't take you for a C-SPAN viewer.

Drew: Avid. When I'm not singing about how much I love nudity. You're wearing a suit!

Me: I figured you'd make fun of me for that.

Drew: I was tempted to, but you look really good in a suit. It's my new favorite outfit. Though I was mostly imagining you removing it while I was watching, TBH

I picture Drew on a hotel bed, watching me as I tug off my tie, sliding a skirt higher and higher while her thighs spread wide. *Fuck.*

Me: Well, now you've got me imagining it too.

Drew: Imagining yourself undressing? I'd think that wouldn't be a novelty at this point.

I laugh.

Me: You're there too.

Drew: Come to New York and I could be.

I suddenly feel breathless, my heart beating hard, this weird surge of testosterone like I'm a teenager again. It's been a very long time since I've blown off my obligations for a woman.

It would be unbelievably irresponsible. And I already know I'm going if she's serious about this.

I could, I reply and then wait, holding my breath, watching those swirling dots as she phrases her reply.

Drew: Peninsula. I'll leave you a key under the name Sexy Viking. DO NOT remove the suit until I get there.

34

DREW

Talk shows are normally the bane of my existence—obstacle courses filled with landmines and quicksand. They entail skirting around all questions about my love life and my childhood, and the implied questions about how I made it big when a thousand more talented women did not. I can speak ill of no one and have to act abundantly grateful to people and entities I hate: my manager, my family, my record label. One wrong step and within hours it will be circulating over the news and social media.

Tonight was different. Because messing up wasn't the worst thing that could happen. Instead, I worried something might delay Josh, or delay me so I couldn't get back to Josh. If we'd been under nuclear attack during the show, my primary concern would have been its impact on the train schedules.

Don't get your hopes up, I tell myself. *He probably came to his senses.*

But my hopes are up anyway. I rush through the interview, distractedly decline the host's invitation to some after-party, and practically run all the way to the waiting car.

I'm dialing his number before I'm fully seated. "Are you at the hotel?" I demand.

"No," he says, sounding aggrieved. "There was something on the tracks near Philly. We got delayed. Pulling in now."

"I'm in the car on the way back to the hotel. Are you at Penn Station? We'll pick you up."

"You don't have to do that," he says. The background noise changes from quiet to chaotic and echoing. He must be at the station. "I can just catch a cab."

I can't explain the weird trip of anxiety I feel. I can't explain that I don't want to be separated from him for even one minute if I don't need to be, that I panic at the idea of him wandering outside Penn Station at night, though I've been outside Penn Station plenty of times without feeling worried once. Is this how he felt when he saw me leaving to run in the dark in Waikiki? It can't possibly be.

"We'll be there in two minutes," I say, making eye contact with the driver in the rearview mirror. He nods. "Send me your location. And don't get mugged."

He laughs. "I could fight ten guys at once. At *least* ten. All at the same time. Tarantino movies are a pale imitation of my fighting skills."

"You," I reply, feeling unduly aggravated, "sound absolutely ridiculous."

We arrive at the entrance near 8th and 31st and I stare at the sea of people there, willing one of the dark shapes roaming around to suddenly materialize into Josh.

When one of them suddenly does—in a suit and overcoat, bag slung over his shoulder—it feels like I'm suddenly made of confetti and champagne, all of it bubbling and fizzing inside me at the same time.

I roll down the back window. "Hey, big boy. You looking for a good time?"

His face lights up with a lopsided grin and he walks toward

the car, opening the door and sliding in beside me in a burst of winter air and warm skin.

The driver has thoughtfully put the privacy glass up. "Hey," he says, turning his head toward me, linking icy fingers through my warm ones. His lips press to mine, hard and fast, as if he can't help himself.

When he pulls back, I place my palm on his jaw because I just want to keep looking at his face. He doesn't seem to want to look away from mine either.

"You're actually happy to see me," I whisper.

He raises a brow. "I just sat on a train for three and a half hours simply to spend the night with you. Is that really a surprise?"

The answer is both yes and no. When I think of the guy I ran with, the guy who watched me like a hawk the whole muddy, treacherous climb down the Kalalau Trail and who kissed me like he'd die without it at the airport—then no.

But when I think about Joshua Bailey, MD, cold and brilliant and intimidating, rattling off facts in front of senators with barely hidden contempt, generous and selfless and far too good for me—yes, it's a little surprising.

"I guess not," I reply. "I do give a really good blowjob." I crack a smile but his is muted in response.

"That's not why I'm here," he says, holding my eye. Something in his expression, in his tone, chastens me: *Don't make this cheap. Don't make this out to be the same bullshit you have with everyone else.*

I swallow. "Yeah, I know. Sorry."

He tips my chin up with his index finger. His lips glance off mine once then press again, just holding there while he breathes me in and out. "Don't apologize. I'd be lying if I said I didn't hope there was a blowjob somewhere in the next seven hours."

I glance from him to the privacy glass. "I could ask him to circle the block."

His eyes fall closed. "Fuck. Now I'm hard. All you had to do was offer and it happened that fast, Drew." My hand unlinks from his and travels, hip to groin. He wasn't lying. It's lovely and long and firm. I manage to give it one solid squeeze before he removes my hand.

"Not here," he says through gritted teeth.

"No?" I ask.

"I have a pretty specific fantasy involving you doing that, and you'll probably want to be undressed when it happens."

Joshua Bailey has specific, filthy fantasies about me. The muscle in my core clenches so hard it hurts.

In the hotel room, he pulls me against him the minute the door shuts behind us. We shrug off our coats, and his hands slide to my thighs as I kick off my heels.

I tug at his belt and then stop myself. "Wait," I command, then go to the bed and lie back against the pillows. "*Now* undress."

He grins and slowly, seductively pulls off the jacket, his eyes on me. His button-down is smooth as glass, molding to the curves of his chest. He raises a brow. "Are we good?"

I laugh. "Hell no. Now the shirt."

His mouth tips up at the corners. "I'm feeling objectified," he says, making quick work of the buttons.

The shirt falls open. He tugs at the belt, undoing the buckle without instruction, and pulls the zipper down on his neatly pressed pants, watching me the whole time with that slow smile on his face.

The shirt flutters to the floor. The pants follow. There's a bulge in his boxers that makes me dizzy.

"Now—" I begin, and he shakes his head.

"It's my turn, Drew," he says, walking toward the bed. "Pull the dress up."

It's a short dress. There is little pulling required. I remove the panties without being asked and let my legs fall open. His lids flutter closed for a moment and then he kneels on the edge of the bed. His lips go to my left thigh, and begin to work their way up.

"I—" I begin.

"Shhh," he says. His tongue sweeps over my center. "Your time in charge is over, for the moment." His mouth closes over me. My hands fist the bed sheets at my sides, and all I can do is hold on for dear life.

~

IT's the middle of the night and I'm lying with my head on his chest and his hand on my hip—just like we did when we were camping except, you know, *naked*. He really ought to get some sleep and so should I, but this is it. The last time I'm going to see him. "What's the rest of your week look like?" he asks.

I list it out for him—more interviews here, a two-day press junket in London for a charity thing beginning the moment I arrive, a performance, interviews in Paris, another charity thing, more interviews, a single night off, and then the tour continues as planned.

He runs a hand over my back. "That's a lot." His brows are pulled together in that way they are when he's worried. My heart melts a little.

I smile. "I just spent two weeks in Hawaii, so it's hard to argue I don't get enough *me time*."

"Do you need to argue it though? How are you even going to function in London all day if you haven't slept on the plane?"

I look at him. I already know he won't like the truth. That

he will look *down* on me for the truth, which is that when I can't keep my eyes open, Davis will locate some cocaine or anything else that might work and prop me up. That I get through a lot of these things like the corpse in *Weekend at Bernie's*, dressed up and carted around while someone else moves my limbs. I want him to be the one person I don't lie to, even if the truth is ugly, but I find in this moment I'm not quite ready.

"I'll manage," I reply.

"I still don't see why you have to," he argues. "You've never said a single word about this guy Davis that makes him sound like someone you'd want around."

I shrug. "Davis made me what I am. If it weren't for him, I'd still be playing guitar in a dive bar somewhere, sleeping on friends' floors."

"From the sound of it, you'd be happier if you were."

Maybe I would be if I hadn't come this far, but going backward now would be a huge failure. "It's kind of like when you're driving and you make a wrong turn, but there's no way to get off the road," I explain. "I keep waiting for my chance to exit and it never comes. Just like you at the camp. You could do just as much good here, you know. You were so persuasive yesterday. If I had one iota of useful knowledge, I'd have been signing up to help."

He flashes me a dimple in the dim light. "I think you might be biased," he says, and there's something so sweet in his gravelly voice I don't doubt he's right. I'd go anywhere he asked me to based on his voice alone. For that dimple, I'd go twice.

"Well, you'll never know unless you try," I say. "How about this? You leave your vital work saving lives, and I'll record a song on acoustic guitar that my fans might not like."

He laughs. "Yes, that sounds fair."

I knew I wasn't going to change his mind, and it's not as if we would ever be a couple even if I did.

Nothing is going to change. And I'm so sickeningly disappointed by that.

35

JOSH

I'm the one who drives my mother to the oncologist. My father—who has spent years blathering to Joel and me about *honor* and *being a man*—is too busy with work and screwing the woman who manages his practice.

Moving as far away as I could and becoming the furthest thing from my father—it was my own, quiet *fuck you* to him. And now my mother is dying and I'm the one who's fucked. I'm the one who's going to be thousands of miles from her, unable to help.

I waited to confirm it until we were home, but I already knew. I knew it the moment I stepped into the Honolulu airport and saw that desperate look in her eyes. It said *Let me have this last vacation with you all. Let me pretend.*

And so we pretended. Now we're here to face facts.

The oncologist comes in. He wants to cut out the diseased parts of her liver and put her in an experimental trial. She says yes to all of it. She knows she will die, but she simply wants more time to set us all straight before she goes.

Once again, I allow her to believe something that isn't likely to happen.

"I was able to get a little more leave," I tell her on the way home. "I can take you to get the port put in."

She squeezes my hand. "I wish we were doing something slightly more fun, but thank you."

My jaw grinds. I hate that I can't stay.

"Have you heard from Drew?" she asks suddenly.

My tongue prods my cheek. Ever since New York, Drew and I have been texting a hundred times a day. It's as if that was the moment we took the cork off the bottle, and I don't see how it could ever go back on. I wake thinking of her, I run thinking of her, I eat thinking of her, I jerk off thinking of her.

I've never experienced anything like this obsession. And it isn't just sex, though God knows when she video calls from an interview, whispering from the bathroom and wearing the thinnest possible tank top, those are the thoughts that come to the fore.

I want to know how her day is, I want to know why she looks so troubled at the thought of going on stage. I want to know why I hear her repeating numbers in her sleep every time we're together. I want to unpeel her, layer by layer, until I get to her heart, and then put everything back together once I know it's in good shape.

"Drew," I repeat, doing my best to look blankly at my mother. "Why would I have heard from her?"

"You two got along so well by the end of the trip. I just thought..." She stops, shrugging, and for a moment I find that I'm hoping for a reprieve.

I just thought something might happen with you two, she could say. *I just thought that maybe if she wasn't dating Joel, the two of you might...you know.*

"I hoped she might confide in you," my mother says instead. "I still think she and Joel will get back together. She could be like the sister you never had."

My hands grip the steering wheel. "Mom, I can assure you, that's not going to happen."

I would do almost anything for my mother, but I will not give her this. I just can't.

36

DREW

I arrive in London on no sleep. It's the middle of the night back home but here it's a dreary gray morning and rush hour, and I just don't feel ready to face the day ahead.

It's not entirely the lack of sleep. Yesterday, Josh told me Beth's cancer is back and that it doesn't look good, which seems like doctor speak for *definitely fatal*. I can't stop going over the trip in my head now, remembering Beth's determination to do things she wasn't up to, her tears when Six arrived and her obsession with seeing her sons paired off. It all makes sense now, but her selflessness just makes it hurt more. At a time when anyone else would be thinking about themselves, Beth was thinking of her sons, and she had enough love left over to extend it to me.

I fish sunglasses out of my purse and put them on, doing my best to surreptitiously wipe away tears before the driver sees.

Josh wants his mom to die secure in the knowledge that he and Joel still have each other to lean on. I want to give that to her, too, but the weird thing is that Beth is the one I want to talk to about Josh. When she texts to say she saw me on TV, or to anything, I want to say *I'm crazy about Josh. I think he's the best man I've ever known and you did such a good job with him.*

In another life, inexplicably, I think she'd be thrilled.

I dry my eyes and steel myself as the car pulls up to the Mandarin Oriental. Davis and Ashleigh are the first people I see when I walk inside. I'd prefer they were the last.

"I've got you an appointment with a colorist," he says. "She's up in your room."

I blink at him. A part of me is ready to concede, the way I always do, but a newer part shouts *Who the fuck do you think you are?* The news about Beth puts things in perspective a bit. It's a reminder that there are harder things to live through than Davis's fury.

"Then *you* can tell her to leave," I reply.

His jaw locks with rage, and he's clearly itching to threaten me, but my hair color is not in our contract. There isn't a doubt in my mind, however, that he'll find a way to make me pay.

HE IS nothing if not consistent. To punish me for the grave sin of wanting my hair to be its natural color, Davis swamps me. He squeezes in extra interviews, an extra meet and greet. My head doesn't hit the pillow until two in the morning, and at five AM, he's got hair and wardrobe knocking on my door to ready me for more of the same.

By the time we get to Paris on the third day, I'm so exhausted I look drunk and I'm acting like it too, stumbling over my answers.

"How is anyone supposed to think you're *not* on drugs," Davis snaps, "when you don't recognize the name of your own goddamn album?" He takes out a tiny silver vial and puts it in my hand. "Do a line in the bathroom and pull yourself together."

My eyes squeeze tight, so frustrated and despondent I'm on the verge of tears. My entire life seems like an endless cycle of problems Davis has created, which he then fixes in problematic ways.

But I do the line because right now I need a solution, and I do more before I go on stage that night, because—as always—nothing matters more than the appearance of having my shit together.

I'm so tired I forget what city I'm in. "Thank you..." I shout at the end of my set. I very nearly say *Berlin*, but it feels wrong so I leave the words hanging and somehow get myself backstage.

I blow right past the crew members and waiting fans and head for my dressing room with Ashleigh at my heels. She feels more like a *minder* these days than an assistant, but as long as she got a brioche from my favorite place over on the Champs-Élysées—the one thing I've asked of her all day long—we're good.

I missed dinner, I missed lunch, and I've been running since early this morning with no break, but if I can get these shoes off my feet and a little brioche in my mouth, I'll make it to the finish line.

I enter the room backstage, ready to collapse on the long black leather couch at the far wall, but come to a dead stop when I only see a bottle of water waiting on the table.

"Where's my brioche?" I ask, unstrapping a heel.

"Oh," she says, unable to meet my eye, "Davis said not to get it for you."

It's such a minor thing but I feel like I'm going to burst into tears. "Did he say why?" I ask between my teeth. I'm barely holding it together.

"He thinks you gained weight in Hawaii," she says. "No pastries, no sugar until we get through this." Her words are hesitant but it's clear who's in charge here and it isn't me.

Anger burns in my gut. I pinch my lips together, clenching my jaw. Tears threaten to fall, but I squeeze my eyes shut and push them back. I should no longer be surprised, but I am. Is there really nothing about my life I'm allowed to decide for myself?

I take off the other heel and sink onto the couch, pressing my face into my hands and trying to hold it together. I know I'm just tired, and exhaustion makes anything seem worse than it is. But I just don't have it in me to snap out of it tonight.

Ashleigh's gathering stuff around the room. She glances over at me as if surprised I'm still seated. "Are you ready for the party?" she asks. "The car's outside."

"No one ever said anything about a party."

She sighs. She's probably thinking I'm just too careless to have listened before and she might be right. "Someone high up at LVP is throwing it," she says. "It's a big deal."

Except it's *always* a big deal. And I'll be expected to smile and pose and try to stay awake for hours just like I am *every* night. I'm done. And there's only one person in the world I want to talk to right now.

I pick up my phone.

Can you talk? Are you free? I text Josh.

Josh: For you, absolutely.

Me: Give me ten minutes.

Maybe I'm leaning on him a little, but how much harm can it do? He leaves for Somalia in a day. It's not as if I'll suddenly decide it can be more than this.

I turn to Ashleigh. "I'll meet you in front in a minute."

"We've really got to go—" she begins and then sees the look on my face and shrugs. "I'll wait outside."

I give her a thirty-second head start before I grab my phone and my purse and start walking, and then running, the other way.

I exit through the back with my heels in h...

the street and jump in a cab. Ten minutes later I'm entering my hotel room, dialing his number.

His voice, his quiet exhale—they're like a warm bath I could soak in for hours. I can't explain why just the sound of his breathing on the other end of the line is enough to make my ridiculous anger about the brioche crack open. I finally let the tears I've been holding in fall.

"Are you alright?" he asks, as if he already knows I'm not.

"Yeah," I reply, but my voice has that rasp it gets when I'm upset.

My feet dig into the plush carpet as if gripping it for balance. I'm here now, alone at last, and I have no idea why I called him. Maybe I shouldn't have.

"You're exhausted," he says. His tone indicates that denying it isn't an option, and I don't think I could anyway, not to him. Everything just feels like too much, and I don't even know what *everything* is. I can't seriously be this upset about a pastry. "Are you crying?"

"No," I whisper. I drop the heels on the floor. "I don't cry."

"Of course not." He laughs, but it's a gentle laugh and for some reason that makes the tears drip faster. "Tell me why you're *not crying*."

I swallow and turn the lock on the door behind me. "I don't know. I'm just tired. It was nonstop today, and then I had to perform, and I just...didn't want to."

"Okay," he says. "Except that's every day for you. Why are you *not crying* this time?"

I give a strangled laugh. "I'm crying over a fucking brioche. There's this place here, Brioche Dorée, which is like the 7-Eleven of pastry shops." It's so stupid that I'm crying over a pastry. With everything that's happened to me, this shouldn't even make a dent. That it *does* makes me feel crazy. "And I told my assistant to get one for me and Davis told her not to because I'd gained weight in Hawaii and—"

"He said that?" Josh asks. His rage cuts through the phone line like a knife. "Tell me he did not make that about your weight. Jesus Christ."

His outrage makes me cry harder because I am seeing how insane it is that I'm in this position at all. How utterly fucked up must I be to have let this whole situation evolve? I'm so untethered without Josh. I had no idea I felt so alone until that trip to Hawaii, and now I can't stop feeling it.

"I haven't slept," I tell him. "Davis kept giving me coke just to keep me awake today and I—"

"Get on a plane," he whispers. "Just come back."

And I'll take care of you. He doesn't say it aloud, but I hear it anyway.

"Come back where?" I ask. "I don't even have a home."

"Come to me."

"I can't," I whisper. "You have no idea how badly I wish I could, but I can't. There's another press call tomorrow, and a charity thing tomorrow night, and then I leave for Berlin. And you're leaving anyway."

He sighs. "Where are you now?"

"In my hotel room," I tell him. "And I'm supposed to be at some party, and Davis is going to be such a dick about this tomorrow and make my life so much harder to punish me."

"Get undressed. Keep me on the phone."

I laugh through my tears. "This is taking an unexpected turn."

"I'm not taking advantage of your exhaustion to have phone sex, I promise. Get undressed and climb into bed."

I still have all my makeup on and my hair is like a shellac helmet on my head, but I'm so tired and...fuck it. I'm here for whatever he's about to suggest, the makeup and hair be damned. I unzip the side of the dress and exhale in relief when it's off. The strapless bra that's been digging into my rib cage for hours soundlessly follows.

"Put me on speaker," he says, "and turn out the lights."

I pad across the carpeted floor, flicking out lights as I go, and then climb into the bed at last. They're the smoothest sheets I've ever felt in my life.

"Oh my god, it's such a comfy bed, Josh. I wish you were here."

"I wish I were too," he says.

I smile suggestively in the dark. "What would you do?"

"Given that you're still crying, I wouldn't do anything especially exciting," he says with a quiet laugh. "I'd lay down with you, and I'd pull your back to my chest, and I'd wrap my arms around you and stay just like that until you fell asleep."

Does anyone but me know how sweet he is? How much goodness lies under that cranky exterior? I lay the phone on my pillow and roll to face it, as if it's him there beside me.

"You would totally get a boner," I reply. "I'm naked."

"I'd think about amputations to prevent it, if necessary."

I grin. "I always wanted a guy who'd think about amputations when I'm naked next to him."

"Then apparently I'm your prince," he says with another small laugh. "Okay. You're in bed? The lights are off? Close your eyes."

His voice and this soft bed are lulling me to sleep, but I'm not ready to go yet. I feel like I just got him.

"I don't want to stop talking to you," I whisper.

"I'm going to be right here, just like I would be there."

It's afternoon in California. I guess he's packing to leave for Somalia and once he's there, whatever this is with us will be over.

"I wish we had that whole two weeks back, from Hawaii. I wish it had been different."

"I do too," he says, "but it was pretty perfect in its own way."

I smile. "You mean the little replica of the Washington

Monument in my back during the camping trip? The moment I realized you kind of liked me?"

"I don't love the fact that you're calling it little, baby."

I laugh, but my heart warms at the endearment. I doubt it's one Josh gives out lightly. And then I fall silent and sleep is overtaking me, whether I want it to or not.

"I miss you," I tell him. "I wish you were here."

"Me too," he sighs. "You have no idea."

When I wake in the morning, the hotel phone is ringing and my cell is dead. I wonder if he'd still be on the line if it wasn't.

I shower and am hustled into hair and makeup. When my phone is charged, I text Josh to thank him, but he doesn't reply. He's on his way to Somalia by now, so that makes sense, but it leaves me feeling exposed. As if I gave away something last night, asked for too much, leaned too hard.

I find myself blanking out, again and again, throughout the day. I'm an adult now, cossetted and sought after. But whenever my eyes close, I'm eleven years old, riding on a bus that's getting farther and farther from home with no idea how I'll ever get back.

The performance in the evening is relatively easy. I'm one of several acts, thank God, so I put my five songs in and then I'm led to some room where I'm stripped of one tiny dress and clad in another, pushed into a limo—an umbrella overhead to protect my hair from the fat snowflakes descending over the city—and delivered to a charity event in a plush hotel ballroom.

The event is packed with wealthy adults in cocktail attire, people who are here to meet me but older and unlikely to be fans. I'm simply the lure to get them through the door, the modern-day equivalent of a bearded lady or a twelve-inch man, the thing they'll pay good money to ogle and discuss later.

I'm hugged and grasped and grabbed and tugged. My dress is too small, my heels are too high. I smile, smile, smile and all the while I'm wondering how I allowed this to happen. Not simply tonight, but *everything*. I've turned into something less than human and I don't even know why. To earn my mother's respect? To vindicate my father? If those were my goals, they haven't worked. They were never going to work. How did I not see that until now? My reasons for putting up with all of this now seem so juvenile and pointless. My chest aches and I rub it, trying to get it to stop.

I sign one photo after another and let overdressed strangers wrap their arms around me, but inside I'm feeling colder and colder.

I picture Josh on his flight—wearing his khakis, pecking away on his laptop. So very boring. I have no idea why such a boring thought has me looking at the clock on the wall, wishing he'd text.

Which he won't—because he's on a flight but also because this is over. I know this and yet, as I am being shepherded from one group of people to another, I pull out my phone for the hundredth time anyway to see if he replied.

He did. And all it says is, **I'm outside.**

I'm almost scared to take it literally but my heart is leaping, ready to thump right out of my chest. Josh is *here*. For *me*.

Two seconds ago, I was empty and despondent and now it's as if fireworks are igniting in my veins, hot and cold at the same time, so thrilling it almost hurts.

"I need a minute," I tell the girl assigned to me. Her eyes open wide—apparently me needing a minute is not on her schedule. "And I have a friend at the door, Josh. Can you please have the doorman send him back?"

"Y___ '_ll h___ d_n___ who want to meet you," she says.

I'm doing this whole thing out of the goodness of my heart, or whatever I have in place of a heart, and I have put in two hours. I don't know what was promised to all these people, but is there really no limit to it?

"I need a break," I repeat, more firmly, "and until I get it and have seen Josh, I am not meeting anyone else."

"So I can tell everyone you'll be back in five minutes?" she asks.

"You can tell them whatever you want," I reply. She looks satisfied by this, not realizing what I'm really saying is *I don't give a shit what you tell them because I am going to do what I want right now* and what I want, more than anything in the entire world, is to lay eyes on Joshua Bailey.

I'm back in the green room for less than thirty seconds when there's a knock on the door and he walks in wearing a heavy coat, snow still melting in his hair, looking like the most delicious thing I have ever seen in my life. I'm already shaking with the desire for him to touch me. "I was in the neighborhood," he says. He hands me a small white bag and his mouth curves upward. "I heard you wanted brioche."

I stare at him for a moment, blinking back tears. I've been given crazy gifts. I've been given diamonds and designer dresses. I was once given a car. But I've never loved anything as much as I do this brioche in a white paper bag.

I fling myself at him, jumping up to wrap my arms around his neck and my legs around his waist. He catches me with a pleased smile, a quiet laugh, and then I'm kissing him. His face, his hair, anything I can reach.

"I hope these are good tears," he says, brushing one off my cheek, and I'm too choked up to do anything but nod.

He cups my jaw and then we are kissing, and neither of us is laughing or crying anymore. I reach behind him to lock the door and slide to my feet, opening his coat, letting my lips graze his collarbone. He's in jeans and thick-soled boots. I never dreamed that combination could inspire so much lust.

He pulls me closer and finds my mouth once more, his hands digging into the small of my back. I feel small and safe like this, wrapped up in the cocoon of him, with his overcoat falling around us, his erection digging through the thin fabric of my dress.

"I have five minutes until they start banging on that door," I warn him.

His ridiculously large hands palm my hips. I feel tiny in his grasp. "That's not nearly enough time," he says.

I pull him down to me again by the lapels of his coat. "I love that you came here to see me."

"It didn't feel like a choice," he says, his mouth ghosting over mine, sliding to my jaw. "I couldn't fucking stay away."

"Can you wait for me?" I ask. "I can be done here in an hour, tops. Less if I'm rude."

"Sure. But I fully support rudeness."

I reach down to his jeans and undo his belt, untuck his shirt. There's something about the sight of him like that—dressed, zipper beneath my fingers slowly sliding down, that I find irresistible. "Drew," he says, a warning in his voice, "fuck. Don't. Not if someone's coming in here in a minute. I don't have a condom anyway."

I slide to my knees, dragging the jeans down with the boxers beneath them. His erection springs up, swollen and lovely, begging for my mouth.

Which I provide.

"Oh Jesus," he says. I look up to see his head fall backward as if it pains him, but only a moment later he's opening his eyes again to watch. Dark, drugged eyes at half-mast, mouth slightly ajar, watching as I lathe his cock from top to bottom, before dragging it into my mouth, letting suction do the work.

I'm so wet my panties stick to my skin. I don't know how I'm going to get through the next hour aching like this.

His eyes start to fall closed. His head sways back as if he's drunk. "Drew. God. I'm gonna come."

My fingers sink into his hips to hold him in place and with a gasp he lets go. His body sags against the door with a groan he can't stifle, his thighs trembling. I rise to my feet, wiping the corners of my mouth like the classy little lady I am.

"I feel like I got the better end of this deal," he says with a shaky laugh.

I take his hand and pull it between my legs, beneath my panties, so he can feel what it did to me. "You *did* get me the brioche. But you'll be making it up to me, I promise."

That drugged look is in his eyes again already. He pushes my panties to the side, spears me with his longest finger, pressing it to exactly the right spot.

"*Oh,*" I whisper.

"I can probably make it up to you right now," he says, dropping to his knees, pushing my legs apart. He looks up at me from the floor, eyes hooded and hungry and it's the hottest thing I've ever seen in my life. He buries his face between my parted legs, his tongue flicking in small, hard strokes against my clit while that incessant finger of his slides in and out.

Someone bangs on the door. "One minute!" I cry, my voice regrettably strangled. He laughs against my thigh. It's the exact kind of situation in which I would normally be unable to come —people right outside the room, pressure, chaos. Instead, it all seems to swirl around me, and the sight of him groaning against my skin is my only focus. "Yes, yes, yes," I whisper like a prayer, and somehow he knows this means *more, faster, harder*. I fly right over the edge, tugging his hair, my knees giving out until I'm on the floor, too, and the two of us lie down on the carpet and laugh.

He's already hard again. "You have no idea how bad I want to fuck you right now," he whispers in my ear.

"No condom," I remind him.

"I'd fashion one. I'd turn into fucking MacGyver and create it from a shoe lace and my driver's license."

I laugh. "Sounds hygienic."

The doorknob rattles aggressively. A fist strikes it. "Drew, it's Davis," a voice announces unnecessarily. "I need you out here now. The natives are restless."

"I'd like a quick word with your manager," Josh says, his nostrils flaring.

I smile. Though part of me would love to watch him put Davis in his place, it will only make things worse. "No thank you. I've seen how your *quick words* work out. I don't need another *Come repeat that on shore, asshole* moment right now."

Slowly, his mouth curves and he looks at me, his palms on either side of my face. It's different than his previous smile. It's not as if I'm the girl he just went down on, but someone he adores. I want to stay here forever.

This must be what it's like to fall in love, I think. *Huh.*

We stand up and Josh fixes the straps of my dress, tucks my hair back behind my ears.

"Your mission, if you choose to accept it, is to buy condoms," I whisper, moving toward the door. "And Josh? Buy a *lot.*"

37

JOSH

S he snuggles against me, tiny and soft. "Hey," I say.

"Hey," she replies. Her eyes are still closed but she smiles. And then she laughs.

I don't even have to ask why. She met me last night at her hotel and promptly grabbed one suitcase and her guitar and told me we were leaving. Apparently, Davis would just stroll right in, otherwise, which still enrages me.

It was only once we'd checked in across the street under a different name that she left Davis a message, canceling her interviews for the day, and she's been laughing about it ever since.

"Davis is, at this exact moment, exploding," she says. "Like, I think his brain might be *literally* exploding."

I push the hair back from her face. "I have the somewhat troubling suspicion that you'd like to watch that."

She hitches a shoulder. "Don't act like it comes as a surprise. You know what I'm like."

"Yeah," I say, rolling her on top of me. "I might need a reminder though."

THE MIDDAY LIGHT IS THIN. Through the windows we look at the rooftops of Paris, covered now with a fresh layer of snow. "I could live here," she says, pushing the room service tray away.

"In this hotel?" I ask. "Let me reiterate: this wouldn't count as *living off the land.*"

She laughs. "Fuck off. I meant in Paris. I could be, like, a barista maybe. I think I could do that. I'd get fired for having an attitude back home, but here I'd fit right in."

I press my lips to the top of her head. "What about me? What would I do?"

She taps her lower lip, thinking. "You're...hmmm. You work as a gravedigger."

"A *gravedigger*? That's the best you can do?"

"Regular nine-to-five job and it would keep you in shape. I'd need a lot of attention when I get home from the coffee shop. Foot massages and such."

"I'll check to see if anyone's hiring before I leave," I say and then regret it. I've referenced leaving and though her smile holds, I feel the way it turns a little jagged. I fly out tonight. It was the best I could do, but it's not enough for either of us.

"We *can* actually go outside the room, you know," she says. "If I'm all bundled up and not wearing makeup, no one will bug us. Just please don't say you want to go to the Louvre. You know how I feel about smart people shit."

I laugh, running a finger down her sternum. "Yes, I remember. For a girl who can recite criminal statutes on demand, you're weirdly opposed to letting anyone think you're smart. But don't worry. I have other ideas."

I lean over, pressing a kiss to the space between her ribs.

She purrs, arching toward me. "I think I know what your ideas are. I'm fine with staying in if you are."

I lower myself on top of her. "Don't worry. It's not sex. Well, it is, obviously," I say as I reach for a condom. "But it's not *only* that."

38

DREW

In the afternoon, the snow stops suddenly. "This is my plan," says Josh, holding my coat for me. "We are going to walk."

I raise a brow. "Just *walk*?"

His mouth twitches. "Just walk."

Outside, the world is strangely silent and peaceful, the roads mostly empty. We buy cheap gloves and hats at a kiosk and then he links his fingers through mine and pulls me close. When we kiss, our breath hovers between us like a small white cloud.

We head over toward Île Saint-Louis, an island that sits right in the center of the Seine, just past Notre Dame. He pulls me inside a café and we order *chocolat chaud*—hot chocolate, but nothing like the drink I know from home. This is thick, velvety, bittersweet. Something you sip. Maybe an acquired taste but on this weird, offbeat day, it feels right.

We sit with our drinks on a bench he's cleared for us. The sun's dying rays descend upon the Seine, painting it in splashes of orange and crimson and gold. My arm rests against his and I let my head lean on his shoulder. If it weren't for his looming departure, I'd be so weightless right now I doubt gravity would keep me on this bench.

"I'd do anything to feel this free all the time," I tell him.

His lips press to the top of my head. "You don't *need* to do anything to feel this free, though."

He's right. This outing has barely cost us a penny—we could easily afford it in my barista/gravedigger fantasy—and I've never been happier. I certainly wouldn't need *more*, but I doubt it would hold up if he wasn't here with me.

"I'm not sure my mother has ever had a moment this peaceful," he says, wrapping an arm around my shoulders. He's already told me she's probably got two years left, maybe three. It weighs on him, that ticking clock. He wants to fill it with all the things she won't have, and it's too late for some of them. "If she did, the shit my dad's done has tainted it by now."

"Why does she stay with him?" I ask.

"Because of us," he says. "I found out when I was a teenager and it was already old news to her at that point. She was willing to pretend things were fine, for our sake, so we'd feel like one big happy family."

She just didn't realize what a strain it would be on her oldest son. Or what a strain she puts on him now, with that all-encompassing love of hers, and the way he struggles to live up to it. I might be the one wrong thing, the one deceitful thing, he's ever done.

When dusk falls, we link hands again and head toward the hotel. "How long do you have?" I ask. My voice sounds small and childlike. I wish he could stay. I just want one more day with him. It seems like so little to ask and yet I know it's impossible for either of us.

His hand tightens around mine. "A few hours."

We stop at a bar on the way back to the hotel. He orders us mussels and frites and two glasses of red wine.

"I could listen to you speak French all day," I tell him.

He grins. "If you worked at Dooha, you probably would. I promise it wouldn't seem so exciting then."

"Pretend I'm your nurse," I say, tipping my head up and closing my eyes. "Say something."

"*Je pense qu'il y a une hémorragie interne.*" His voice is soft as velvet. My nipples tighten under four layers of clothing.

"That sounded sexy," I tell him. "What was it?"

"*I think there's internal bleeding,*" he replies and I laugh.

Our food arrives and we eat quickly, suddenly famished. We're only half done when the bar grows crowded. The mood is celebratory—it's not every day the city is unexpectedly shut down. We are bumped from all sides and Josh turns us so I'm seated and he's standing, blocking the crowd with those ridiculous shoulders of his.

I take a sip of my wine, savoring it the way I did the hot chocolate. His gaze falls to my mouth and my blood heats in response.

"What are you thinking about up there?" I ask.

His eyes drop to my mouth again. "Watching you drink wine is the sexiest thing I've ever seen in my life," he says. His nostrils flare a little, as if he's trying to breathe me in.

I swallow. I need him undressed right now and looming over me. I need those large hands of his palming my hips, pulling them off the mattress to meet his. "Maybe we should go back to the room," I say breathlessly.

He nods, the check is paid, and the two of us stumble from the bar, walking too close to be graceful. On the street, he presses me against the building's crumbling stone facade and kisses me, the air biting cold, his mouth warm and needy. I press against him, my hands sliding beneath his coat.

"I want to be so far inside you, you'll never forget I was there," he whispers.

You already are, I think, pulling him down the street.

We reach the room and shed our clothes as if they're suffocating us. And then we are on the bed, deliciously naked, and he's above me, pinning me down with his heavy limbs, moving inside me like he'd sooner die than stop.

He wrings the first orgasm from me easily, but then demands another. I can feel it building, a tight ball of heat in my stomach, but it's the sight of him there, trembling on the cusp but refusing to be pushed over as he waits for me, that finally sets it off.

And then he lets go—a desperate, hoarse cry in my ear, his body shaking above mine.

"I'm not going to forget, ever," I whisper against his skin. "I promise."

He doesn't have long after that. He tells me to stay in bed as he gathers his things, so I watch him move across the room, stepping into boxers, tugging a t-shirt overhead.

When he's dressed and his stuff is gathered, he comes to the edge of the bed and presses his lips to my forehead. They hold there for the longest moment and neither of us says a word.

I will probably never see him again. The thought hits me hard and fast, creating a desperate need to hold on to this moment.

It's only when the door shuts that I let myself feel the full weight of my loss. My chest aches. I want to cry but it's as if the tears are stuck there, too painful to be dislodged at all.

When I wake the next day, there's nothing to open my eyes for.

Very soon—in a few hours, in fact—I will need to pay the price for my defiance and face Davis. I was so brave, so joyful when Josh was here because I was leaning on him, even if I didn't admit it to myself, and now is when I fall. Now is when the label comes down on me for blowing off interviews, when Davis tells me I'm in breach of contract and extracts concessions to make up for it: extra shows, extra appearances. He will drive me until I don't know what city I'm in and pass out on stage because I've forgotten anything matters more than keeping the machine running.

I get to the airport that afternoon. We travel by private plane when we're on tour—a luxury, in theory. In reality, it means Davis gets to spend the entire flight bitching at me. I close my eyes and for once I don't see myself sitting on a bus, alone and frightened. I see myself sitting at Île Saint-Louis with Josh, watching the sunset and feeling absolutely free.

I'd work myself to the bone for that feeling, except Josh was right: I don't have to. I was born entitled to it. Everyone has a right to be happy, to feel peaceful. And the most successful third album in the history of third albums won't give me any more of it than I had yesterday.

Maybe it's time I truly consider getting off this particular ride at last.

When I'm in my room, I grab my phone and text Ben Tate, the attorney Tali's been on me about. He agrees to meet me in New York when I'm there next month. I write the info down on the hotel notepad, oddly terrified. It's as if I'm trying to escape a cult.

And as tangled up as all my business dealings are, escaping a cult might be easier.

39

JOSH

I go from snow and Paris sunsets and Drew's breath mingling with mine to armed guards pointing guns at me in a customs line. And this is the *safe* part—if there is a safe part—of Mogadishu.

I used to feel like I wasn't giving up too much coming back here. The work was interesting and I liked my coworkers. Today, though, I'm not interested in the faint pleasures of living within the confines of the camp: getting to know the families, camaraderie with the rest of the staff, the occasional hookup with a cute nurse. The assurance it provided that I'm not like my father is no longer enough.

I want my weekends back. I want a modicum of safety. I want to be able to go to a pastry shop to buy breakfast for the girl waiting back at my place. I want a huge soft bed, where that same girl will be stretched out beside me, suggesting I become a gravedigger.

My shirt clings to my back as I get my first whiff of dust whipping off the dry plains outside the city. The drive to Dooha is the most dangerous part of leaving and returning. I'm normally hypervigilant, looking for signs of trouble, but today I'm just gazing at the picture I took of Drew outside the *patisserie*—steam rising from a cup beside her face, her sweet, surprised smile.

We are in a shitty, unfixable situation. Soon, she'll find someone who can actually see her. Who can actually admit he's *with* her. Cutting this off now would be easier than reading about her and the guy she replaces me with in a week or a month. But when she texts, I'm thrilled.

It means I still exist somewhere in her world.

I'm also thrilled because she says she's meeting with a lawyer about getting rid of Davis. I video call her the second I get to my tent, abandoning any attempt at restraint. She's in her hotel room, smiling wide. I never once saw her smile like that for my brother. "Give me a tour of your tent!" she demands.

I laugh. "That would be a really short tour."

She flops down on a big bed, soft pillow, her hair splayed out around her. "How was your trip?"

I decide not to mention the bombed-out hotel we passed on the way, a hotel I once stayed in, or the illegal road block we encountered. "Uneventful," I reply. "But I missed the sunset happy hour."

"Did everything run smoothly without you?" she asks.

I sink into the chair next to my desk. "Not really. Some supplies were stolen. It's a problem." I don't mention that there was also a bomb threat, or that whoever took most of our pain medication from the supply closet must still have a key and it will take another week to get a replacement lock.

"It really doesn't sound safe there," she says. Her top teeth worry her bottom lip.

She doesn't know the half of it. The situation has gone dangerously awry over the past year. But it's not the danger that has me thinking of leaving, and it's not my mom's illness. It's her. It's the thought of her moving on without me, when I wouldn't have anything to offer her even if I was there.

I can't believe I'd consider abandoning people who need me for a woman I can't even admit I'm dating.

It sounds exactly like something my father would do.

40

DREW

I somehow manage to complete two more weeks in Europe. Talking to Josh is the highlight of every day, the one part that makes me feel like there's a point to all this, though I'm not sure what that point would be. Growing close to someone was never on my bucket list. Nor was growing close to someone I'd have to keep a permanent secret.

I call him late in the evening after my show is over. It's the only easy time for both of us to talk. When he answers, it hits me right in the center of my chest how much I miss his beautiful, tired face. He is lying on what appears to be a cot—he wasn't exaggerating about the conditions there. I climb into bed and turn out the lights, just so it feels like we're there together.

"Where are you now?" he asks.

I actually have to think for a moment, glancing out the window to get my bearings. "Rome. Have you been?"

His eyes close. He looks exhausted. "Long time ago. Summer after I graduated."

"You should be here," I tell him. "We could go down to Sorrento and drink limoncello and shop."

His eyes close again, but he smiles. "Drew, if I flew to Rome, we would not be leaving the hotel room."

Heat flares to life at the idea of it. An entire weekend with him in this very bed, not leaving once. I can't imagine anything better. And it makes me almost bitter that other people get so much and we have so little. How long will he be willing to be my long-distance buddy before he finds someone there to take my place? If he hasn't already.

"Get on a plane," I tell him. It's phrased like a joke, but if I thought I could persuade him I'd be begging right now.

His eyes brush over my face. "I miss you," he says. "It's never been as hard to be back here as it is this time."

It's more than he's ever said, and I don't say it back but I feel guilty when I hang up the phone, as if I should have. Why is he the only one who ever puts himself out there? I can name a hundred things he's done for me since we met, but can I name one thing I've done for him? At a certain point, it looks less like caution and more like selfishness.

I take a deep breath. Those dreams about the bus ride, they've been happening again ever since he started getting past my walls. I think maybe they've been preparing me for this moment. I know what I have to do, and it terrifies me.

I have to say *yes* to the unknown.

I'm going to Somalia.

"No, you're not," says Jonathan.

He is Tali's best friend, Hayes's assistant, and the one person who can figure out how to get me a visa. I should have known he wouldn't make it easy. I love him, but he was a constant thorn in my side when we were planning Tali's bachelorette party. I still think the private island off the coast of Dubai would have been *way* more fun than Vegas.

I wander to the window of my hotel room and pull back the curtains with one hand, holding the phone with the other. In the distance, Zurich's snow-capped mountains gleam, reflecting the bright sunlight. A river winds lazily just beyond the window. If he could see my view, he'd *really* wonder why I'm so eager to leave. He'd probably suggest I go to Vegas instead.

"Somalia is deadly," he says. "People *don't* get into Somalia."

"Sure they do," I argue. Josh left and returned without a problem, and I've been in way too many nice, uneventful places deemed *dangerous* to take warnings too seriously. "There are embassies and tons of aid organizations traveling in and out. If they can manage, surely a woman with the money to buy the world's best transportation can."

"Drew," he says with a sigh, "do you know anything *about* Somalia? You'd need to hire multiple armed guards just to get you anywhere in the city. And you might not even be safe *then*. If you want to earn yourself some good PR, there are easier places to go."

I'm embarrassed to admit I'm going there for a guy, but I'm not sure Jonathan will help me if I *don't* admit it. "I have a friend there," I tell him. "Someone I've been seeing."

He laughs. "It's kind of cute...I wondered what you'd be like when you fell in love and now I know."

"I never said I was in love with the guy."

"Drew, honey," he says, "you're flying to Somalia to see him. I'm pretty sure that's love. Or you're insane."

I'm way more comfortable with the idea of being insane.

IN EARLY MARCH, I return to New York to film a cameo on a sitcom I don't especially like. Davis and Stephanie claim it will raise my profile. I suspect they're more concerned with raising their own.

When the first day of shooting is over, I sneak off set while Davis is trying to get people to go out to dinner. From there I take a cab to the Ritz Carlton where Ben Tate is waiting in a private room with another associate from his firm.

It took me a while last summer to persuade Tali that Ben and I were never going to happen because tall, hot guys in suits didn't do it for me. Little did I know.

And Ben *is* hot, that part is non-negotiable. I just only seem interested in wildly unavailable doctors at this exact moment.

He shakes my hand and introduces me to his associate, Amelia. We make some small talk about Hayes and Tali and the baby, and then his hands steeple atop his notepad.

"So," he says, "I understand you want to break up with some people."

I nod. My heart is racing and I press a hand to my chest, waiting to feel air slip in and out of my throat. "I'm terrified," I admit.

My phone buzzes on the table. Davis is calling me. "Do you need to get that?" Ben asks.

I shake my head. "Do you know how crazy this situation is right now?" I ask them quietly. "I don't even know if he's traced my whereabouts. There's literally nothing in my life he doesn't know more about than I do. He arranged this phone purchase. He hired my publicist and my accountant and my assistant and they all answer to him. I keep picturing that door opening and him walking in."

Ben leans back in his chair and shrugs off his jacket. "Then before we do anything else," he says, "maybe you ought to turn the phone off, just in case."

I'd worried that I sounded paranoid. Now I wonder if I was paranoid enough.

Ben and Amelia ask questions and take copious notes. They're so incredibly assured and thorough that I begin to hope they can actually get me out of this mess. But Ben says I needs to see my contracts and all that hope whistles straight back out of me.

Every contract is in the possession of Davis or other people Davis hired. I know of no way to get Ben a thing without alerting them all.

I tell them this, feeling like an idiot. "I was twenty when I got signed," I explain, "and I was dead broke. I was just thrilled someone was willing to take charge and handle all the details, and anytime I need something, Davis has always just offered to take care of it."

"Yeah," Ben says. "I bet he did." I hear in his sigh the words he kept to himself. *Of course he offered to take care of it—he wanted to make sure no one was checking up on him.* For a girl who insists she can't lean on anyone, it strikes me that I allowed myself to just lie *flat* where Davis is concerned.

"As far as those contracts go," he continues, "how do you feel about pretending to buy a house?"

I laugh. "What?"

"You're going to decide to buy a house. An amazing, very expensive house somewhere in LA." He turns to Amelia and she nods and pulls out her phone, already researching. "And I'm going to approach your accountant and whoever else for copies of those contracts, because obviously any bank would want to see them before they give you a loan."

Amelia holds up her phone. "This one's nice," she says, showing us a twenty-two-million-dollar mansion with multiple pools overlooking the lights of the city.

I laugh. "I live in a one-bedroom right now. That's quite the upgrade."

Ben's smile is brief. "Great. But I've got to warn you—there's a strong possibility he's been mismanaging things."

My stomach sinks. "Mismanaging them...how?"

He frowns. "Drew, even decent people are seduced by
power, by someone else's money. Even decent people ratio-

nalize skimming off the top. And Davis doesn't sound like he was ever a decent person."

"So you think he's been taking my money," I whisper. I'm sure I sound impossibly naïve to him right now, since I've clearly painted Davis as an asshole. But there's a vast divide between an asshole and a *thief*.

"I'd stake my life on the fact that he's been taking your money," he says. "It's just a matter of how *much* money, and how many other people have been helping themselves alongside him. He's gone to great lengths to keep you out of the loop, and there's probably a reason for it."

"Are you really going to be able to figure all this out, though?" I ask, feeling winded. Sure, I have money. I have a *lot* of money. But most of my revenue from the last tour and the most recent album is still "out there" somewhere, theoretically being held until venues and the crew and a thousand other entities have gotten their cut. I wouldn't know where to begin trying to separate out the truth from the excuses.

"With some help, yes," he says. I like that he's so sure of himself—one of us needs to be. "But if my suspicions are correct, he's going to fight you tooth and nail to hang on to control, and you're really going to need a backbone when it happens. He's going to try to convince you to let him handle everything with the house, and he'll go out of his way to make you back down."

I want Ben to be wrong about all this, but what he's describing sounds exactly like what Davis has done all along.

"WHY THE FUCK are you buying a twenty-two-million-dollar house?" Davis demands when I arrive on set the next day.

I shouldn't be surprised but somehow I am. Ben contacted

my accountant, and my accountant ran straight to Davis. That, to me, is the first nail in the coffin for them both.

"Why shouldn't I?" I reply. "I can afford it, right?"

I see the way frustration twists inside him. There's a momentary flare of his nostrils, a curl of his lip. "You're famous," he says after a second's pause. "You don't need to go through a bank for a loan like you're Bob and Betty Sue of Butt-fuck, Nowhere, hoping to qualify for a new condo. We've got people who can take care of all that for you."

"I don't want it taken care of for me, though," I tell him. "I'm twenty-six and buying my first place. I want to do it myself like any other adult would."

"*Normal* adults do things themselves. The benefit of being a celebrity is that you don't have to. I need you focused on your job—you know, the one you haven't exactly been crushing of late."

My chest is growing tighter and tighter the longer this conversation goes on. Exactly how much does he have to hide?

"Except I've already handled it," I reply. "You're the one wasting my time arguing. And why would my accountant be calling *you*?"

He's flustered then. I'm sure he anticipated I'd hand this over as readily as I have everything else. "He was just concerned. He didn't understand why you'd be dealing with a stranger for all this."

"*Everyone* I deal with is a stranger," I reply.

He sighs heavily, as if I'm being childish. "A stranger to *me*. You should only be going with people I've vetted. I'll find you someone else."

"*No*," I reply. "Just tell the firm to give Ben whatever he needs."

"I'm very uncomfortable with bringing in outsiders," he says.

Yes, I think. *I bet you are.*

~

BETH and I chat on the phone the day after my meeting with Ben. I don't reference her cancer, since I'm not supposed to know, but I do ask how she's doing and she dismisses the question, wanting instead to know how I am. I stammer through a conversation about the tour, about the sitcom I'm filming. It's hard when the most exciting thing in my life—the *only* exciting thing in my life—is my relationship with her son.

We make plans to get together when I'm back in LA, which is when she asks if I'm going to see my mother before I leave.

I blink in surprise. Beth and I have never really discussed my family before. "I hadn't planned on it," I reply, gazing at Central Park through the hotel room window. It's March, but still fully winter here. There are lots of things about New York I don't miss, and the weather is high on the list—but not first. "We don't really get along all that well."

"How could any mother not get along with you?" she asks. "You're an angel."

My throat swells. Obviously, I have to take what Beth says with a grain of salt—she'd say the same of Six, I'm sure—but the simple fact that she still likes me, even after I broke up with her son, feels like a gift I can never repay. "I'm not really an angel," I say quietly. "I'm frequently kind of a jerk."

She *tsks*. "I can't see that. But even if it's true, I'll bet you have your reasons. And I bet your mom has her reasons too, and they probably don't have much to do with you at all. Give her a chance, honey."

I smile and tear up at the same time. Beth is trying to fix her boys' lives before she dies. And I get the sense she's trying to fix mine too.

"Life isn't black and white, Drew," she says. "And you have to learn to live in the gray a little, accept that it can be perfect in all its imperfections."

Because she asks me to do it—and only because of that—I meet my mother for lunch the day before I return to Europe to finish the tour.

She's already waiting at the restaurant when I arrive.

Sometimes when I see her on a week day—her hair pulled back in a neat bun, clad in her annoyingly corporate attire—it's hard to picture the woman my father fell in love with. Today though, I catch a glimpse of her in an unguarded moment, before she's seen me, and there's something wistful in her expression, something that's gone unfulfilled—and I find the woman I remember once more. The mother of my early childhood, who made forts out of pillows and blankets with me and laughed as my father sang ridiculous songs in Russian. Before she ruined it all.

I move toward the table. She smiles and stiffens, simultaneously, as if I make her happy and she's bracing for me to take that happiness away at the same time.

"I like your hair," she says.

Of course she does. I could walk into her law firm now as a junior associate and no one would blink an eye. The teenage rebel in me wants me to go to the bathroom and shave it off, pronto.

"Thanks," I say grimly, taking the seat across from hers.

"*And* you're sober," she says.

"Tell me something, Mom," I reply, looking over the menu, "are we always going to throw our worst moments in each other's faces? Because you're not cheating on my father right now either, but I managed not to bring it up."

I look at her just in time to watch a wealth of emotions pass over her face. Shock, anger, sadness, resignation.

"You're right," she says for the first time in her life. "I'm sorry."

The waitress asks in a hushed voice if we'd prefer still or

sparkling water. I say one and my mother says the other. We cannot even agree about water, apparently.

"How was Hawaii?" she asks once we're alone again.

Already the trip has become a blur in my head, a few images, a snippet of conversation left to represent hours and days and weeks. Mostly, it's now just an overall feeling of warmth, and hope, of being made new. "It was really good." I suppose I should ask about Steven, or my asshole step-sibling, or her job, but I don't give a shit about any of them. I give negative shits about them. And I'm so sick of doing things just to be polite or because someone expects it of me.

"They're saying in the news that you broke up with that guitarist."

I don't want to tell her the truth because she hated Six the one time they met and it would thrill her. That I've fallen for a doctor would thrill her even more. One of many reasons she'll never know. I sigh. "Yes."

"Good," she says. "I never liked him."

"Really, Mom?" I ask with a bitter laugh. "Gosh, you were so subtle about it."

She frowns. "He has a drinking problem," she says. "You understand why I wouldn't want that for you."

"Because they're so hard to be faithful to?" I ask. It's a low blow, even from me.

Her mouth pinches. "I thought we weren't going to throw things in each other's faces?" she asks.

"Sorry," I mutter. I return my gaze to the menu. This is the kind of place *she* likes. Fancy salads ruined by things like beets and quail eggs. So neither the food nor the conversation will be enjoyable.

"I was working all day," she says, breaking the silence, "going to law school at night, trying to get us into a better neighborhood and you into a better school and then I'd come home to your father resenting me for it. I spent the last year of our marriage trying to study and work and take care of you while your father went out and got drunk. I know I made mistakes, but back then, Steven was the only one telling me I was doing okay, who was impressed at how I did it all."

Of course he was, I think sullenly. *He thought you'd wind up fucking him, and he was right.*

But then I think of Josh. Josh, the only person who's impressed with what I take on. Josh, telling me I deserve more. It's seductive, having someone on your side for once. "We don't have to rehash it all."

She stares straight ahead, as if I haven't spoken. "I will never try to tell anyone I handled it the right way. Steven won't either. I just wish you'd try to understand that even if I'm the villain in this story you've created, I'm not the only one."

So I guess we're doing this here, over our gross lunch of water and quail egg salad.

"You could have sent Dad to rehab or something," I say.

She gives a short, unhappy laugh. "You have forgotten some significant parts of your father's personality if you think he was going to let anyone force him into rehab. Where do you think you got that stubborn streak of yours?"

I have over a decade of accusations inside me, the same ones I've been making all along, but there's not the same vigor behind them. Something has changed in me these past few weeks. Maybe I just have some empathy now for moral gray areas, given how I've ventured into one. "Maybe you're right. I guess I just wish things had been different."

She presses her palms flat to the table and stares at her lap, swallowing hard. "I'll never forgive myself for that day," she says. I stiffen. This is something we do not discuss, ever, and I want to stop her but I can't. "I was in court when the school called to say you hadn't shown up and I let it go to voicemail. If I'd just checked, maybe—"

Her voice cracks and she stops talking.

I feel an ache in my chest, as if my lungs are squeezing tight. I didn't know she was blaming herself for what happened all this time. Of all the things she did wrong, this isn't one of them.

"That wasn't your fault," I tell her. I know in my rare honest moment that my father was no saint. He broke my nose, for God's sake. It's all the years *afterward* I blame her for. "But you took me from my home, Mom, and from my school, and from my father, and you just—" My throat clogs. "*Left*. You were never there. Everyone in that household treated me like I wasn't welcome and wasn't even *human* and you just looked the other way."

I wait for her denials, her arguments. She's a lawyer, after all. It's what she does best. But when I look up at her, her eyes are damp. "I know," she says, staring at her hands, her voice raspy. "And that's harder for me to live with than anything else, because I can't get those years back and I don't know where we go now."

It's more than she's ever said before. I swallow hard and then force a smile. "Hopefully someplace with burgers. You know I hate salad."

Her eyes finally find mine and we both laugh. Something feels like it's shifting. Things aren't perfect and they never will be, but maybe I can learn to live in the gray area just a little.

41

DREW

Ben, after much prodding and a few threats, finally receives the requested documents. They arrive so woefully incomplete he thinks I need a forensic accountant to figure out what's gone on.

I'm back in Europe finishing the last few dates of the tour when he calls to discuss it. I have to go shut myself in the bathroom to talk. "If they're being this cagey about a routine document request, there's almost no chance they're not hiding something major," he says.

I perch on the counter as my stomach tightens into a knot. "Davis will go ballistic."

"He will," Ben says, "and wouldn't Davis going ballistic over something that in no way involves him set off some alarm bells for you? Because they were buzzing for me the moment you said he'd hired *everyone* in your circle and that you don't even have copies of all this stuff. And when he tried to cut me out of this by handling your bank loan himself...that was all the alarms at once, right there. What exactly do you think he can do to you?"

"He knows stuff, Ben," I whisper. "Stuff I'd rather not have made public. I want out of everything, but if I come after him, he'll come after me too." Davis knows I have panic attacks and he knows how my father died. None of it is such a big deal, but I don't want to discuss it in every interview and I don't want to read about it every time I see my name online. Mostly, I just don't want to make an enemy of Davis because he's already terrible when he's on my side.

There is disapproval in the half-second of silence before Ben speaks. But he likes to fight, and it's not his life we're discussing. "Then you need to decide how much you want to keep it all to yourself," he finally says. "Just know that the way you're living now—where you're answering to him for everything and miserable—that situation is permanent until you do something about it."

And if this situation is permanent, it means Davis shoves another three-record contract with the label under my face, full of stipulations about world tours and promo. Am I really willing to sign away the next ten years the way I have the last five?

I tell him I'll let him know, but there's a weight on my chest when I hang up the phone. There's only one person I want to discuss this with and before I think too much about the fact that maybe I'm leaning on Josh and what a bad sign it is, I video call him.

He answers on the third ring. "Drew?" he asks, looking concerned. He's in a massive tent, the kind you might hold a wedding in, and it's the middle of the day because I've messed up the time. There aren't even curtains dividing most of the people. There are just bodies lying on gurneys and it looks like chaos.

"I'm sorry," I tell him. "I didn't realize you'd still be at work. With the time change my hours are all messed up. I can call back."

He smiles and the thing in my chest eases. "I've got a second," he says. "Where are you?"

Before I can answer, a woman approaches him, also in scrubs. She's pretty—high cheekbones, jet black hair. She speaks to him in French and I have no clue what she's said but she *sounds* elegant and smart, the kind of woman he *should* be with, probably.

He replies to her in French and it makes me ache. First, because it's so goddamn hot, him and his perfect French accent, and second, because he is just so much. So smart, so accomplished, so much more of everything than I am.

"Who was that?" I ask. Does he hear this tiny bite of worry in my voice?

He looks over his shoulder for a moment as if he cannot even remember who he just spoke to. "That was Sabine. One of the nurses. I have to go in a minute, but tell me why you were calling."

I can't. Now that I see a room full of people behind him, I cannot possibly sit here in the comfort of the *Canalejas* suite at the Four Seasons Madrid and tell him how trapped I feel by my terrible life of travel and designer clothes and adulation, how I'm scared to have Ben help me get out of it. "It was nothing," I reply. "I just wanted to talk."

He looks at me hard, that assessing look of his, the one I used to misinterpret. I know he's trying to find the truth in my lies, but this isn't the time to let him succeed because I feel like I'm about to cry. "Someone's at the door," I lie, "I'd better go."

"I miss you, Drew," he says and then the line goes dead before I even have a chance to say it back.

"I miss you too," I reply to no one at all.

And maybe it's hearing him say he misses me or maybe it's just straight-up jealousy of pretty French nurses, but I decide it's time to pull the trigger.

That night after the show I tell Davis I need a week off. We are supposed to be returning to California in two days. I'm sure there are things planned but I'm just done. I need a break.

A break I plan to enjoy in Somalia.

His face barely moves as he shakes his head *no*, like a father ignoring an unreasonable toddler. "You've got interviews."

"I really need some time off," I reply.

"Yeah," he says, "so do we all. That's life. And I've booked the studio to start work on the next album after the interviews, so deal with it."

"The *next* album? We don't have a single decent song."

"That's part of what you'll do in the studio. Play with those demos I sent you. Make them your own."

"So let me get this straight," I reply, channeling Josh. "You've got me booked for interviews I never agreed to, followed by studio time on demos I didn't agree to."

He rolls his eyes. "If I was going to wait for you to lead the way, you'd still be serving burgers to tourists at Planet Hollywood, Drew. I'm not sure how long it's going to take for you to realize a little hustle is necessary to stay afloat in this industry. And a few hard decisions, also."

"Well, here's a hard decision for you, Davis," I reply, "figure out what happens when I don't show up, because I'm not showing up."

He's still yelling about *breach of contract* when I walk out the door.

42

DREW

Two days later, I leave Dubai for Mogadishu, the capital of Somalia. I have the best armed guards money can buy, a tourist visa that required a small fortune in bribes, and a backpack that holds a few changes of clothes—and lingerie.

I know Josh won't have a ton of time for me, but I've already allowed my imagination to run wild. He'll perform dramatic surgeries all day and I'll find some way to make myself useful. Given my stunning lack of skills—I doubt they need a great deal of singing or posing—I have no idea what I'll do, but there must be something. I can hold babies. I can play with children. I can apply a Band-Aid over a scrape, as long as the scrape is small and not super gross. I'll find a way to stay out of his hair, but the nights will be ours, and we will, I'm sure, make the most of them. Especially once he sees the La Perla *bustier* I bought in NYC.

It's nearly an eight-hour flight but the airport is surprisingly nice, and I'm starting to think Jonathan's warnings were overly dramatic when I see a line of guys with machine guns against

My tour guide, Simon, also carries a machine gun. He is ostensibly the best money can buy. "Welcome to Somalia," he says. "I hope you're wearing a bulletproof vest."

I stare at him and then he laughs. "Just a joke," he says. "But also not. Make no mistake. Nothing about Mogadishu is like the United States. Remember that, please. It might save your life."

I dismiss my nerves. I don't care what I have to endure today as long as it ends in Josh's tent when it's all said and done.

I'm led to a series of armored SUVs. He nods toward the one in the center where four guards with AK-47s stand waiting. "All this is for me?" I ask.

He gives me a small nod. "Anything is possible in Somalia," he says. "You have to be prepared for all circumstances." I take a deep breath, pop a Dramamine in my mouth since I'm not allowed to ride up front, and climb aboard.

For twenty minutes, we bounce over the streets of Mogadishu, which doesn't seem that different from other African cities aside from the stunning number of buildings that are missing half their facades. "Bombs," says Simon.

At a checkpoint, we stop. Money is exchanged and I see the guards looking back toward the vehicle. "It's okay," Simon assures me. "They won't do anything. They just want to see who's here."

I'm relieved when we finally leave the city behind, whether or not I should be. The rubble turns into dirt and shrubbery, desolate under the rapidly dimming sky.

We're driving fast it seems to me, given the state of the roads. When we hit a pot hole the entire truck bounces so hard my head hits the roof. "We don't like to be out this late," Simon explains. "If you think this is fast, you should see us on the way back."

There is only one moment when I am truly scared: another roadblock, but this time there is a great deal of yelling between the first car and the guards. Slowly, the men in the first car climb out and each has his finger on the trigger of a gun. "Get down, lady," says the guard behind me and I do.

I remain on the floor until well after we've passed the checkpoint. Maybe Jonathan wasn't being dramatic after all.

After another thirty minutes, we reach Dooha. I know we're nearing something when I see people shuffling along the sides of the road, looking up through the haze of dust at our cars' approach.

There are guards at the gates who let us pass after a moment's conversation, and inside it becomes another world entirely. A small city of tents and people staring as we drive past.

Simon tells me to stay put while he checks things out. He and one of the guards descend and no one seems at all surprised by the sudden arrival of two men carrying machine guns.

After a moment, he opens my door. "The staff is in the canteen," he says. "This is your stop."

I'm both thrilled and terrified. It now seems like I should have asked Josh first. What if he isn't even here? But I think of the way he surprised me in Paris. How thrilled I was, how busy I was, and how nothing but him mattered once he arrived. Is this really so different? I take my backpack from one of the guards, thank Simon, and descend to find a woman standing there in a sarong with a shawl over her head. She looks me over from head to toe and seems to find me lacking. "This way," she says with a frown.

The canteen is in a large tent, just as the hospital was—one room with long tables. She points to a group in the corner in scrubs and walks away with a shrug. I'm nervous, feeling awkward, but then I spy Josh and it all falls away. He's in scrubs, listening intently to the woman across from him and nodding. My heart swells until I notice Sabine, the pretty nurse, sits beside him. I try not to let it bother me.

One of them turns. And then they all turn. They are blinking, staring, astonished. And Josh looks the most astonished of them all.

"Surprise," I say weakly, hoisting my backpack further onto my shoulder.

For all the low moments we've had since we met, I've never seen him look less happy to see me than he does now. He does not smile as he rises and moves to stand in front of me, as if he wants to block me from view. For the first time I wonder if he might be ashamed to have his colleagues know about me. It was one thing in New York, or in Paris, among strangers. But these are people he likes and respects...and I'm *me*.

"What are you doing here?" he asks, his jaw tight, his voice low enough not to be overheard. Behind us his companions return to their conversation, but they keep sneaking peeks at us.

I feel little and stupid. Like a teenage girl with a crush. The horrifying realization that he doesn't want me here hits hard. The possibility that he's been lying—or I've been lying to myself—follows right on its heels. I look back over at the table and see Sabine watching us with a level of interest that is hardly impartial. Is he as interested in her as she clearly is in him? The mere suggestion of it is enough to make my stomach tighten painfully. "I thought it was obvious when I said 'surprise'," I reply, trying to sound casual and in control when I'm anything but. I try to step backward but he's holding me in place, his hands on my biceps.

His eyes fall closed and his tongue darts out to tap his upper lip. He's either thinking or he's praying for patience, perhaps both.

He glances over his shoulder at his colleagues and then starts pulling me toward the exit. "Come on," he snaps.

His grasp on my arm is iron-tight and I allow myself to be pulled, but my heart is shattering. It's obvious he wants me out of here as quickly and quietly as possible and it really fucking hurts. I thought he was different. I thought there was something between us, and of course I was wrong because I'm always wrong.

We get outside the canteen and I try to pull away from him. "Let me go," I choke out. "I get it. I'm leaving. You don't have to be an asshole about it."

"*Leaving?*" he asks with an angry laugh. "You're in one of the most dangerous places in the world, at nightfall. Where the fuck are you going to go?"

It doesn't matter. It feels as if nothing matters. I can only remember one other time in my life when I've felt this empty, this lost, this broken. The last time it happened, I grew from the experience and came out stronger at the other end. But I don't want to learn and grow again. I don't want to have to rebound from another loss.

Reluctantly, I recall Simon's haste to be off the road and admit to myself Josh is probably right, which means I'm stuck here until daylight with someone who wishes I hadn't come.

He pulls me past armed guards to a long line of tents and then unzips one of them and tugs me inside. It's tall enough for us both to stand in, but there's not much to it: a cot on the right, a small desk at the back with some kind of hanging rack with shelves for his clothes.

If I weren't so upset at the moment, I'd marvel that anyone manages to live like this. No wonder he was so horrified by the excesses of Hawaii.

"Please tell me what the hell you were thinking," he says, his voice tight with anger.

I stare at his chest, unable to face him. I want to be mad but what I am, most of all, is heartbroken and humiliated.

"It's my fault for taking you at your word," I say, my voice hoarse with tears. "I thought you actually meant it when you said you wanted to see me."

He exhales heavily. "Of course I meant it." He doesn't sound apologetic. He sounds *weary*, just like my mother does when she claims the same. "But not *here*. Do you have any idea how dangerous this is? Anything could have happened to you on the way here. They kidnap expats all the fucking time. And if anyone had recognized you...Jesus. There wouldn't have been a *chance* of surviving the trip unscathed."

"No one recognized me and it was fine," I reply in a small voice, pulling out my phone. "But don't worry, I'll get out of your hair. You were clearly *busy*." By which I really mean *You clearly didn't want to be associated with me*, but I'm not about to sit here and beg for empty reassurances from him. We weren't what I thought we were. I hoped for too much and made more of this than it was, and I should have known better. That's all there is to it.

"Stop," he says. For one agonizing second I let myself hope he's going to tell me it's okay I'm here, though I have no clue what he could say at this point to salvage the situation. "I don't trust those guys who brought you," he says instead. "Let me make a call."

I perch on the edge of his cot while he holds a terse conversation with someone about "the primary". He mentions Istanbul, then curses. "Djibouti, then," he says.

It's taken me ten hours and thousands of dollars to get here —for this. To have him kick me out without so much as a hug and a *It was so nice of you to come*. I've never felt more foolish, and I'm suddenly so exhausted even sitting up is an effort. I want to curl into a ball and sleep until this whole thing is over with. And it means we are over. That's what hurts the most. There is no coming back from this, not that it appears he'd want us to.

He hangs up finally and leans forward, elbows to his knees, hands briefly over his face. He looks at me at last.

"What was all that about?" I ask.

His teeth dig into his lip as he hesitates. "I know some guys here. I can't tell you who they're with and you can't ask, but they'll get you to the airport in Mogadishu tomorrow before daybreak. They'll wait with you there until you've boarded your plane. You'll fly to Ethiopia, and leave for the US from there."

The tension in his words makes me pause. Is he simply worried, or can he not wait to get rid of me? I don't know. I only know it hurts. That I feel small and stupid and utterly unwanted. I shouldn't have come. I shouldn't ever have continued this pointless, futile thing with him after Paris.

"Have you eaten?" he asks.

I blink in surprise and then shake my head. I haven't eaten and I haven't slept because all that mattered was him. How excessively one-sided it all was. I'm so stupid.

"I'll get you something," he says. "You'll need to wait here. I can't risk having someone recognize you if they haven't already."

He looks at me for a moment and his mouth opens, then closes. Whatever he was going to say, he thinks better of it and walks out instead, zipping the tent up behind him.

His eagerness to get away from me hurts, but doesn't surprise me at this point. I've invaded his space and now I'm a problem he has to deal with. I've turned into Sloane—the unwanted interloper, inconveniently messing up his plans. I wonder if he'd decide to sleep on the couch, if there *was* a couch.

How did I ever convince myself I was someone he'd want for longer than a few non-consecutive nights? He's a doctor who testifies before Congress, while I'm a living, breathing disaster who never even finished high school. Anyone looking at this situation would have known I wasn't good enough for him, was never going to be what he wanted.

I lie down on the cot. The pillow smells like him and I feel strangled by grief. A tear rolls down my face and I quickly brush it away. I wanted this to be different and I wanted *him* to be different and I can't entirely shake off who I thought he was, even now that he's shown me otherwise.

When I hear the tent unzipping, I sit up and try to pull myself together, drying my eyes on my sleeve. I will survive this situation, but I'm not sure I could survive his pity on top of it.

He steps inside, frowning at the sight of me. It's as if not a minute has passed since the day I landed in Honolulu. I'm back to being the girl he doesn't want on the trip.

He hands me a tray. "There wasn't much to choose from," he says with a sigh. "The kitchen's already closed for the night."

"Thank you," I tell him stiffly. I pick at some rice but I can't stomach anything else. "I'm mostly tired." He crosses the room and takes the tray from me. For a moment, we both hold it. It's the closest we've been since I arrived.

"Lie down," he says, returning to his seat at the desk.

"This cot isn't big enough for two people," I say quietly. "I can sleep on the floor."

"Of course you're not sleeping on the floor," he says. "I'm going to stay up until the transport gets here, anyway."

He's really not even going to touch me. He can barely stand to *look* at me.

I lie down, facing away from him so he doesn't have a clue when the tears start rolling down my face.

43

JOSH

She sleeps and I wait. I could probably lie down, but I'm too fucking *scared*. I know I'd be tempted to do more than lie there, and I'm not willing to let down my guard for even a moment. God only knows who recognized her at the airport or on the way here. At any given moment I expect to see the tent being ripped down the center.

This is all my fault. I didn't want her to know how bad things were, but...they're bad. We have informants all over the camp. Already, I'm certain, someone has left to tell the local terrorists we have a visitor. Even if they didn't recognize her, they'll know she's pretty and young and American, that she looks like she has money. And one of those things would be enough. All of them together—I have to stop thinking about it.

I bury my head in my hands and take a deep breath, trying to stay calm.

It's impossible to quell my anxiety, though. Even if we get through the night, she's still got to get back to Mogadishu. The road is the most dangerous part, but the airport isn't all that safe either. I'm gonna be a nervous wreck until she's safely landed somewhere else.

For the next few hours, I listen to her talk in her sleep—those same numbers. Seven, one-ninety-nine, eighty-eight. I wish she'd tell me what they mean. Usually, I hear them once or maybe twice. Tonight she says them again and again, as if she's trapped in a nightmare that's on repeat.

I should never have kept this going. I should never have started it in the first place. Maybe I've ruined it anyway, with the way I've treated her tonight. That would probably be for the best. Because I can't seem to let her go, and this proves, beyond a shadow of a doubt, that I should.

44

DREW

Josh wakes me when it's still dark.

"Drew," he says, "your ride is here."

He's still dressed. I'm groggy, but awake enough to feel another flush of shame. I've never seen anyone want me gone as badly as he did when I showed up last night.

I rise from the cot, unable to meet his eye, and grab my backpack.

"I'm ready," I tell him, with no emotion in my voice. I'm angry but it's mostly at myself. I should have known better than to come here. I've spent my whole life determined not to do something this stupid again, and look what I did at the first chance that presented itself: I leapt at it.

"Here," he says, handing me his Georgetown hoody.

"It's hot out," I argue. *And I don't want your stupid fucking sweatshirt. I want to forget I ever knew you.*

"You need to wear it," he says, "with the hood up. They need to make sure no one recognizes you."

I do as I'm told. "I'll mail it back to you," I reply coolly. We're right back where we were that first morning in Oahu—Josh reluctantly trying to do the right thing and me telling him, as best I can, to fuck right off.

"Keep it," he says.

"I don't *want* it," I say, and I'm sure he hears the hurt that leaches out of me with those words. My God, I sound more like Sloane with every second that passes.

"Drew," he says, pulling me toward him with his hands on my hips. "Look—"

There is a tap outside the tent. "Hey, Bailey?" someone says. Another American. "We gotta go."

He presses his lips to my forehead. "I'll call you."

I glance up at him for one second, which is as long as I can stand. I think the memory of him is going to break my heart every day for the rest of my life. "Bye, Josh," I say, and I unzip the tent.

He starts to follow me and I shake my head. "Don't, okay?" My voice quavers and after a moment's hesitation, he nods, and that's it.

Two guys in camo wait outside. "This seems like overkill," I mutter quietly when I see the armored truck waiting for us.

One of the guys raises a brow. "Only someone who hasn't spent much time here would say that."

Our ride back to the airport is entirely uneventful, certainly no scarier than sitting in the back of a New York City cab. The worst part of the whole trip is how carsick I am until the medicine kicks in.

I have to wonder, once more, how much of this was actual worry on Josh's part and how much was him just being not wanting to be seen with me.

I guess it doesn't matter. It's over now, either way.

One of the guards escorts me all the way to the plane. "Thank you," I tell him when I reach the door.

"If it makes you feel any better," the guy says, "he called in a favor for you he'd never call in for himself."

What does that mean?

It really doesn't matter, though. It just goes to show how fucking unnecessary it all actually was.

45

DREW

When I finally land in LA, a full day later, there's a text from Tali. The picture she's sent shows Hayes holding a tiny human in the palm of his hand.

It's a girl! it says. **Audrey Bell Flynn.**

I marvel at the photo. While I'm familiar with how people are created, I've never seen one come from people I know, people I've known since the beginning of their relationship, with all its starts and stops. It's...a miracle. Out of their tortured back and forth, this gorgeous little girl was created.

They took the long journey and it paid off for them. Most of us aren't that lucky.

I head to the first-class lounge at LAX to shower and change clothes, since I'm too gross right now to be seen much less be in the presence of a newborn.

I have texts from Davis about the interviews and some movie premiere in a few weeks for which he's found me a date. I guess I've got no reason to say *no* at this point, do I? I also have several missed calls from Josh and several texts asking me to let him know when I'm back in LA. *Responsible as always, our Joshua. Making sure everyone's taken care of.*

I'm back, I type, nothing more, and then I hit send. His obligation is done and so is mine.

I reach the showers and have just closed the door behind me when he calls. "How did it go?" he asks. "There weren't any issues?"

"It was just peachy," I reply. "I'm getting in the shower here so—"

"Drew, wait," he says with a sigh. "I'm so sorry about how that all happened. I know you meant well and—"

"It's fine," I interrupt. "Believe me, I've learned my lesson. *You're* the only one allowed to pay a surprise visit. So I guess in five years or whenever the hell you're free to travel and willing to be seen with me, I'll just wait for a knock on the door and drop all my plans."

"You can't be serious right now," he says. "Do you have any idea how much danger you put yourself in? Do you have any idea—"

"Please stop," I say. My throat aches with the desire to cry. "You made it abundantly clear when I was there that I was nuts to have shown up and I definitely don't need to hear it all over again. More to the point, this is done. So you don't need to worry about me anymore."

"Drew," he says hoarsely, "don't do this. I know it's a messed-up situation, but I'd give anything to—"

I'd give anything to—. Those are the words that bring me up short. I've heard that before. It was bullshit then, and it's bullshit now.

"No, Josh, you actually *wouldn't* give anything, because if that was true you'd be here. And if that was true, you'd be willing to tell your family and you wouldn't have *hidden* me from your colleagues. Let's call a spade a spade: you're not willing to give up a fucking thing."

And then I hang up, block his number, and get into the shower where I cry like a child for a very long time.

A NURSE USHERS me back to Tali's room. She, of course, is gorgeous and radiant, smiling wide when she sees me.

Only Tali would look this freaking cute right after giving birth. Hayes sits in the corner, still in scrubs, holding a baby so tiny in his arms she hardly seems real. There is something soft on his face, something I saw there on the day he and Tali married. He flashes me a quick smile but then his gaze is on the bundle once more, so besotted with tiny Audrey he can barely stand to look away.

"You poor thing," Tali says. "You just landed, didn't you? You look more exhausted than I do."

"I wanted to see her before I sleep for a thousand hours," I reply. "How's the vagina? How ruined is it on a scale of one to ten?"

Hayes shoots us a quick, alarmed glance while Tali laughs. "I wound up needing a C-section, so I imagine things are intact," she replies. She turns to her husband. "Hayes, you have to share the baby."

Hayes gives her a sheepish grin and rises with the baby in his arms. "Do you want to hold her?" he asks.

I blink uncertainly, looking from him to Tali. Does anyone really trust *me* with the baby?

"I don't know," I say. "I've never really... She's so small."

"You'll be fine," Hayes says.

I wash my hands and sit before he places her in my arms. She's the most darling human I have ever seen in my life, with her tiny rosebud mouth pursed, sucking in her sleep as if she's dreaming of being fed. Her fingers are impossibly small, clutched into tiny fists, and I feel something unfurl inside me as I look at her. "She's perfect," I whisper, and to my horror, my voice cracks.

Hayes glances over at Tali. "Do you think she's hungry?" he asks. "She's doing that sucking thing with her mouth."

Tali smiles at him adoringly. "You worry too much," she says. "I assure you she will not just *forget* to eat."

He takes the seat beside her and their eyes meet. For a quick second, it's as if they're the only people in the room. I used to claim that I didn't want what they had, that I didn't want a little girl like the one in my arms, but it was simply that I thought those things were impossible for me.

And it turns out I was right.

But it hurts a lot more now than it used to.

46

JOSH

She's blocked my calls. I have the insane impulse to get on a plane and beg her back, and I fight it every day. She could have gotten killed coming here the way she did, and if she had, it would have been my fault. Just like it's my fault that she got hurt by this whole thing. I knew better than to start this, and I certainly knew better than to continue it.

I get through work every day, but my heart is no longer in it. I find myself wishing I'd never gone into medicine in the first place, simply so that I wouldn't have come, so they wouldn't need me to stay.

I've told the director of operations I need out, and he asked me to give him a year to find a replacement. It'll take every day of that year. We just had another bomb threat yesterday, one of our guards was shot this morning and a refugee camp to the south was attacked while I was in Hawaii. No one with an ounce of sense would choose to come here now.

So...a year. It will be too late to win Drew back by then, but what was I going to do anyway, under the circumstances?

"You look awful," my mom says when I call.

She does too, but I keep that to myself. "Just busy here." I tell her. "How are you feeling?"

"I'd feel a lot better," she says, "if you were home and your brother was okay. Have you spoken to him?"

"We've texted," I tell her, though in truth it was just one text I sent asking him to look in on our mother, to which he did not reply.

"The breakup with Drew has really hit him hard," she says. "I think he's drinking."

I laugh, scrubbing a hand over my face. For once my brother and I have something in common. "Mom, was there ever a time when he wasn't drinking? He spent most of the trip to Hawaii drunk. Aside from the part he spent in jail for drugs."

She sighs. "Your father thinks he needs to go to rehab, but I just think if Drew would come back he'd—"

"Do not suck her into his spiral, Mom," I say. Her eyes widen at my tone. "She's got enough going on. She doesn't need to be dealing with an addict on top of everything else."

"But...he could support her too," she argues. "They could be there for each other. Marriage and a baby would change everything for both of them."

"A *baby*?" I repeat, aghast. Aside from the fact that marriage and babies didn't seem to improve my parents' life much, it's not really ideal for a guy with addiction issues and a very recent arrest record. Mostly, though, it's for selfish reasons I want to derail this entire line of thought.

"He's been talking about it," she says. "The other day he was here. I guess that friend of Drew's, the writer, just had a baby. She posted about it. Joel thinks maybe if he made a grand gesture, she'd come back."

The camp siren goes off for the third time in as many days. "Sorry, Mom, I have to go." I end the call to report to the hospital. We'll probably be on lockdown again all night, my life is likely at risk, and I'm so depressed after the call from my mother that I barely even care.

47

DREW

For the next two weeks, I do what I have to do.

I get through the interviews and get my dress fitted for the premiere and go to the studio, putting in the motions of bringing the demos to life. My performance is so lackluster that Davis finally explodes and tells me to take a few days off and pull my shit together.

I don't feel sad. I simply feel numb. LA is still sunlit and busy and I feel like a ghost as I float over its streets. I have no purpose anymore. Ben is still on me about the forensic accountant and I can't commit to that either. I don't know how my life can be so empty yet feel unbearably heavy at the same time.

Someone has uploaded a video of me performing my new song that last night in Oahu, having finally realized who I was. The comments are equally divided between *That's way better than Naked* and *Tell her to stick with what she knows*. It hurts to watch. There was so much love in my eyes as I sang to Josh. I had so much faith in him, and it's never coming back.

The only bright spot, the only bearable moment, is when I visit Tali and the baby each day. They're at their house in Hollywood Hills, as—to Tali's chagrin—Hayes is temporarily refusing to leave LA.

"Just in case Audrey needs, you know, emergency brain surgery at UCLA," Tali explains with a laugh, pulling the baby to her shoulder and burping her like an old pro. "He's insane."

"It's sweet, though," I tell her, watching as she offers a pinky to Audrey, who grasps it. That's the thing with mothers, I'm finding—they can't seem to stop seeking contact, even when the child no longer needs it. Even when, as in my mother's case, they sometimes do more harm than good.

Tali looks up at me and sees something on my face. "Have you spoken to Josh?"

I swallow. "I told you. I blocked his calls. The whole thing was pointless. It was just going to drag on forever."

She gives me a sad smile. "Not everything that drags on forever necessarily hurts forever, though," she says.

I swallow in polite disagreement. In her life, things work out okay. In mine, even the good things go to hell, eventually.

ON THE DAY of the premiere, I reluctantly rise and prepare for a day I could hardly be less interested in. Getting ready for something like this is a lot like getting ready for a wedding, if that wedding was taking place at three PM and involved millions of people discussing your weight, pores and love life afterward. An entire day wasted in hair and makeup, then a red carpet, then a movie I don't want to watch followed by a party I don't want to attend. A thousand women would kill to trade places with me and there's nothing wrong with that. There's also nothing wrong with the fact that I'd kill to trade places with a woman staying home. I'm tired of pretending to be excited and grateful all the time.

I'm in a suite at the Beverly Hills Hotel because my cottage wasn't large enough for all the people it will take to make me presentable. By nine in the morning the facialist is there, complaining about broken capillaries and blackheads I can't even see. And then the rest of the crew moves in—manicurist, hairdresser, makeup artist, stylist.

Stephanie and Davis are in rooms nearby with friends and family, who pop in sporadically to gawk. The atmosphere is celebratory. There is cheering and laughter and champagne corks popping and the entire time I feel sick, wound so tight that even smiling is a struggle. There's a huge spread on the table and I'm too nauseous to eat.

"Don't be nervous, hon," says the hairstylist. "You're going to look beautiful. That guy you were dating is going to explode when he sees you with Luke Powell."

I want to laugh and cry at the same time. By *that guy you were dating* he means Six, not his brother, which is who actually concerns me. How long will it take for the news to make its way to Somalia? How long do I have before Josh sees pictures of me on the arm of another man, thinking I've moved on? How long 'til he starts dating the pretty nurse, if he isn't already? Not long. The speed of light, really. There are thousands of gossip sites, thousands of places those pictures will post. It just takes one staff member there checking *TMZ* before Josh knows too. Sabine probably has an alert set, waiting for this moment to swoop in.

I'd have set one, too, so I can't really blame her.

Good, I think. *Let me ruin everything*. It was going to be ruined eventually anyway. But my stomach continues to churn.

My hair is blown out, meticulously straightened, and then re-curled. When I check my phone afterward, I see two missed calls from an unknown number that begins with the Somali country code. Is it Josh, calling from a different number because I blocked his?

It's 1:30 in the morning there. Why would he be calling me

so late? I squeeze my eyes shut and take a deep breath, trying to stay calm. I blew off all his claims about the dangers of that camp, but the terrible possibility that he was right makes me feel like I've taken a hit to the chest. I can't listen to the voice-mail fast enough.

For a moment, the line is silent, as if someone didn't know it was recording. And then I hear his voice and my world stops. "Hey." It's a whisper. He pauses. "Hey, I know—"

The line goes dead, leaving open every possibility. Why did he just hang up like that? Did something go wrong, or did he just decide that whatever he was going to say was pointless?

I call the number back, but there's no answer. He doesn't answer his cell either. My hands press to my stomach. Maybe he just wanted to talk, then changed his mind and went to bed. Or maybe something terrible has happened. He was evacuated last summer. I guess things *do* go wrong there.

"You need a drink," says the makeup artist. "It's not like you to be so nervous."

I shake my head, forcing a smile. "No, I'm fine." If I have even one hair less self-control than I have at the moment, I will cause a scene that will make falling off the stage in Amsterdam look like child's play.

I continue to be painted and sprayed and fussed over, fighting myself the entire time not to call Beth. Yes, she'd be the first person contacted if something bad happened, but the last thing she needs is to be needlessly alarmed by me. And how would I explain the fact that the wrong son called me in the middle of the night?

By three PM, I'm nearly ready. I stand in nothing but Spanx while the stylist and her assistant pull the dress over my head —there is no such thing as modesty when you're trying to keep makeup off a borrowed Christian Siriano.

The dress is a sample size two. "Was it this tight before?" I ask as they zip me up.

The stylist laughs. "It's supposed to be tight. If you can breathe easily, that's when I know we have a problem."

Except I wasn't breathing easily *before* the dress was on.

My phone starts to bleat while the safe with the jewels on loan is opened.

"Ashleigh," I call. "Who is it?"

"Someone named Beth?" she asks in response, but she's already setting the phone back on the table. No one named Beth could possibly be important, she thinks.

"I need it," I gasp.

Ashleigh crosses the room. I grab it on the last ring.

"Drew?" Beth cries. There is panic in her voice. Beth, who shrugged off her son being held in a foreign jail and everything else that occurred in Hawaii, is hysterical. "I'm trying to locate Joel. Is he with you?"

"Me?" I reply. "No. Why? Is everything okay?"

She releases a choked sob. "It's Josh," she says, and Jim takes the phone from her.

"We're trying to locate Joel," he says, his voice even but tense. "There was an attack on the refugee camp about an hour ago. We don't know what's happened, but we don't want Joel to hear it from the press first."

I sink to the floor. There's a collective gasp from the room and I don't care. The stylist rushes toward me and I hold up a hand to ward him off. "What else do you know? Is someone trying to get them out?"

"They're not telling us anything," he says. "Sloane made some calls...it sounds like the medical personnel were being evacuated when the attack began and two doctors stayed behind. They think Josh was one of them."

My breath stops. He called me. He called me when it was happening. Maybe because he thought he was going to die.

"What does that mean?" I ask. My hands shake, my lungs can't get enough air. "For him. What does that mean?"

I'm making no sense. Jim somehow understands the question. "It means they probably took him hostage...or worse," he says quietly. "We're trying to get ahold of the embassy in Ethiopia since that's where they went the last time they were evacuated."

My brain is spinning. I can't focus. "We have to go to Ethiopia," I tell him. "We need to—"

I stop and press my hand over my face because I have no idea what we need to do. I have no idea who to pressure to find him. The one person I want to lean on in this moment is Josh. With that thought, I burst into tears.

"I'll call you back," I whisper.

I would give up my entire fortune for this not to be happening, to be back where we were the day before when he was safe and I was merely heartbroken.

Davis and Stephanie come barreling in, summoned by Ashleigh, no doubt.

"What's the problem?" barks Davis.

"We may need to iron the dress," says the stylist as I push myself off the floor. "How much time do we have?"

"No," I say quietly. "I'm not going."

"Not going?" Davis yells. "The hell you're not going. You're supposed to perform. You can't just *choose* not to go."

I look at him and feel utterly clear for the first time. "Of *course* I can," I reply. "Ashleigh, I need a private plane out of LA. One that can go a long distance. *Now*."

She looks at Davis and does nothing. My laughter borders on hysteria. "Ashleigh, are you *serious*? I'm the one who's paying you."

"I—" She looks from me to Davis. "You have to be on stage in two hours."

And again, it's so clear. It was *always* clear. I was just scared I'd make things worse, but there's nothing these people could ever do to match the terror I feel right now.

"You're fired," I reply, turning for the bedroom. Davis grabs my dress so hard it tears from the back. Everyone in the room gasps in unison.

"You are not going anywhere," he says, gripping my arm. "This is breach of contract. They can sue you and so can I."

I look at his hand on my arm. "You just tore my dress and grabbed me inappropriately. There are fifteen witnesses. I'm pretty sure I can sue you right back."

I pull away and march into my room, reaching for my inhaler as I wrench the dress off. And then I call Ben. "Pull the trigger. On all of it. Also, do you know how I can get a plane?"

FROM THE CAR, I call Beth and Jim and tell them I've got a plane ready to go. We'll leave for Ethiopia in ninety minutes, sooner if we get there faster and the pilot does too. I'm calling everyone I know to make sure this is being taken seriously.

"This is so kind of you," Beth says. "You really don't have to go there. I know you're busy."

She still thinks I've done all this simply because I dated *Six*. It kills me that I can't tell them, but maybe it's for the best. Because if they knew, I'd have to tell them he tried to call me, and the fact that he got cut off doesn't seem good.

"It might help to have me there," I tell her. "There might be people I can call."

"You're right," she says, and then she's crying again. "This is so kind of you. I'll never forget it. I'm still trying to reach Joel. Hopefully he can come with us."

Normally, I'd think Six's presence would make a bad situation worse. Except this situation can't get worse. It might already be over and we don't even know.

I go online and look up kidnappings in Somalia, and I wish I hadn't. Josh wasn't exaggerating about the dangers. Kidnappings are routine there. Kidnapping of *doctors* is routine. An optimist would see that at least half of them survive. A pessimist, me, sees that of the other half, many die, and many are held for years before they are rescued. I close Wikipedia. I don't want to know any more.

The plane is ready to go by the time Beth and Jim reach the airport. "I reached Joel," Beth says, squeezing my hand. "He's flying out tonight."

She looks so hopeful about us. I feel all the blood drain from my face but I say nothing. It doesn't matter. Nothing at all matters as long as Josh is okay.

I let Jim and Beth take the actual bedroom at the back of the plane. I'm sleeping fitfully in one of the reclining seats when she takes the chair beside me. Her face is drawn.

"We just heard from Sloane," she says, tears rolling down her face. "They've been found, but several people are injured and an American is dead."

The tight knot in my stomach becomes a hole and I feel as if I'm falling right through it. There were other Americans there, but the bulk of the staff was French. And I know how little good hoping for the best does at times like this. Beth begins to sob and I join her, my face in my hands, my shoulders shaking.

"What are they doing with the survivors?" I ask when I can finally get the words out. "When will we know?"

"They'll be flown to Ethiopia once they're medically stable," she says. "The rest of the staff is already on their way there."

My eyes squeeze shut. Even if Josh isn't the one who died, that still doesn't mean he's okay. And if he is okay, if he did survive, I need to know this can never happen again. Beth goes back to the bedroom and I pick up my phone.

"Hey, Ben," I say to his voicemail, "when you're drawing all this up, can you do one more thing? I want to give fifteen million dollars to this refugee camp in Somalia." I know I've got that much liquid right now and I'll send more later. "And half of it has to be earmarked for security."

I'm somewhere over the Atlantic Ocean right now—groundless, without a manager, without a record deal or an assistant, and soon to be without most of my money. None of it matters. Josh is the one thing, of all the things I had, that I wish was still mine.

IT'S early evening when we arrive in Ethiopia. The air is sweltering, Beth seems exhausted, and just as I'm kicking myself for not arranging transportation, I see a driver holding a sign with the names Bailey/Andreyev on it. Ben has taken care of everything.

Beth's been told that some of the survivors of the shooting are already on the plane to Ethiopia, so we go straight to the hospital. The first person I see when we enter the emergency room is Sabine. Her eyes go wide and then she launches herself at me, as if I'm family. "Thank you for coming," she says and she starts crying. "They won't tell us anything. Please. Do you have news? Please."

That small, terrified voice inside me thinks: *She doesn't sound like a friend or a colleague.* But this is about Josh, and I just want him to be happy, even if it's not with me. "I don't know anything."

She buries her face in her hands. "I should have stayed with him," she says and she starts to cry. Her friends console her and I walk away with Beth.

"Who was that?" Beth asks. "Is she his girlfriend?"

My stomach sinks. Even *Beth* thinks there was something there. "I don't know," I reply, my heart so heavy it hurts. It doesn't matter. "She's someone he works with, I think."

I know Six has arrived when I hear Jim's disgusted exhale. I resent him for it, but I understand it as well—even from a distance it's clear Six is worse for wear. He's wearing sunglasses inside and I can smell his pot-and-beer odor from five feet away. He hugs his mother, then me.

"Thanks for helping my parents," he says against my ear. "Can we talk later, once we know the deal with Josh?"

"There is absolutely nothing to discuss," I reply, detaching myself. "I didn't do this for you."

There's a commotion at the door before he can even react. A gurney is coming in, led by two guys in flight suits. The patient is on oxygen, has lines going everywhere. I clutch Beth's arm until the guy's face comes into view.

"It's not him," I whisper, relieved and devastated at once. I don't want Josh to have been badly hurt, but I'd take that over other alternatives. Suddenly, Beth's legs start to give out. I catch her and Jim sprints across the room to help me get her into a chair.

"I'm sorry," she cries with her face in her hands. "I was so scared and then it wasn't him and now I wish it was. He's still my baby." Jim places a hand on her back and my eyes tear up yet again. I've only known Josh a fraction of the time they have and I'm devastated. I can't imagine what this must be like for them.

The next time the doors open, I brace myself. *It won't be him. Don't get your hopes up.*

And then I stand to get a better look and clutch the plastic waiting room chair beside me to stay upright, covering my mouth to hide the strangled sob that leaves my throat.

Josh.

He's bare-chested and there's a makeshift bandage around his shoulder that's soaked in blood. He's being pushed through the doors in a wheelchair, but he's alive. Tears roll down my face at the sight of him, pale and exhausted, barefoot, covered in dirt. But *alive*. Thank God.

His family surges forward while I stay behind, watching as he rises from the wheelchair—ignoring the outcry from the soldier pushing him. He hugs his mom, his father, even Six. Sabine and the other two nurses have rushed toward him as well.

I want to stand here and stare at him until I've had my fill. I want more than that, but I'd settle simply for the sight of him. Except, my part in this is done. I wanted to know he was safe, and that will have to be enough. I'm not going to make an awkward situation worse.

I take another step backward and look for an exit. It was always my plan to leave once we got news. I just didn't realize how much it would actually hurt to see him and walk away.

Suddenly, his mother is pointing toward me and his head jerks my way, astonished. His eyes lock with mine, and it makes me so happy and hurts so much at the same time.

I give him a small, pathetic wave, accompanied by a small, pathetic smile. One that says *Hi there* and *I'm glad you're okay* and *I get it, this is weird, but I'm playing along.*

And then he's pushing past them, breaking through the crowd to reach me. He stops when he's a foot away and I'm frozen, uncertain how to be this near him without pressing my face to his chest, without throwing my arms around him. I was right, I guess, when I said it would never work. It still doesn't work.

"You came all the way here for me," he says.

I swallow. "Of course I did," I say roughly, and then there are tears rolling down my face.

"Because you love me."

I nod. "Yes. But your family—"

He steps closer and reaches toward me. One hand lands on my waist, the other cups my jaw. "And you're in this for the whole ride, wherever it takes us?"

My eyes widen. "Yes," I whisper in a choked voice.

In the distance someone shouts *What the fuck?* But Josh is smiling. The world is falling apart around us and he's smiling.

"Me too," he says and then he kisses me. In front of his entire family and all the people in this waiting room, he kisses me like he thought he might never see me again. And then I start to cry once more, because I never dreamed I'd end up with everything I want from this, and I have.

48

JOSH

There's a time to worry about being diplomatic, about handling everything in exactly the right way. But this isn't that time. Not after nearly dying and realizing I didn't want to leave the world without letting her know how I felt.

"I love you," I tell her. I know I should let her go, stop kissing her long enough to get this all out, but I want too many things at once right now. "I love you so fucking much."

"I love you too," she says, sounding like she is laughing and crying at the same time. "And I was so stupid. I didn't know it was that dangerous and—"

"Not stupid," I tell her. How could she have known? I went out of my way to make it sound manageable. "I hurt you. I was so freaked out that I didn't think at all about how it made you feel."

"I should have given you a chance to explain it," she says. "This might have escaped your attention, but I'm a little messed up."

I smile against her mouth. "You hid it so well." But inside I think *Not messed up. Resilient.* She's a tiny fighter and I love that about her. I love everything about her, the bad and the good. I want to tell her this, and tell about that bleak moment when I was certain I was going to die, and she was the only thing in my head. I want to make her a thousand promises and then go somewhere with her alone.

But it'll have to wait, I guess. I owe a few people apologies, after all.

I hold onto her and turn back to face my family. My dad is at the front door where he—and a security guard—are holding my brother back, while my mother walks toward us.

There were times when I hoped maybe she *knew*, and was trying to push us together—by insisting on lunch in the hotel Drew was staying in, for instance. But there is pure shock on her face right now. Apparently, she didn't have a clue.

"Mom," I tell her, "I'm sorry. I love her. I just couldn't help it. I'll work things out with Joel eventually."

There are tears in her eyes and then she smiles. "That's okay," she says, wrapping her arms around us both. "I knew she was meant to be part of our family. We'll figure it out."

A small sob comes from Drew and I know my mother's words have hit her hard. I pull her even closer and press my lips against her hair. *Family.* I'm going to do my best to give her everything she's never had before, but I'm glad my mom is still with us to give her this too.

～

THE BULLET WAS REMOVED by a medic in Somalia, but I still have to get my wound checked out before I'm free to leave. My family stays in the lobby, while I wait to be seen in an examining room. I bring Drew with me, of course, because her presence here still feels too good to be true.

I sit on the examination table while she takes the only chair, and we discuss the past day. She tells me about their trip here, about some unfounded rumor that an American had died. I offer her as few details about what happened as I can. I still have to go back, after all. She doesn't need to know how close I came to not making it out alive.

"You're sure you're okay with this?" she finally asks. "I mean, with us."

I laugh. "Are you really asking me that? I just got everything I wanted, and my mother was fine with it."

"Your brother isn't. Sabine wasn't either."

My brow furrows. "Sabine? The *nurse*?"

She grins. "Are you serious? She just ran across the lobby to hug you. She was sitting next to you when I showed up in the canteen. You cannot possibly be surprised by this."

"Surprised by what? I have no idea what you're talking about."

She stands up and starts to cross the room and I ward her off. "Drew, you swore you'd remain in your chair."

She kisses me once, closed mouth, and returns to her seat. "That's all I wanted. I wasn't planning to blow you."

I groan. "I think you have no idea how little it takes to excite me." I'm wearing scrubs, for God's sake. This doctor is gonna walk in at any moment and see way more of my anatomy than I'm interested in sharing.

"I'll talk about my feelings," she says. "That kills any erection."

I grin. "Don't be so certain about that. I've been waiting a very long time to hear about your feelings."

The doctor checks out my shoulder and prescribes some painkillers and a lot of rest, though he's clearly aware, having *seen* Drew, that I have no intention of resting. "Do your best, anyway," he concludes. I'm given scrubs and hospital slippers, and then Drew and I walk out hand-in-hand to find my parents waiting in the lobby. Joel is gone, and it worries me only because I'm sure it worries my mom. At the moment, however, she's so delighted about Drew and me that nothing can touch her.

My dad suggests we all go to dinner, but my mom looks at our linked fingers and suggests we meet up tomorrow. My father is complaining about this as they walk away—*We flew all night to see him*—but she waves him off.

"I want grandchildren," she replies. "Let's not get in their way."

Drew hears it and laughs. "I think your mom might be getting ahead of herself."

I picture Drew pregnant, and I picture the child we might have. I smile and tug her closer. I'm not sure my mom is all that far ahead of herself, but I'll take baby steps for now.

49

DREW

When we get to the hotel—Ben somehow arranged this too—I help him remove the shirt over his bandaged shoulder. Standing there shirtless, scrubs hanging low around his waist, he looks so good I can hardly bear not to touch him.

"I need a shower," he says. He comes closer, his mouth at my ear. "I might need help. You know...bum shoulder and all."

I let my palms rest against his chest. "Yeah?"

He nods. His eyes have gone all hazy, the way they do when he is *not* thinking about cleanliness, and there's a bulge distorting the front of his scrubs. "The doctor said you should rest," I remind him.

He leans down, finding my mouth. "Even *he* knew that wasn't realistic. It would take a lot more bullets to make rest a priority right now."

He strips me of my hoody and the t-shirt beneath. It's not easy with only one good arm, but with my help he manages just fine. I push the jeans down myself. He tugs me against him then, like he can't stand not to touch me. "I've missed you."

"I've missed you too," I sigh. More than I would ever have

let myself admit. His nipple is level with my mouth. My lips close over it, taking it between my teeth.

"God," he groans. His hips reflexively arch toward me, seeking friction. "Shower." It comes out more as a plea than a demand. I let him lead me, shedding my bra and panties on the way, watching with breathless anticipation as he tugs the scrubs down over his narrow hips.

His cock is thick and long and shows no sign of needing any rest whatsoever. It needs the *opposite* of rest. I reach for it but he evades me, stepping into the spray with a laugh. I follow, taking the hotel soap and lathering it in my hand.

"Hmmm...where should I start?" I ask.

He laughs again. The last time I saw him this free, this unburdened, was the day we reached Kalalau Beach. It's as if he's suddenly got everything in the world he wants.

"You'd better start at the top," he replies. "Otherwise this will be a very brief shower."

I lather his neck first, letting my hands run over his chest and his back, avoiding his shoulder. I don't miss his small intake of air every time his cock slides against my stomach, the way he tenses as if it's so good it hurts. My core clenches in response. I go down to my knees to get his legs, slowly working my way up and over his skin.

"You're torturing me right now," he says.

Finally I rise, moving behind him, running my hands from his back down to his ass, reaching through his legs to cup his balls while my other hand roams over his hip to stroke his cock. Air hisses between his teeth at the contact. I move to face him and when I reach for him again, he stops me.

"Fuck," he groans. "No condoms."

"I'm...clean," I whisper. "And I'm on birth control."

This is something I never, not once, gave his brother.

His eyes slowly close. "Drew, I'm not gonna last two seconds without one."

I smile. "If memory serves, you'll be ready for round two fast enough. I can wait."

He moves us so I'm completely out of the spray, my back against the wall. "You're going to get your bandage wet," I warn.

"That's okay," he says with a half grin. "I know a guy."

His palm glides down my leg, hooking his fingers under my knee to pull one thigh around his hip. He bends his knees to get the right angle, rubbing his hardness over my core, hitting my clit with just the right amount of pressure and then he's inside me, hissing at the feel of it. "Oh God, that's so good," he whispers. I arch to get closer to him as he tugs my hips toward him and begins sliding in and out, the tempo even and perfect.

I didn't think it would be so different. After all, it's the same amount of friction, the same amount of force. But it's slicker, hotter, more real. When he thrusts inside me hard for the first time, my feet nearly leave the floor.

One of his hands is on my hip as the other trails over my neck to my breast, then my rib cage, then lower. His fingers slip between my legs.

I laugh. "This is going to end so fast if you do that."

He groans. "This is going to end so fast in either case. That's *why* I'm doing it."

He is stiff with the effort to restrain himself, to not push faster and harder and take what he needs.

"Faster," I demand.

"Drew," he says with a warning in his voice but I arch toward him and he complies, his hips bucking hard and fast, almost involuntarily. My blood heats and leaves my brain entirely. That thing in my stomach starts to wind tight and tighter. "I'm close," I warn him.

"Thank God," he grunts, and his next thrust is pitiless and entirely selfish and it sends me right over the edge. I cry out and then he pushes once more, hard, and I hear his own muffled cry as he buries his face against my neck.

Eventually, we dry off and find our way to the bed where we repeat everything at a more leisurely pace, sleep like the dead for a few hours, and then wake and do it again.

It's dark when he rolls toward me and says, "Tell me about the numbers."

I frown. We're happy now and it's not a happy story. "Was I talking in my sleep again?" I ask him.

He shakes his head. "No. Not here. But in Dooha, you were. All night long."

I try to think of a way I can distract him, a way I can turn it into a joke, but I guess the time for that has passed. At this point, failing to answer would feel like a lie.

"They're bus lines," I tell him, staring at his chest. "From the last time I went to see my dad."

He stiffens. "I thought he died when you were young."

"He did," I reply, and then I close my eyes and let the story spill free, each piece of it a little uglier than the one before it.

My father was distraught after that bottle hit me in the face. I told my mom the truth because a stupid part of me thought she'd understand how lost my dad was, how much he needed us.

"She said she was taking away his visitation rights, instead," I tell Josh. His hand slides over my arm, encouraging me to continue. "And he said he was going to do his best to fight it."

I believed him, little idiot that I was. I believed him and I packed a bag and memorized the bus schedules and left New York, alone. And I was so scared the whole way. I'd never taken a city bus in my life and I was sure someone was going to ask why I wasn't in school, or that I would get off on the wrong stop, or forget which bus came next. M7 to the 199 to the 88. And I dream about it again and again, those moments before I knew how it would all turn out, when I still was full of blind, stupid hope.

"Did you make it?" I hear concern in his voice, as if this is a story that's still evolving, that can still change.

"I did," I reply. I take a single deep breath. "He'd shot himself in the head."

He stiffens. Maybe he isn't sure if I'm making another wildly inappropriate joke. Lord knows I've made enough of them. I hear the air leave his chest in an audible rush. "Jesus, Drew."

I shake my head. "I don't really remember it," I tell him. "A neighbor came in behind and got me out of there." What's left, mostly, is the feeling of being blindsided, of being stunned that he didn't try like he said he would. He was never going to try, and I truly believed every word out of his mouth until that moment.

Josh holds me for a long time after I conclude. I'm not sure if it's for me or for him or for us both. "I think it's why I reacted so badly when I came to see you in Dooha," I admit. "It just felt like it had all been a lie." I cut him out of my life because it felt like the least painful option. Until I realized how much more painful things could be.

"I wish I could go back and fix it all for you," he says. "What happened then. And how I acted when you came to visit."

"I'm not sure we'd be where we are if it all hadn't happened just the way it did," I tell him. I close my eyes. "It's all gonna come out now, though. Davis knows. Once he discovers I wasn't bluffing when I fired him, he's going to tell the whole world, and he'll find a way to make me look bad. I think I probably need to get it out there first."

It still terrifies me, but not the way it did before. Those hours I spent thinking Josh might be dead make any other outcome pale by contrast.

"I'll be there with you, at the interviews, if you want me there," he says, pressing his lips to the top of my head. "I've got two weeks off now, but I'm going to find a way to get out of

Somalia permanently. I already put in the request but now I'm going to demand it."

I blink up at him, my throat swelling a little. "Really? But...I thought it was impossible? What changed?"

"What changed is that I fell in love," he says. "And I don't ever want to spend a single night away from you again. It might take a while, but Drew, even if we're apart, you're not alone anymore."

I press my face to his chest and cry. Not about my father, really, or the scare we've just had. But about all the lonely years that existed between those two events.

And how relieved I am to discover it's coming to an end.

50

DREW

Nine Months Later

Our new terrace looks spectacular.

Fairy lights are strung haphazardly overhead. The long plank table is laid out with ten place settings punctuated with wine bottles and vases full of hydrangeas. And Josh stands on the other side of it, which might be the thing I like most.

He grins at me now while helping Audrey, Tali's daughter, take uncertain, lumbering steps across the grass. Gemma, Jonathan's oldest child, is trying to teach her somersaults, which might be a little advanced given that Audrey just started walking a month ago.

Tonight we are celebrating several things at once—our new home, the release of Tali's book, Jonathan and his partner's newest child.

And perhaps most of all, Ben's first but significant victory over Davis—and therefore mine as well. It took many months to sort out all of Davis's mismanagement. This week, he finally freed up the eleven million they owed me, and now we go after him and my former accountant for the ten million they embezzled. I don't need the money, but I'm looking forward to ruining them both—or ruining them *more*, anyway.

The interviews I gave about my father's death, with Josh by my side, highlighted Davis's role in hiding it all, and the way it kept me silent and compliant as well. His company's other clients fled once the stories came out, but the best part for me was simply getting out from under it. That story held a lot of power over me for a very long time, and letting it out broke the spell. If I had to continue rehashing it in interviews, I'd probably be okay, but my new publicist terrifies everyone into good behavior so it doesn't come up.

"You did an amazing job," says Tali, coming up beside me.

I shrug. "Thanks, but Beth did most of the planning." She wanted me to cook for this—she keeps trying to teach me how to make Josh's favorite foods—but my domesticity has its limits. "Have you met Ben's date, by the way? I couldn't get a straight answer about what she does for a living."

Tali rolls her eyes. "I think she just goes around being *hot* for a living, and taking pictures of herself. Who can we set him up with? He needs to settle down."

Ben shows no signs of *wanting* to settle down, but now that Tali's happily married she's hell-bent on marrying everyone else off too. Between her and Beth the number of daily hints I get about weddings is staggering.

"You have two sisters, right?" I ask.

"One of them is married and one of them is *barely* twenty," she replies. "What about that friend who's been helping you with the album...Juliet?"

Juliet has been a godsend now that I'm finally free of my

obligation to the record label. It's her label and producer I'm working with, and she even came in and sang backing vocals on two tracks. But I can't see her with Ben.

"She's hung up on someone else. And she's more of a *Six* sort of gal, anyway."

Tali's nose wrinkles. "Ugh. *Six*."

I laugh. Six has been trying to clean up his act a little these past few months, ever since he learned about Beth's cancer. And he's going to need people in his corner when his mom is gone. I plan to be one of them.

"He's not so bad," I reply. "He even played on one of my new songs since I am, and I quote, 'about to be a member of the family'."

Her eyes light up. "*Member of the family*, huh? Does he know something I don't?"

"No," I say firmly. "He's just been listening to Beth, who—like you—keeps putting the cart before the horse."

"Says the woman who claimed she and her boyfriend were going to *take things slowly* when he got back from Somalia then moved in with him a week later."

I smile without a hint of shame. We *did* plan to go slowly, but after waiting three more months for the refugee camp to replace Josh, I was done with being away from him. Even living together, I still feel like I don't see him enough—only Josh would move from one wildly understaffed medical facility to another. On the bright side, the fact that he is "wasting his talents" at a free clinic aggravates his father to no end, which we both enjoy.

"Oh God," Tali says, her attention focused across the yard. "Hayes just took the baby from Jonathan. We've got to get over there."

I laugh. "He's the most overprotective father I've ever seen. The baby is fine."

"Sure, the *baby* is fine. I'm worried about myself. If Hayes holds that kid for more than thirty seconds, he's going to want another one."

We cross the yard. Tali deftly "borrows" the baby from Hayes, Josh returns Audrey to her father and wraps an arm around my waist. He's currently telling the guys about my latest foray onto Twitter, which I've discovered is the perfect place to mess with people who irk me. After Richard, my stepbrother, sent a text saying he wasn't surprised I'd been "dropped" by my label, I put out a one-line tweet about the white-collar criminal he was in the process of defending, a guy he was trying to get a plea deal for.

Suddenly the case was in the news, and not in a good way. It was something along the lines of *another rich guy is escaping justice*. As it turns out, having your client's wrongdoing become the focus of national attention does not help grease the wheels of justice. Who knew?

Ben covers his face with a hand. "Please don't start encouraging people to do that, Drew," he says. "Not everyone I represent is, uh, as deserving as you."

"It gets worse," Josh says, pressing his lips to the top of my head. He has enjoyed the hell out of my Twitter revenge. "Her stepfather sent a text scolding her for it and Drew tweeted about one of his clients too."

Ben groans aloud while everyone else laughs. Weirdly, my mother didn't seem to mind all that much. She told me the firm was in an uproar, and when I told her I wasn't sorry, she said *I didn't figure you would be. Let's get lunch the next time you're here. It can even be burgers.*

Dinner is served, toasts are made. It's a lovely evening but it ends pretty early given that there's an infant, a ten-month old, and a toddler all falling apart by nine PM.

When everyone's gone, I climb into bed and wait for Josh.

"I think it went well," he calls from the bathroom.

"It did but Ben seemed kind of...wistful when he left. Do you know anyone we could—"

Josh wanders out with only a towel wrapped around his waist, skin still damp. My thoughts turn carnal in a second flat. "Well, *hello* there, nearly naked stranger."

He grins. "I've got something for you."

"I was hoping you'd say that," I reply, throwing off the covers. "Remove the towel."

"It wasn't *that*. I mean, it will be obviously, in about thirty seconds," he says with a chuckle, "but not just yet."

He goes to the dresser and pulls out a sheet of paper. "Remember that reporter who came to the studio when you were recording? She just published a story about it."

I stare at him for a moment, and then I start to laugh. "An online blogger wrote an article...and you *printed* it? You are *so old*."

He raises a brow. "You never know how long that stuff will stay up—"

I'm still laughing. "Yes, you do. It stays up forever. I don't need to read it, but that's very sweet of you."

"She makes Davis sound like an asshole," he says. "Obviously, not the hardest job in the world. But she also says really nice things about the songs she heard you working on."

I don't really care what anyone says about Davis, or what anyone says about the album, but I love that *he* cares. I love that *he* likes my new songs. And I love that he printed the article out like someone who still thinks the internet is a passing fad.

He crosses the room to put it away but stops in place when I pull off my t-shirt. He stands there, blinking, as if he's forgotten for a moment what he was doing, and then he slowly turns away, putting the printout in his sock drawer next to a black velvet box I'm trying very hard not to peek at. And I *wasn't* snooping. I do his laundry sometimes.

"Come here," I tell him. His eyes already have that dark, drugged look they get when he's thinking about sex. I stretch out on the bed, relishing the outline of him now bulging under that towel. My work here is done.

He climbs beside me and I wrap my arms around him. "Tell me something," I whisper. "Tell me something no one else knows."

"I'm madly in love with you," he says, pressing his lips to my neck.

I smile. "Everyone knows that. And of course you are. I'm adorable. Tell me something *else*."

He laughs and rolls on his side, his hand on my hip. "I was thinking we ought to take a trip to Maui," he says. "My mom has a book that says it's the most beautiful of all the Hawaiian islands."

"Sure, but how's the medical care?" I ask.

He pulls me closer and bites down on a grin. "I don't know, but they apparently have several good places to hold a wedding."

My heart thuds in my chest. "Yeah? Do you know someone planning to get married?"

His lips brush over my temple, my cheekbone, down along my jaw. "I might. Depends on if she says yes."

I remove his towel. "I bet she'd say yes. It sounds like she'd be crazy not to."

"You're sure?" he asks. I arch up to help him tug off my shorts. "It's a pretty long trip. I know you have an aversion to that."

I pull him toward me. "I'm sure. I don't mind a long trip every once in a while."

It makes all the difference when you're not taking it alone.

The End

ACKNOWLEDGMENTS

When you decide, at the very last minute, to scrap the book
you've written and start fresh (based on one page you wrote
about Hawaii a year before)...some help is required.

First and foremost, thanks a million times over to my friend
Sallye Clark, who's been letting me tag along on her work trips
to Hawaii for years. We've stayed in places I could never afford
on my own and have seen sights I'd never have found if she
hadn't been there to direct me. (When I tell people about these
trips, they always ask if Sallye needs another friend. The
answer is *No, she does not*. I like things exactly the way they are.)

Thanks next to the wonderful Sali Benbow-Powers, whose
brilliant suggestions and love for this book gave me the confidence to move forward with it. Sali, I will never publish
anything that hasn't been placed into your hands first.

Thanks to my amazing, last-minute beta readers for taking this
on at the eleventh hour to help me perfect it: Michelle Chen,
Christine Estevez, Katie Meyer, Jen Wilson Owens and
Tawanna Williams. Your suggestions and confidence in this
book made all the difference.

Thanks so much to Staci Frenes at Grammar Boss for
squeezing me in for editing and Julie Deaton and Janis
Ferguson for squeezing me in for copyediting, to Lori Jackson

for another HOT cover, to Nina and everyone at Valentine PR for their endless help, and the amazing Christine Estevez for handling all the stuff I'm terrible at so I can write.

Finally, thanks to my kids and extended family for not rolling their eyes every time I say "I can't, I'm on a deadline". I'd like to promise this frantic, last-minute behavior will change, but we probably all know better by now.

**Some people marry the
enemy in Vegas . . .**

Keeley managed to get knocked up by him too.

Available now.

PIATKUS

ACKNOWLEDGMENTS

When you decide, at the very last minute, to scrap the book you've written and start fresh (based on one page you wrote about Hawaii a year before)...some help is required.

First and foremost, thanks a million times over to my friend Sallye Clark, who's been letting me tag along on her work trips to Hawaii for years. We've stayed in places I could never afford on my own and have seen sights I'd never have found if she hadn't been there to direct me. (When I tell people about these trips, they always ask if Sallye needs another friend. The answer is *No, she does not.* I like things exactly the way they are.)

Thanks next to the wonderful Sali Benbow-Powers, whose brilliant suggestions and love for this book gave me the confidence to move forward with it. Sali, I will never publish anything that hasn't been placed into your hands first.

Thanks to my amazing, last-minute beta readers for taking this on at the eleventh hour to help me perfect it: Michelle Chen, Christine Estevez, Katie Meyer, Jen Wilson Owens and Tawanna Williams. Your suggestions and confidence in this book made all the difference.

Thanks so much to Staci Frenes at Grammar Boss for squeezing me in for editing and Julie Deaton and Janis Ferguson for squeezing me in for copyediting, to Lori Jackson for another HOT cover, to Nina and everyone at Valentine PR for their endless help, and the amazing Christine Estevez for handling all the stuff I'm terrible at so I can write.

Finally, thanks to my kids and extended family for not rolling their eyes every time I say "I can't, I'm on a deadline". I'd like to promise this frantic, last-minute behavior will change, but we probably all know better by now.

He might not be the devil, but working under him for six weeks is my idea of hell.

Meet the temp assistant and the British boss she loves to hate . . .

Available now.

It's all fun and games until your work nemesis tells you to beg.

You don't want to miss meeting Ben Tate . . .

Available now.

PIATKUS